THE BRIDGE OF BONES

Book 5 of the Vatican Knights Series

By
Rick Jones

ALSO, BY RICK JONES:

Vatican Knights Series
The Vatican Knights
Shepherd One
The Iscariot Agenda
Pandora's Ark
The Bridge of Bones

The Eden Series
The Crypts of Eden
The Menagerie
The Thrones of Eden
Familiar Stranger

TABLE OF CONTENTS

PROLOGUE

Port of Ploče Container Terminal
Croatia

The last of the freight containers were loaded onto the deck of the *Александра* (the *Aleksandra)*. The ship was a converted cargo vessel registered with the Croatian Register of Shipping (CRS), under the guise of a reputable shipping merchant, which was a dummy corporation for the Croatian mob.

Standing along the rail of the 133-meter ship and overseeing the last freight container loaded squarely on top of another by hook and crane, stood Jadran Božanović, a high-ranking contributor within the organization. He was known for his brutality when dispensing a certain brand of justice with the keen edge of a knife, which also happened to be his weapon of choice since it never ran dry. His signature hallmark was to leave behind a corpse so brutalized that it appeared to have been mauled by an animal, the message behind his actions a testament to his raw and unbridled viciousness.

At six-three and weighing close to 220 pounds of lean muscle, and with body fat that could be measured in the single digits, Božanović was as intimidating as his appearance. His face was hard-looking with a mild flaring of cheekbones, a carryover from Mongolian genes that had been diluted over generations. His eyes were the color of onyx, dark and non-expressive. But what dominated his features and made his face so memorable was the scar that ran laterally down his cheek to the top of his lip, the scarring pulling down the corner of his lower eyelid enough to expose the glistening pink tissue under it.

He was also a man who played a key role in the pecking order of the mob's hierarchy.

As streamers of light began to surface along the horizon, and as the shadows of the night started to dim and wane, the cranes continued to work under the bank of lamps that were fastened the ship's headers and beams. Once the last container was loaded and secured, Božanović waved his hand as a gesture to move quickly before the members of the CRS began to second-guess his onboard stock.

The Croatian fell back from the railing and headed for the main deck, as the horizon grew brighter in set colors of oranges and reds, the morning light inching and lengthening over the docks.

When he reached his stacked supply of containers, there was a man of tiny stature taking inventory with a pen and clipboard. When standing next to Jadran Božanović, the man appeared small and insignificant. And to Božanović, like with all men beneath him, this man was nothing more than a working asset to the company, someone who was nameless and faceless and could readily be replaced at a moment's notice.

"Are we good to go?" Božanović asked him. "I count eight containers in total."

The smaller man nodded. "Eight crates carrying," he checked his clipboard with the point of his pen, "seven hundred and six assets."

Božanović cocked his head. "Seven-o-six? There's supposed to be seven hundred and twenty."

"I'm afraid fourteen didn't make it, Mr. Božanović." When the smaller man spoke, he did so with the greatest air of caution. To Jadran Božanović, every asset was money. And money lost was inexcusable. In time, the Croatian would hold someone accountable and make a messy example of that person with the blade of his knife. Prudence was supposed to be taken with all of his properties; this had been the paramount rule of handling.

"I want a full list of those responsible for the treatment of my assets," he said.

"Immediately, sir."

Božanović gave a cursory glance to the east and noted that the upper rind of the sun was beginning to show itself. "How much longer before we depart?"

"Immediately, sir."

"See to it then."

"Yes, sir."

Božanović went to the railing and scrutinized the dock area as stretches of daylight were crawling along the portside, providing light to areas that had been steeped in dark shadows moments before. From the edge of his downturned eye, he caught movement—a glimpse. Somebody was taking shelter behind a wall of stacked crates.

The person was not alone.

Božanović slapped the heels of his hands repeatedly against the railing in frustration. His operation had been compromised.

Where there is one, there is always another…

He quickly ran across the ship's deck crying out to move the *Aleksandra* from its mooring, as members of an international task force closed in from all points, their weapons raised and directed. They were adorned in black gear, wearing specialized helmets and composite armor, their weapons high-grade armaments.

Božanović continued to bark out orders as he ran across the ship's level. *"Pomicanje! Pomicanje! Pomicanje!"* Move! Move! Move!

Božanović's shipmates tried to detach the mooring lines from their bollards, only to be cut down by strafing gunfire, as bullets stitched across bodies, causing blood founts to jettison in arcs and red mist.

Bodies fell as boneless heaps all over the deck, as the international unit pressed forward along the gangways.

Božanović tapped his palm against his sheathed knife. It was hardly a formidable weapon against such an arsenal, so he pulled his Glock, instead.

He took aim and fired in rapid succession, the bullets hitting their marks. A soldier wearing composite armor went to a knee for a quick moment before recalibrating and redirecting his weapon on Božanović. A quick volley of bullets soon followed and pinged against the metal bins behind the Croatian, the projectiles caroming in all directions, as Božanović ducked beneath the hail of gunfire. In vain he raised his hand and blindly fired off several shots, hitting nothing, while running to the stern of the ship.

He had six shots left.

Military enforcers swarmed and fanned out across the deck of the *Aleksandra,* firing in 180 degrees of direction—left, right, east, west. Božanović's men fell as they were judiciously dispatched by the team's advancement.

But when Božanović heard the cries of his men, he felt absolutely nothing—no remorse, no contrition, and certainly no sense of gratitude for their sacrifice. In Croatia, where people often romanticized ideas of becoming a member of the Croatian mob, replacements were always bountiful.

When he reached the ship's stern, he came upon a one-man submarine that was tethered to the deck by metal clamps. On the one-man pod was a numerical keypad, bearing a code only he knew. With deft fingers, he began to type in numbers on the keypad. Bullets pocked the area around him. Holes appeared around him as though by magic as bullets zipped close his ears with as waspy hums, then lodged in the wall behind him. And then the sub's hatch opened and lifted with the whoosh of escaping air.

Bullets pinged off the sub's hard titanium shell, as Božanović slipped inside and locked the latch. With the pull of an internal cord, the clamps holding the sub to the deck lifted with metallic noises. The torpedo-shaped sub then slid cleanly down a ramp and to the surface of the sea, where it bobbed like a cork for a quick moment before righting itself.

Božanović quickly engaged the sub's electronics. He initiated the driveshaft and propellers, worked the flaps, and filled the buoyancy tanks with water. Within moments the sub vanished beneath the waves, as bubbles rose from the point of its descent.

Members of the international team grouped around the railing with their weapons pointed downward at the churning froth.

Jadran Božanović was gone.

John Majors, who was the team leader of the English task force from the London Group, and former head of the British Special Forces, lifted his face shield over his composite helmet, then he watched the last of the bubbles burst along the surface as Božanović made his escape.

"Bloody 'ell," was all he said, looking at the waves. They'd had Božanović trapped; they'd had him hemmed in, his crew offering marginal resistance against a much better team. Yet Božanović had slipped their grasp.

Majors closed his eyes and fought for calm, as the muscles in the back of his jaw worked.

This was the third time they had closed in on the Croat within eighteen months. The man had escaped through the grips of American, Spanish, and English forces.

Majors visibly huffed in anger and frustration at missing the kill. To

9

take away the life of Božanović would have been a justifiable act in the eyes of the international court of opinion, the man's death already having been adjudicated as a green-light 'go' by those who sat upon the thrones of worldwide justice.

Then: "Colonel?"

John Majors opened his eyes. "Yeah?"

"Sixteen crew members of the *Aleksandra* are dead, sir."

"Survivors?"

"None."

"And the cargo? Is it safe?"

"Yes, sir. Safe and secured."

Majors led his team to the main deck, where armed units of British commandos congregated around the freight containers.

"How many bloody crates this time?" Majors asked a soldier, who by his striping served as a sergeant.

"Eight."

Majors shook his head and walked past the soldier; his eyes fixed on the shipping crates. "That's eight too many."

Majors lowered the point of his weapon as he neared the first container, a transport crate one would find on the back of an eighteen-wheeler. "Open the bloody door," he stated firmly. *And pray that we don't find what we're supposed to.*

A soldier with a welder's torch sparked the tip and placed the flame against the lock, the metal melting as easily as a hot cake of butter. When the lock fell free from its hasp, the soldier lifted the latch and opened the door.

The smell was nauseating as the stench of human waste overwhelmed them. There was also an accompanying wave of heat like a wafting fever that was real and alive—that of sickness and disease, as people coughed with phlegm-like wetness and viruses coursed through their veins.

Majors stepped back. *Damn you, Božanović.* "For God's sake, get these people out of 'ere! And get them some bloody 'elp!"

"Immediately, sir."

People coughed sickly upheavals from burning lungs, all between the ages of twelve and twenty-five, victims of Jadran Božanović's pleasures, as a merchant of human misery.

Majors took note of the other crates with hard appraisal, knowing that each one contained the same cargo as this one: human livestock.

10

He shook his head in complete and utter disgust, wondering how people like Božanović could even exist. He tried to comprehend what possible element in life could make a man so horrifically miserable that he would readily accept the devil as his ally and be comfortable with that alliance.

Damn you, Božanović.

Damn you to bloody 'ell.

CHAPTER ONE

London
Approximately One Month Later

When Colonel John Majors returned to his flat in London for R&R, he could not exorcise the images of the children on the *Aleksandra*, or the way their flesh held the awful color of grayness instead of a healthy glow. In fact, they carried that haunted look of detachment.

Once again, Jadran Božanović had proven himself to be as slick as an eel.

And this sickened Majors to no end, because he had been so close to capturing the Croat, he could smell the man's foulness in the air.

After pouring himself a tumbler of cognac, Majors went to the balcony of his fourth-floor flat, which offered a view of Hyde Park in the distance. From there he could see a spread of trees and open fields. But the reason he cherished the park so much was because of the podiums that were seated along the pathways. He would come to listen to those who spoke of hot-button topics that mattered, things that could change or alter the mind and one's philosophy. But lately, at least from his interpretation, the podiums had been taken up by weirdoes and cranks who spouted off nonsensical rubbish.

Times were changing.

Downing his drink, Majors went to the bathroom and looked at his reflection in the mirror. His eyes were red and raw. And the lines and seams along his face were growing deeper and longer.

When he was the head of the British Special Forces things had seemed so different because his mind and body were in sync due to the blessings of youth. But now that he was aging, his body was telling him that he was in the twilight of his service, even as a task-force leader. The constant aches in his knees and shoulder were becoming a testament to what his mind was beginning to register: *you're getting too old.*

But he wanted to do *one* last thing that meant something good in his life—the one thing that would make him a legacy. He wanted to be known as the man who took down Jadran Božanović.

He grunted as the pains in both knees were too great even for the cognac to numb. So, he opened the mirrored door of the medicine cabinet, grabbed a bottle of painkillers, and shut the door. When he did, there were two images reflected in the mirror: his and Jadran Božanović's.

Major's eyes didn't even start. Nor did he turn to confront the intruder. It was as if he'd been expecting this moment all along.

In the mirror, he watched the scarred face of Božanović looking at him with features that did not betray his emotions, a look of neutrality. His eyes, however, held something deep and cold to them, their blackness impenetrable.

And Majors had come to realize that Božanović was a man of subdued rage, who had come to collect a toll from him for compromising the operation on the *Aleksandra.*

Božanović raised a knife. Its point was sharp and wickedly keen, with its polished blade reflecting clean light from the overhead bulb. In malicious play, he toyed with it by turning it over in his hand in simple rotations to give Majors a good look from all angles.

And Majors conceded with a nod, knowing there was nothing he could do against this man alone.

Three days later, when the body of Colonel Majors was discovered, the *London Times* would equate the murder to the likes of Jack the Ripper.

CHAPTER TWO

Office of the Monsignor
The Vatican

"I kill people. It's what I do. It's what I'm good at."

Monsignor Dom Giammacio was the Vatican's counselor for clerics who floundered in the self-doubt of waning faith. But today he was not listening to a priest at all. He was listening to a soldier of the Vatican, a seasoned warrior who served in the capacity of protecting the sovereignty of the Church, its interests, and the welfare of its citizenry.

This morning, he was listening to someone who was simply known as 'the priest who is not a priest.'

He was in session with Kimball Hayden, team leader of the Vatican Knights, who was always in search of salvation and sought deliverance from a dark past that clung to him like cancer.

"Kimball, what you're telling me is beginning to sound like a hollow mantra. We've been down this road many times before."

Kimball fell back in his chair, his startling cerulean blue eyes never losing their focus as he stared into the copper-hued eyes of the monsignor. "Then what's left to talk about?"

The monsignor looked at the curls of smoke rising from a cigarette that was wedged between his long and thin fingers. He watched the delicate loops of smoke as they rose and dissipated. "We need to talk about your unwillingness to accept the fact that you have achieved God's good graces by serving as a Vatican Knight."

Kimball leaned forward. The muscles in his forearms were considerable and became electric with movement. "Can God forgive a man who has killed innocent women and children for the sake of duty?"

"It all depends. Are you a man of contrition? Do you feel repentant for committing such actions?"

"Repentant?" Kimball slowly fell back into his seat. "The hardest thing for any man to do, Monsignor, is to forgive himself. You know that."

"So, is that the bottom line, Kimball? You can't forgive yourself?"

Kimball sighed. "No… However, if I wait long enough, then I can justify my actions no matter how heinous they may be. After a while, I learn how to live with what I've done by making myself believe that what I did was right, that my actions were justifiable in the end. It's so easy to make yourself believe anything over time."

"But apparently, you don't. Not if you come in here today and tell me that God continues to forbid your salvation. You cannot justify your actions, then feel ongoing culpability. You either feel absolved of those actions or you don't. So, tell me, which is it?"

Kimball closed his eyes and immediately recalled the moment he killed two children in Iraq. He could see the images. He had killed them out of a sense of obligation. Not only had he committed murder, but he also committed theft. He had robbed a mother of two sons, siblings of two brothers, a father of children to forward the family line, and future generations from those he killed. He could see everything move in his mind's eye with the slowness of a bad dream, the way the bullets ripped into their bodies, which had caused the desert air to suddenly become the color of red mist.

It was then that he had had an epiphany, a pang of guilt and regret as he had buried the boys in the desert sand. During the night, as he lay on the desert floor staring up at the countless pinpricks of light in the sky, he sought for the face of God and saw nothing but star-point glitters.

It was then that he knew that God had turned His back on him.

He opened his eyes. It had been several years since that kill. Yet he continued to see their faces as he slept, forever witnessing that final moment when the innocence of their eyes had vanished. The moment he canceled their lives.

Then: "I haven't been able to justify my actions," he said. "Not yet. Not what I did to those boys."

"After so many years, Kimball," the Monsignor quickly stamped his cigarette out in the ashtray, "you're not going to justify this one particular act, because it is exactly as you said: The hardest thing for any man to do is to forgive himself. And you need to find a way to do so. The struggle for your salvation is not God's struggle. He accepted you into His embrace the moment you donned the uniform of a Vatican Knight. The problem lies within you, Kimball. You are a creature of imperfection and good moral character, who needs to best these demons of self-guilt on terms that can only be your own."

"Then why does He continue to remind me every night when I go to sleep, by showing me the faces of those children? Why do I continue to see their blood drain upon the desert floor night after night after night?"

"Your dreams, Kimball, are manifestations of your conscience mind, and not from God. You know that. The obstacle here is to somehow get you to forgive yourself for an action that you cannot readily justify because it was wrong. But since then, you have made incredible strides, by saving numerous lives. You have, in some circles, become a saint to those who cannot defend themselves…and a demon to those who have been so corrupted that their souls are forever lost, and they wish to do nothing but untold harm.

"You've come full circle, Kimball. We just have to somehow get you to overcome that one obstacle of not being able to forgive yourself, which is a mountain that needs to be climbed." Monsignor Dom Giammacio maintained a steady eye, waiting for a response that never came.

Then: "Time's up. But I want you to think about this." The monsignor reached for another cigarette. "I want you to think about how you can climb to the peak of that mountain and get to the other side."

"Isn't that your job? To see me through?"

The monsignor nodded. "I can only show you the way, Kimball. It's up to you to chase away your demons. That has always been the answer to everything."

When the monsignor lit up, Kimball got to his feet and full height. He was a massive man, standing at six-four and with a bodybuilder's physique, his muscles sculpted and developed by hours in the gym. "Next Monday, then?"

"And please don't be late—like you always are."

When Kimball left the monsignor's office, he could not picture in his mind a viable way to best the obstacle of his self-guilt, the feeling of this particular emotion that ate away at him like slow-moving cancer. It was deeply rooted, something that was now a part of him, like a dark pall that constantly followed in his wake.

Tonight, he told himself, like every night, he would see the faces of the two boys he had killed.

But the dream would not be the same.

He did see *their faces as he lay asleep in his spartan chamber.*

He could see the agony in their eyes, the abject terror, knowing that their lives were about to end. Everything moved too slowly, the pumping of their legs across the sand as the soft desert landscape slowed their chances of escape. And then came the sprays of red mist, the bullets punching through their flesh, as gouts of blood erupted, the bodies falling to the terrain as they bled out. Their eyes were open, then dimming, the ember of life finally disappearing as the air became scented with the smell of copper.

In his dream, he had somewhat of an omniscient point of view, looking downward through a celestial eye and seeing himself standing over the two bodies.

He then looked skyward, appraising the heavens, perhaps looking for an answer.

But nothing came.

The bodies began to move, reanimating themselves to give Kimball another chance at salvation by allowing them to live and move on.

But Kimball shot them again…

…And again…

…And again…

The man was incapable of changing or letting go.

And the mountain of an obstacle grew increasingly taller and increasingly distant.

It was here that Kimball awoke with the final images remaining in his mind. He was looking downward through a heavenly eye, as he continued to riddle their bodies with gunshots, killing them over and over again in his mind.

As his eyes began to focus, he saw nothing but the stilled shadows of his chamber. He could see the outline of the votive rack standing across the room, as well as the podium that seated the Bible—a book he rarely opened.

He knew he'd been granted a conscionable opening by giving the boys a chance to move toward the Light. But Kimball had given in to the lifestyle for which he had been groomed and cut them down repeatedly in this recurring dreamscape, always denying them the right to Glory while preventing his path to Salvation.

He closed his eyes.

I kill people.

He opened them.

It's what I do.

He shook his head disapprovingly.

It's what I'm good at…

He fell back into his pillow and stared ceilingward at the pooling shadows, at the unmoving shapes, while trying to make sense of their odd designs.

He would not sleep again that night.

CHAPTER THREE

Two Months Later
Paris, France

Shari Cohen had always romanced the idea of visiting the city of Paris. Now her idea had become reality as she, her husband, and their two children walked along the Avenue Gustave-V-de-Suède beneath a blue sky. The entire scenery was idyllic, and perfect for an artist's canvas, with Parisian gardens that bloomed in a riot of colors, and with endless rows of trees that were full, green, and plush.

They absorbed everything as they walked along the Pont d'Iéna Bridge, which spans the River Seine, and eventually links up with the Eiffel Tower on the Left Bank. As they approached the cultural icon, their eyes appraised the structure from bottom to top, as if watching the slow trajectory of a rocket, following up to its highest peak of the tower's observatory.

Even the girls, now ages fourteen and sixteen, were astonished.

"Amazing, isn't it? Now you have something to tell your friends when you go back to school."

Stephanie rolled her eyes and tried to mask her appreciation with feigned indifference. "What...everrrrrrrr." At sixteen, she was deeply rooted in the stage of knowing everything. She constantly pushed the boundaries with her parents. It was a phase that Shari and Gary had come to expect but didn't have to appreciate—the moment where a teenager just 'hated' you overnight for no reason at all. But they both regarded it as a test of patience. They needed to ride out the storm, no matter how tumultuous it could get. There was yelling and slamming of doors when things didn't go a certain way for Stephanie, who constantly regarded house rules as being 'lame.' Terry on the other hand, who was fourteen and beginning to exhibit similar traits, was waiting to cast her wings and test the same grounds on which her sister was treading. The idea brought a cold chill to Gary's stomach. One was bad enough, he considered, but two? He was hoping that whatever genetic disposition that drove teenagers to live life in such a sarcastic manner, would simply hurry along.

"Come on, Steph," he said. "Can you at least *try* to enjoy yourself? At least for a little?"

She rolled her eyes and clicked her tongue. *What...ever.*

With a preamble of a smile, Shari took out her digital camera and started to click away, catching breathtaking images.

But as the day wore on, so did their endurance. As the sun began to set and the old Parisian lampposts came to life, they finally headed back to their hotel after eating a meal at a sidewalk café.

The room was elegant, with French-styled furniture conceived with curls and sweeps and lots of paisley designs in the fabrics. Pictures and watercolors adorned the walls in soft colors and hues, promoting an air of comfort. And an attached mini-suite for the girls—which Stephanie strongly verbalized against since she needed to be alone, and that sharing a room with her younger sister was 'lame'—had a small tub in the room's center, with all the working jets to soothe the body. Within a moment that was too quick to note, sister or no sister, Stephanie had fallen in love with the room.

Why can't we have something like this in our house?

Then as the days wore on, with the rules becoming less 'lame', with laughter becoming more of the norm, life in Paris was wonderful. The kids became kids again by making believe they were French by speaking a language that wasn't French at all but had made-up words that supposedly sounded pleasing to the ear. But they weren't. The consonants were too hard and the vowels, at best, were painful pronunciations. But in the end, they laughed and giggled like the schoolgirls they were. And Gary couldn't have been more pleased.

Everything was simply perfect, he thought.

Everything was fine.

In the eyes of Jadran Božanović, the girls were prime stock.

The taller of the two, somewhere between the ages of sixteen and eighteen he guessed, resembled the mother, who possessed more of an exotic look with copper-hued skin and eyes the color of cinnamon. The

20

younger one was striking as well, with resemblances shared from both mother and father. Her hair was raven, her complexion cream-colored, and her limbs were long and gangly, like her father's. Both were edging their way toward the build of mature women. Already Božanović was calculating the number of Euros in his head, anticipating a cumulative amount close to a half-million American dollars at auction between them.

After the debacle on the *Aleksandra* two months ago, and with an estimated cost of losing more than twelve million dollars worth of live goods, Božanović was rebounding with another haul. He had teams in Italy, girls mostly, recruiting female victims by planting dreams of far-off places that bled riches, enticing them with false hopes of attaining the unattainable, of garnering wealth beyond comprehension, only to corral them into a world of dark corruption, where dreams were truly living nightmares, horrific and unimaginable. So far, the haul of Roma girls mounted close to sixty, the French girls closer to four dozen— easy pickings since the world was filled with dreamers, with Božanović himself a dreamer in his right.

As a minority Muslim living in the town of Vukovar, at the time Croatia declared itself to be an independent state from Yugoslavia in 1991, Božanović was the son of a well-to-do attorney who had lived a moneyed lifestyle. He was spoiled and secure if not overly so. And because he'd had a never-ending well of financial resources to tap, he had believed himself to be the center of everyone's world, everyone's life, including his own. In his mind's eye, Božanović was *it*—the man, the myth, and the legend by the time he reached his seventeenth birthday. It was also the day the JNA, the Yugoslav People's Army, began its heinous campaign of war against the town of Vukovar and its people.

Distant mortars and gunfire had erupted the moment he blew out the candles of his cake. Though the sound was far away, it was close enough to cause the floors and walls to tremble and the crystals of the chandelier to clink together in a melody of chimes.

Being people of wealth and privilege, they chose to turn a blind eye to the effects until several black-gray plumes of smoke rose from the city.

The Serbs, who had taken umbrage with Croatia proclaiming their

21

independence, viciously attacked their political opponent in the first step of a civil war, something Jadran's father had known was brewing. But the man had believed—or wanted to believe—that the political powers would resolve the matter judiciously rather than by using force.

Within eighty-seven days the Baroque town had come under siege, and it eventually fell to Serbian and paramilitary forces who fought off the brave defensive unit of the Croatian National Guard (CNG). The town was destroyed in the end, with the Božanović estate laid to ruin.

'Ethnic cleansing' became the proverbial household phrase, as the international community watched Serbian forces under the command of Slobodan Milošević purge and clear the township of more than 31,000 people, either by slaughter or deportation.

Božanović ultimately lost his self-centered state of mind, as he saw his life crumble as quickly and easily as the walls of his home. Immediately he took up arms alongside his friends, the teenager fueled by intense anger, as his life disintegrated into dark misery. The moment he hefted the antiquated rifle in his hands he felt an unbridled sense of untold power, the firearm giving him the choice of taking away life at the pull of a trigger. He was elated, ecstatic by the fact that he was once again the center of the universe, as the man who wielded the power and choice as to who lived or died by his decision. Whoever had the fate to cross his path was surely by the design of a higher presence, he considered—he was a vessel to command and power.

Prisoners were laid at his feet before him, cowering, the act in itself making Božanović feel all-powerful and incredibly infallible. He rested the point of his weapon against the skulls of Serbs and pulled the trigger time and again, feeling no pang of guilt, the act always becoming a sense of catharsis as he stood and watched the victims bleed out.

He had lived in squalor with his teammates, becoming a leader amongst men, as they fought bravely against overwhelming odds, the JNA more than twenty times their numbers. But on the seventy-third day, his unit was surrounded. Božanović found himself kneeling before a Serb officer who was holding a pistol that gleamed with a mirror polish to its barrel.

They stared at each other, their eyes refusing to break, a testament to their wills.

The Serb holstered his firearm and removed his knife, a wickedly sharp-looking weapon that held the same mirror polish as the pistol. He had held the blade up to display without breaking eye contact.

This knife has killed many of your kind, he had told Božanović, rotating the blade. *It will kill more.*

The Serb placed the blade against the young Croatian's face until the point caused an indentation against Božanović's skin, just below his eye. Božanović refused to break contact, something the Serb had to admire but didn't have to acknowledge. So, he applied enough pressure to the knife and broke the skin, drawing a bead of blood.

Božanović winced, which drew a simple smile from the Serb.

I will kill you. And I will kill your entire family.

But Božanović's family had already been slain by the Serb's invading forces, his entire family removed from the house and slaughtered in the streets, the house then razed by fire. Although Božanović had escaped, he could remember the Serb's gunning down his mother and father, and his brother and sister with such malicious glee, he was sure that they would celebrate by drinking his family's blood from jeweled goblets—the image unlikely, but so strong in his mind.

Anger had consumed him.

Hatred had filled him.

And murder had given him hope, albeit a dark one that had led him on a path that he would never surrender.

After I kill them, then I will kill you, yes? The Serb began to trace the point of the knife gingerly along Božanović's face.

Božanović could not take the taunting any longer, so he turned to the side and spat, the action an ultimate display of courage and defiance, or perhaps one of stupidity depending upon who was watching. To his brethren, he became a god at that moment. To the Serbs, however, it spelled a foolish finality to Jadran Božanović's life.

The Serb grabbed Božanović by a hank of hair and forced his head back, exposing a smooth and open throat. *Do you think you're brave?* the Serb had fumed angrily, his face growing a shade of crimson. *Do you think that what you do will make your friends think differently of you?* He searched the surrounding faces of the Croats and would have seen the admiration for Božanović in their eyes. Then to Božanović: *You and those like you are no better than the scum beneath my boots!*

With the point of his knife, he drew a deep groove along the side of Božanović's face, from the lower edge of his eye to the corner of his lip, opening a wound that pared back enough skin to show the bloody protrusion of his cheekbone.

Božanović cried out in agony, his bravado gone. When the Serb looked upon the faces of his comrades, he saw whatever sparks of admiration had been in their eyes quickly diminished with flickers of terror.

The Serb was back on top.

So, he had smiled—another small victory as he pulled back the knife with its point tipped with scarlet.

In a macabre and sick display, the Serb licked the point and made a face, as if he relished the taste. *Now Croat*, the man had said, *it's time to die.*

Božanović had closed his eyes and waited.

Then came a volley of loud gunfire. Numerous shots cracked the air in rapid succession. The smell of gunpowder was everywhere, as Božanović opened his eyes to see a contingent team of Croats moving forward with their weapons raised. The team of Serbs was dead, dying, or writhing in misery against the broken pavement.

Božanović didn't hesitate. He got to his feet, grabbed a weapon, and summarily executed those who remained alive, with the exception of the Serb leader, who lay there with a hip wound, the man gritting his teeth against the pain.

Božanović grabbed the man's knife and held it before the man's eyes in the same manner of display the Serb had used. He showcased its magnificent point and the sharp running edge of its blade.

Do you think you know pain? he had asked the Serb, and then he kicked the man at the point of his injury, the man screaming at length. *I'll show you pain.*

The young Croat got to a bent knee and with the knife he began to cut away at the fabric of the Serb's uniform, exposing the man's legs. Božanović then motioned for his team to hold the officer down, each man grabbing a limb, arms and legs, so that the soldier could not move.

He held the knife up long enough to see terror detonate in the man's eyes.

Then: *This is pain.*

Božanović brought the edge of the knife against the man's upper thigh, from left to right, and then he began to draw the blade downward, filleting the man. The skin curled up like shaved wood from thigh to knee, a piece he then cut off and summarily discarded to the side, as food for the curs that ran the streets at night.

The Serb fought with futility against his attackers as he looked at the wound, at the fiber of muscle now showing, screaming louder than Božanović thought any man could ever scream.

Božanović had smiled, the blade his new friend, one that returned to him his power of invincibility. Once again, he had the choice as to who lived or died. And certainly, the Serb had sealed his fate, as blood dripped copiously from Božanović's wound and onto the soldier's uniform.

The Croat then peeled back a second strip from the man's leg, then a third, the man in such white-hot agony that he passed out. But Božanović would not be denied. He had his team remove the man to a broken-down safe house, where the Serb slipped in and out of consciousness, only to awaken to the smiling and ravaged face of a Croat who never seemed to sleep. The face was poorly stitched, a fieldwork practice by an unskilled hand that gave Božanović somewhat of Frankensteinian appearance in its display. It was something that was horribly twisted and evil about the face, with its downcast eye and upturned lip, his mouth forever in a constant sneer.

After a startling moment of recognition for the Serb, that it was Božanović who stood over him with the knife on display again, Božanović would then run the edge of the blade along the man's torso, stripping him clean until the Serb finally died from his wounds three days later.

It was then that Božanović established himself as one to be feared, a man who articulated his power by posting communication through others, using their bodies as the canvases on which he sent his messages. The knife now served as the paintbrush that provided the broad strokes of his personal and artistic meaning.

And he never surrendered that knife, having used it over and over again until he had perfected his craft, becoming a Picasso in his field.

These thoughts, these images, drove him to become stronger and richer and more powerful—to become omnipotent and omniscient at the same time. This was his dream. This was his goal.

So, he strove for greater heights in 1995, when Croatia won its independence, by becoming a 'cleanup man' working for the Croatian mafia. His determination and perseverance eventually caught the attention of mob leaders who saw reckless propensity within

Božanović's makeup and deemed him a perfect asset when it came to getting specific messages across—especially with the blade of a knife.

In Croatia, the mob was a single unit split between three families, who had become the major kingpins in Afghani heroin trafficking, human trafficking, and money laundering. They also had strong ties to the Italian Mafia and the IRA. Within three years inside the organization, Božanović had his hand in every jar, profiting from every vice. He killed with impunity, whenever someone skimmed from mafia profits.

He became admired and then feared, the man eventually becoming exalted as an elite killer within the hierarchy. Whenever jobs of major importance needed to be performed or when trails of bodies needed to be left behind to send messages, Jadran Božanović was the taskmaster to make it happen. He had become so ruthless in his dealings that his misshapen face eventually mirrored his blackened soul, the man becoming corrupt from the surface of his flesh to the essence of his inner soul.

He was evil personified.

As he sat in the van watching over his new prospects, Božanović issued a terse order to the passenger sitting beside him. "Follow them," he said. "Learn what you can. If they're tourists, I want to know."

"Yes, sir." The passenger exited the van and closed the door behind him.

Other than recruiting victims through others, surveillance was also crucial to the industry. They often chose those from other countries, who had no umbilical ties to the area. The inability to speak the language and the unfamiliarity of the locale often delayed any progress target's families had with local law enforcement and prevented an immediate search.

Through the open passenger-side window, Božanović spoke. "I have another matter to attend to," he told his companion. "Find out where they're staying, then contact me. I'll send a team to maintain a perimeter. When the time is right, we'll act."

The Croat nodded. "Yes, sir."

"Do not lose them."

Božanović started the van. And with his down-turned eye that sparked evil incarnate, he gave the man a hard stare a moment before he set the vehicle in gear and sped off, leaving his foot soldier behind.

For hours, the man trailed the family: the mother, the father, and the proposed targets of the two girls. First, they went to a sidewalk café and ate. And then as the day grew late, they headed back to their hotel on the Rue Cler.

The foot soldier tried to appear as inconspicuous as possible as he entered the lobby moments after the family, maintaining distance, and keeping an eye on them from behind the dark lenses of his glasses. After the family entered the elevator, the man contacted Božanović via cell phone. The conversation was short, the answers between them clipped.

Jadran Božanović now knew where his prospects were.

Though the foot soldier could not see Božanović, he knew the Croat was smiling due to the Euro signs floating about his mind's eye. It was always about the money.

Once the children were taken, once Parisian officials finally galvanized themselves to locate them, the trail of the young foreigners would have grown so cold that they would never be seen again.

CHAPTER FOUR

Shari Cohen and her family were staying at the Hotel de La Motte Picquet on the Rue Cler, the area a well-renowned marketplace in Paris.

The night had grown late, and the girls were in bed in the adjoining suite.

Gary looked exhausted, with gray half-moons under his eyes as he slipped beneath the covers next to Shari. "The girls are away," he said. "Off to la-la land."

She sidled up beside him and traced the tips of her fingers in circles over his chest. "You look tired," she said.

"Tired isn't the word. I'm exhausted. It was a long day."

"I think the girls are having fun," she added.

"They are. Steph is just being difficult. I know that. I keep telling myself that it's just a phase. But she's starting to warm up a bit."

"We have to be patient," she told him. "It's part of being a parent."

Now it was his turn to roll his eyes. "Kids," was all he said. He turned to her with his eyes laced with red stitching from fatigue. "I want to ask you something."

She shrugged. "Go ahead."

"The girls are getting older now—you know, teenagers starting to spend time away. So, I was wondering, since being a stay-at-home dad is no longer as useful, about doing something different."

"Like what?"

He turned his eyes turned toward the ceiling and looked at the wonderful carvings of celestial beings and angels. "I want to go back to work," he told her. "I think it's time."

She continued to trace her fingers in circular patterns over his chest. "If that's what you want to do, go ahead. I agree. The girls are fledglings, starting to spread their wings."

He turned back to her. "I want to go back to the CIA," he told her squarely.

She didn't say anything for a long moment. Prior to the kids being born, Gary was a Company man who had harbored many secrets with his high-security clearance. His hours were long, the job stressful. But he had been happy.

"If that's what you want to do, then do it. You know I won't hold you back."

Shari understood his position, because she was the FBI's leading Hostage Rescue Team (HRT) responder in D.C., who was called to negotiate in extreme cases—especially those of high-profile. One such case took place several years ago when she had orchestrated the release of Pope Pius from domestic forces that had ties to Capitol Hill, a secret she was never to divulge.

Though the hours were also long and her job stressful, she was like her husband in the sense that she was quite happy.

"I want to work," he said. "It's time."

She tapped her fingers steadily against his chest. "If that's what you want to do, Gary Molin, then do it."

He smiled. "I was talking to Dennis about three weeks ago," he said. "I'll have to go through training at Langley again, which is no big deal. It'll last about six weeks to get me current."

"I think it's a good idea," she told him.

He turned and kissed her forehead. "So, what's on the agenda for tomorrow then?"

"Well, the girls want to do the marketplace alone, which is negatory. And then we're off to the Louvre. And if time permits, off we go to the Notre Dame Cathedral."

"Sounds like fun."

"Tell that to the girls."

He chortled. Not his department.

She leaned closer and kissed him, Gary returning her response with a passionate kiss which, in turn, led to incredible lovemaking.

Outside their windows, the City of Lights continued to burn.

CHAPTER FIVE

Jadran Božanović lay in his hammock surrounded by spartan fixtures, a small table with two chairs, a refrigerator that hummed with a waspy drone, and a TV that had four workable channels. As he lay there, he became fixated with the spinning revolutions of the fan blades above him, one wobbling because it was loose.

He'd left his foot soldier behind to deal with the surveillance of the new assets because he had to clean up a situation. He needed to stage a punitive matter before others, due to what had happened onboard the *Aleksandra* two months ago. Even though the operation had been compromised, fourteen people died during the custody of *his* caretakers. He groomed these people to watch over his profits. But they had failed in their endeavors to keep those profits alive, which was unacceptable. Though the entire batch of profits was lost due to invading forces, fourteen people lost their lives to poor handling procedures before the auction. If they had survived long enough to stand upon the blocks, he would have made two million euros. But with his windfall lost, a statement had to be made: *Do not let my assets die!*

He raised his hands to the air as he lay there, turning his arms over and examining them. His hands and forearms were bloodied up to the elbows with the blood drying to reddish-purple, that of burgundy wine, with the man wearing the stains like a badge.

He had two men imprisoned in the hull of an aged boat, which was docked at an old graveyard slated for ships. Their hands were tied by flex cuffs, the men weeping, each one knowing his fate. Božanović stood over them with a heavy audience surrounding them, a classroom in which he was the professor teaching an unforgettable lesson.

The men wept and pleaded, as they made promises to conform, but Božanović felt no contrition or remorse. Removing his knife and holding it on display, he'd begun to carve the first man by stripping his flesh, the bands of skin coming off easily, simply rolling off his bones.

He then did the face, the chest, and the abdomen, the man looking horribly mutilated by the time he died, a slow death.

The second man screamed for forgiveness before the blade had touched his skin, the tears streaming along his cheeks. With a smile of malicious amusement, Božanović had looked down upon his soldier, as if deliberating his fate, then telling him that his actions were irresponsible, and that life was money.

And then he'd proceeded to cut the man, stripping him clean, too, each cut a message to those watching that unreliability would not be tolerated. Božanović was all about messages. The knife his brush, the man's body his canvas.

When it was all done, Božanović had asked if there were any questions as to what he wanted in the future. And as expected, no one had had any. The message was quite clear: *Money was optimum, and mistakes would not be tolerated.*

He allowed his arms to fall idly by his sides as he lay there. Above him, the blades continued to rotate in slow revolutions, with one blade threatening to wobble loose from its mounting.

Tomorrow, before he went to work, he would wash his arms and clean himself. But for now, he would sleep with the comfort of knowing that he was covered by the warmth of another man's blood.

CHAPTER SIX

The Rue Cler Marketplace
Paris, France
The Following Day

Both Shari and Gary kept a watchful eye on their daughters but gave them enough distance to make themselves believe that they were independently shopping on their own.

The girls giggled, feeling a sense of liberation. Here they were, two girls, shopping in a foreign land and buying items with Euros, each one feeling adult and mature.

But they weren't the only ones watching. Božanović's man was tailing the family, the man watching the parents and the girls at the same time. The problem was, they were in a crowded marketplace and separated by a fair distance. So it was hard to observe everyone at the same time.

Removing his cell phone, the man dialed a number already programmed into his phone.

"Yeah."

"We're at the Rue Cler Marketplace," he told Božanović. "It's too crowded."

"I'll send a team and a van. When the family leaves the marketplace, direct the handlers and have them follow. They'll know what to do."

"Yes, sir."

After hanging up and placing the phone in his shirt pocket, the man meandered about, looking at items while trying to keep a steady eye on the prize.

The girls were ecstatic, buying French trinkets and baubles, things to adorn the shelves of their bedrooms when they got back home.

Three hours later and finding themselves low on cash, they scouted their parents down and discovered that they were just a stone's throw away.

"Now what?" asked Stephanie. "We're almost out of money."

"Well, we were thinking about taking a trip to the Louvre, and then to the Notre Dame Cathedral," said Gary. "They're very historic places, you know."

She rolled her eyes: *Whatever.*

At this juncture, Gary had to smile. He just had to. Stephanie was no doubt enjoying herself, but she was *so* adamant about keeping up appearances by flexing her attitude muscles. He couldn't hold back any longer and showed the fine whites of his teeth.

"What?"

He nodded. "Nothing."

In time, they got on a bus with none of them wise to the fact that they were being trailed, as Božanović's man took a seat in the rear and kept his eye on them.

Once at the Louvre, the bus driver announced their arrival in three different languages: French, Italian, and English.

They disembarked by the Grand Louvre Pyramids and entered the Sully Wing to the east.

Božanović's man kept pace, blending in with the crowd and coming so close to the girls that he could smell their perfumes.

When he fell back, he got on the cell with Božanović. "We're in the east wing of the Louvre," he told him. "I heard them say that they had to meet the bus in four hours on the Cour Carrée et Pyramide du Louvre."

Božanović hesitated a moment on his end, then, "The Carousel will be busy with cars," he finally said. "Too many witnesses."

"They also mentioned a trip to Notre Dame Cathedral afterward."

"Better. I'll send a team to the Cour Carrée within the hour and have them follow the bus to the cathedral. Once they arrive, we'll act. Stay close, Tolimir. If there's a change in plans before the team gets there, let me know."

"Yes, sir."

"They will arrive in a black van, very nondescript. You know the routine."

"I do."

"They will call you when they arrive."

Before Tolimir could respond, Božanović had hung up.

They could only appreciate so much art, so many statues and displays. They left the Louvre one hour before they were supposed to and began to tour the side streets.

The day was sunny and warm, the overhead sky blue. But the canopy of trees along the sidewalks provided a wonderful shade.

"Do you see him?" Gary said softly, almost under his breath.

She nodded.

They had first seen the man inside the Louvre by the Mona Lisa. He was hard looking, with a face that was deeply lined and craggy, his hair unkempt. He wore clothes that were not in tune with the tourists or the French, but someone who dressed outside the box. He wore faded jeans, military boots, and a well-worn jacket—hardly the artistic-looking type.

Gary looked at Shari's purse. "Did you leave the money in the safe back at the hotel?"

"Most of it," she said. "Keep the girls close."

"Girls!"

They turned.

"Stay close," he told them.

They took the next right, planning to maneuver quickly around the block and back to the bus.

The man was on a cell phone and hung back at an even distance, then took the same right turn they did.

"He's following us," Gary whispered.

"You think he's got a weapon?"

He shrugged. "If he wants whatever you have in your purse, give it to him. I don't want to put the kids in jeopardy."

They quickened their pace.

Tolimir was in constant communication with the van, which was moving quickly to their location. "We are circling behind the Louvre on the side streets, moving west. They know I'm following, so hurry."

The van was as nondescript as Božanović had stated, as it rounded the corner and came into Tolimir's view. It rolled behind him at a pedestrian's pace. As described, it was primed with flat-black paint with no windows and wheels that had no caps.

"You see them?" asked Tolimir.

"Yeah. We got them."

"You know what to do." Tolimir closed the phone and crossed the boulevard. He then headed down a side street, picked his pace up into a jog, and headed south.

Gary felt an incredible sense of relief. "He's gone," he told Shari.

"I don't care. We need to get back to the bus."

As the last word escaped her lips, tires skidded to a halt beside them, a van door sliding back on its track as four men rushed out and overwhelmed them. Two immediately grabbed the girls, the other two stalling Shari and Gary with assailing hammer blows and well-placed punches.

Gary doubled over and fell to his knees, his eyes witnessing his girls being whisked away inside the van. Another punch was thrown, this time clipping him on the shoulder as he saw it coming and juked to his left, the blow a mere graze. The men were wearing ski masks and were well-muscled, their fists coming fast and furious, delivering blow after blow. Shari took the brunt of the force and it sent her to the ground, screaming for her daughters. Gary reacted by swinging out his leg and kicking his assailant's legs out from under him, sending the man hard onto his back and knocking the air out of his lungs.

Gary quickly got to his feet, his attacker down for the moment. He confronted the other man.

Shari was down as well, injured, yet her hand reached imploringly out to the van.

The man turned on Gary, came forward, then went into a skilled boxer's mode, coming up and across with a series of blows that Gary could hardly defend. He took a right cross, a stinger that sent a cluster of internal stars sparking inside his head, then a follow-up left that sent him crashing to the ground, his vision suddenly blurred.

The attacker helped his partner to his feet, aided him inside the van, closed the door, and gunned the engine. The tires screeched until they finally picked up traction.

Shari got to her knees. Her face was bloodied at the nose and the corner of her lip. She cried out in a pitch that was as keening as the wail of a banshee.

When the van skidded out of view around the corner, Shari's hand dropped in defeat, its backside hitting the pavement hard, as the indescribable pain of a mother's loss consumed her wholly.

Her babies were gone.

As Tolimir walked along the street, his cell phone rang. "Yeah."

"We've acquired the packages."

"Any problems?"

"Nothing we couldn't handle."

That was all Tolimir needed to hear, as he closed his phone and pocketed it.

At the end of the street, a sedan was waiting for him. He opened the door and got into the backseat. The two people sitting in the front never acknowledged him.

"The packages have been acquired," Tolimir said. "So, deal with the matter accordingly. Once the issue has been dealt with, let me know immediately, and you will get paid as always."

The driver and the passenger said nothing, didn't even move.

Then from Tolimir: "How long before you can get back to me on this?"

The driver hesitated a moment as though deliberating, then said, "Two, maybe three hours."

Tolimir nodded. "Call me when the matter's complete." Tolimir eased back into his seat. "Now drive," he told the man. "Take me to the Place de Varsovie and drop me off."

Neither the driver nor the passenger spoke, as the vehicle eased back into traffic and headed north.

None of them were aware they had been captured by a traffic cam.

CHAPTER SEVEN

The interrogation room was small and dingy and spartan, the walls peeling chips of khaki and off-white paint. A small window rode high on the wall, its glass pane embedded with chicken wire. And the table and surrounding chairs held slight wobbles to them.

A lieutenant entered the room holding three cups of coffee and dispensed them across the tabletop; one for Shari, who didn't touch or acknowledge it; one for Gary, who followed Shari's lead; and one for himself.

The man was somewhat on the thin side with stringy and wispy limbs, the beginnings of a receding hairline, and a mustache that was grown to cover an obvious harelip. His eyes, however, were bottle green and sparkled with genuine compassion. When he spoke, he did so with the lilt and flair of a French accent intermingled with English words. There was something poetic in the way he talked—smooth, kind, and gentle.

"Madame Cohen, Monsieur Molin, I am Lieutenant D'Aubigne . Please accept my apologies for what has happened to your daughters."

Shari's eyes were red and raw from too many tears. Gary had never seen Shari like this before. It was a side of her that was completely alien to him. She had always been rock-solid with her emotions, always kept in check under the most severe conditions. But this was something different. This was personal.

"How many were there?"

"Four," she answered.

"And the vehicle?"

"It was a black van," Gary stated. "It was primed. No windows. No hubcaps. No dents from what could see. We told you this before. Why aren't you out there looking for them?"

"We are," said D'Aubigne. "Sometimes we re-ask questions

because when time passes and the mind begins to settle, the victims will remember something they initially omitted the first time around. Often it is something that will aid us in the search."

D'Aubigne took a seat. "I understand that you work in law enforcement, Madame Cohen?"

She nodded. "The FBI."

D'Aubigne gave off the impression that he was impressed. "And you, Monsieur Molin?"

"Former government employee."

"I see."

"What exactly are you doing about our daughters?" he asked, his voice rising.

The lieutenant raised his hands and patted the air. "Believe me, Monsieur Molin, we have all our resources looking for them as we speak. I know it's hard. But we have to be patient in such matters."

"Such matters? This happens all the time, does it? People get lifted off the streets by strangers?"

"Monsieur Molin, I know it's difficult—"

"Do you have children, Lieutenant?"

"Four."

"Are they all at home?"

"Two. Two are away at school."

"So, they're all right, then? No problems?" Gary was beginning to tax D'Aubigne, he knew. He could tell by the way the man was chewing on his lower lip as if to bite back his words. But he was angry and needed to vent.

Then in an even and steady measure that was almost without feeling, D'Aubigne said, "There are no problems."

"Then you don't know what *difficult* is until you go through what my wife and I are going through right now."

"Yes, of course, you are right, Monsieur. But as I sit here, and because I am a father, it doesn't take away the fact that I feel complete sorrow for your situation. I do. Most fathers would. But I'm trying my best to reach out to you and make things right. We're trying our best."

Shari reached across the table and cupped the lieutenant's hand. "Thank you," she told him. With the cuff of her sleeve, she wiped away tears that were brimming along the edges of her eyes.

"Trust me, Madame; we're doing all we can. Unfortunately, there are no other witnesses other than yourselves. And Paris is a large city."

She bowed her head and let out a sob, causing Gary to sweep her into his embrace.

"So, what usually happens at this point?" asked Gary. "Will they call the hotel for a ransom? What?"

Lieutenant D'Aubigne turned toward a camera situated at the upper corner of the wall, raised his hand, and made a motion as though he was beckoning someone. "Monsieur Molin, Madame Cohen, I think there's something you need to know. Something you're not going to want to hear."

The door opened and two men entered the room, each one a facsimile of the other. They were both smartly dressed—same black suit and red tie, with each man carrying waxy appearances and conservative haircuts. At first, they conversed in French with D'Aubigne, who gave them an accurate outline of communication up until this point. When he was finished, he got to his feet with his eyes cast downward in a solemn manner. "Madame Cohen and Monsieur Molin," he pointed to the men, "these fine people will assist from here on in. So please, and I mean this candidly, I am terribly sorry for what has happened, and we are doing everything possible to locate your children." Without anything further, Lieutenant D'Aubigne exited the room as the two men took the vacant seats at the table in his proxy.

One man extended his hand to Gary, who accepted it. The other man remained idle.

"Monsieur Molin and Madame Cohen, please accept our apologies as well. We are looking for the van as we speak," said the idle man. "I am Inspector Beauchamp, and this here is Inspector Reinard. We are from the Direction Centrale de la Police Judiciaire."

"What about Lieutenant D'Aubigne?"

"Lieutenant D'Aubigne will no longer be handling this case," he told them. "We will be."

"Why the switch?"

"Kidnapping, Monsieur Molin, is our department. It is our chief field of investigation."

"We told the police at the scene, we told Lieutenant D'Aubigne, everything we know."

"Yes, we know."

Shari turned toward the inspectors with her eyes, and especially her heart, already knowing the truth. "We're never going to see them again, are we?"

Inspector Beauchamp met her eyes straight on. "Madame Cohen—" He cut himself short, the sudden inability to tell her the truth difficult. But it was something that had to be said. "Madame Cohen, I am told that you are FBI, yes?"

She nodded.

"Then you know that such kidnappings, almost all kidnappings…involve ties to cartels that deal with human trafficking. The profit no longer lies with contacting individuals who may or may not have the funds to pay off the bounty of a loved one. The profit now lies with the victims being auctioned off to those in need of certain laborers. It's guaranteed money."

Gary leaned forward. "Are you telling me that my girls were abducted by a human trafficking ring?"

"All I'm saying to you, Monsieur, is that the probability of this happening…it is the most likely scenario."

Shari lowered her face into her hands and sobbed. *She knew all along*, thought Gary. *That's why she's a mess.*

"Your wife works with the FBI. So, she knows the reality of today's world and the statistics involved in such cases."

"What statistics?"

Inspector Beauchamp looked at Shari. "That we have to find your children within ninety-six hours."

He shrugged. "What happens after ninety-six hours?"

Shari's sobbing became louder.

She knows, Gary thought. But he had to hear it for himself. "What happens after ninety-six hours?" he repeated.

"After ninety-six hours, Monsieur Molin…the trails as to the whereabouts of your children will grow cold, and they will disappear from the grid entirely."

"What do you mean by entirely?"

"They will never be seen again."

Shari finally broke, crying uncontrollably.

"Are you telling me that we only have four days to find them?"

"We are already looking for the van," he proposed.

"That's not good enough. You must have an idea as to who heads up these crazy organizations."

"Monsieur Molin, Paris is a big city with lots of places to hide. Crime here is no different than crime in the United States. Like your country, the numbers are high, and our resources are limited. But we *are* looking."

Gary sounded drained. "Limited resources. What exactly does that mean?"

"It means that we can do only so much with what we have." The inspector then shrugged in a manner that suggested *isn't-it-quite-obvious-what-it-means?*

Gary was becoming more animated, his hands moving wildly about. "Are you telling me that your resources are so limited that you're simply going through the motions? Is that what you're telling me? What you're telling us?"

Beauchamp shook his head. "Of course not, Monsieur Molin, not at all. I'm saying that I can only do so much with what I have. And right now, all I have are the vague descriptions of a van and the four men who were inside that van, all wearing ski masks, no less."

Tears were beginning to well in Gary's eyes too. "These are my children we're talking about."

"I understand that, Monsieur Molin. And I am so sorry."

"That's all you have to say?"

"Monsieur Molin, more than five hundred children disappear from the streets of Paris every day. *Every...single...day.* I'm sorry for what has happened to your family. But you have to understand that every parent feels the same way as you do, that they deserve exclusive assistance in such matters. And as much as my department would like to aid them by doing so, we just can't accommodate everyone with what we have. We try. We really do. But all I can guarantee you and your wife is what I can guarantee everyone else who happens to be in your position: that we will do our best with what we have to find your children. This I promise you."

When Beauchamp got to his feet, it was also a cue to Reinard that it was time to leave.

"Go back to your hotel," Beauchamp told them. He then left them a card. "Call my department should you remember anything else. Anything. I'm sure Lieutenant D'Aubigne will assist you with a ride back to your hotel."

Beauchamp turned on his heels and left the room with Reinard walking with a gait and manner that was oddly similar to Beauchamp's.

Gary watched them leave. And then he pulled his wife close.

At least they had each other.

CHAPTER EIGHT

"She's FBI!" said Beauchamp.

"It matters not," said Tolimir, who was sitting in the rear seat of the inspector's vehicle. Reinard remained vigilantly silent as they parked in a vacant lot that had a panoramic view of Paris in the far distance. The Eiffel Tower was shrouded with late-afternoon smog.

"'It matters not'? Are you serious?"

Tolimir handed Beauchamp an envelope by tossing it over the seat and into the inspector's lap. Reinard, from his position, gave a sidelong glance at the money-filled packet without turning his head.

"That is your normal fee," said Tolimir. "You know the routine. Slow the progress of the investigation for four days. By that time the products will be moved."

Beauchamp whipped around and looked Tolimir in the eyes with a hard and steely gaze. "Did you hear what I said? She's FBI. Do you know what that means?"

"I suppose you're going to tell me."

"It means that she's most likely going to call in liaisons to hasten the matter. You're asking me to put my head on the chopping block by prolonging the investigation."

"Monsieur Beauchamp, sometimes there are obstacles. And obstacles were made to be conquered. Jadran Božanović has paid you handsomely over the years, for your assistance in prolonging investigations for the four days necessary to move our products. Once the products are moved, you have nothing to worry about. You have done well in the past, so I'm sure you will do just as well in the future."

"Are you not listening to what I'm saying? Regardless of what I do, the agency will move on this. And that's my point. My hands are tied on this one. You chose poorly."

42

"Božanović never chooses poorly. He's a man with a keen eye for detail and profit."

"Then I'll need more money," said Beauchamp. "I'll need to grease more palms to see this through."

Tolimir smiled. "So, this is what it's all about, is it? To raise your price?"

"I can't do this alone. Not this one."

"Then pay them with what I gave you."

Beauchamp swooped up the thick envelope and held it up. His face appeared red and angry. "This is not enough!"

"It's more than enough," Tolimir told him. "You will not receive one Euro more for your efforts."

Beauchamp tossed the envelope into Tolimir's lap. "Then you're on your own."

Tolimir said nothing as he waited the man out with their eyes holding steady. Then: "Do you really want to do this, Monsieur Beauchamp? Is this...*really*...what you want to do?"

Beauchamp faced forward, pretending to look over the landscape of Paris without care, often giving nervous and periodic glances to the rearview mirror.

In the mirror's reflection, he could see Tolimir reaching for his cell phone. "Who are you calling?"

"Who do you think?"

Beauchamp whipped around. "All I'm asking is for more money to see this through. That's all I'm asking."

"Fine. Then you can tell Božanović yourself. But I think you already know the answer."

At this moment, Reinard left the vehicle, walked a good distance away, and lit a cigarette.

"Even your partner knows," Tolimir told him evenly. "He's trying to distance himself from you."

Beauchamp closed his eyes, sighed, and held out his hand. "Give me the money," he said. "I'll do it."

Tolimir smiled and handed him the packet. "Four days. That's all we need."

"I'll try."

"There is no trying. Either you do or you don't. And you know what happens when you don't."

Beauchamp knew exactly what would happen. He didn't want to

become one of Božanović's extraordinary pieces of artwork. Beauchamp laid on the horn and beckoned Reinard to get back into the vehicle.

After stubbing out the cigarette and getting back in the unit, things remained quiet back to the city as Beauchamp realized that he had made his deal with the devil. There was nothing he could do about it.

Nothing at all.

Inwardly he sighed, having no choice but to resign himself to his fate.

CHAPTER NINE

Shari had not said a word since they left the station, their hotel room holding a tomblike silence as Gary stood on the balcony overlooking the city of Paris. He wondered where his girls were, thinking that he should be out there looking for them.

In the meantime, Shari had grown cold and distant with a stoic detachment about her. Her face was unemotional, the tears were now gone; leaving Gary to wonder whether the fortitude of the fighter in her was beginning to die inside.

He looked at her as she sat statue-like on the couch. Her eyes were fixed on nothing in particular. It was the look of wheels churning.

"Honey?"

She looked at him with indifference.

"They'll find them," he told her. Even his tone lacked conviction.

She looked away.

We'll find them.

Shari suddenly moved into action by picking up the phone. She asked to be connected to Larry Johnston, who currently served as the FBI Director of Field Operations in Washington, D.C. She even provided the man's number.

On the fourth ring, he picked up. "Hello."

"Larry, thank God you're there."

"Shari... How's Paris?"

"They're gone," she told him, her voice beginning to crack. "They took my babies."

"What... Who?"

"My babies," she said. "The police think they were taken by a human trafficking ring."

"What? Are you serious?"

"Larry, please. I need your help with this. The inspector overlooking the case says they're doing all they can, but they have limited resources. And we both know what that means. Is there any way you can send a team to expedite matters?"

"You know that answer to that, Shari. The FBI has no jurisdiction in foreign countries. The only way we can get it is if the hosting country agrees to our intervention, and it also needs to be approved by the congressional body. And for that to happen, it needs to be something cataclysmic, like a nine-eleven event."

Her voice began to crack. "Please, Larry."

"You need to contact the American Embassy," he told her. "That's our liaison there. I'm sure they'll do whatever needs to be done to get this investigation off the ground with both barrels blazing."

"Anything, please."

"In fact, I'll call them. Where are you?"

She gave him the hotel and the room number. "They said that we have four days until their trail grows cold," she added.

"I'll do what I can," he told her. "And I'm so sorry."

"Thank you." She hung up the phone by placing it gingerly onto its cradle.

There would be no team coming, no outside help. Protocols had to be followed no matter who you were or who you knew. The marginal spark of hope that had kindled inside her was all but snuffed out. She knew the embassy had limited powers, no matter their effort to light a fire under the carcasses of foreign law enforcement. No matter what, she knew, the situation would be forgotten by day's end, as newer and more important issues surfaced.

She closed her eyes.

My babies...

...they're gone forever.

And then she wept long and hard, with an incredible sense of loss and emptiness.

Božanović and Tolimir were sitting outside a Parisian eatery enjoying their cups of latte, while the surrounding patrons endeared themselves to the pages of *Le Monde*. As Tolimir spoke, Božanović listened as he was updated about Shari Cohen, a potential problem since she was

FBI. But in the end, Tolimir assured the Croat as promised by giving them a few days for the trail to run cold before they would start to examine the case.

Božanović was not disturbed by this news at all. He knew that the American Embassy would get involved, but he had greased so many palms, proffered so many messages with the blade of his knife to keep law enforcement compliant to his needs, that their requests would fall on deaf ears. "And the girls?"

"They're fine. They're sedated."

"Very good. Keep them well, Tolimir. Should they or any of my stock grow ill, I will hold you solely responsible. You know I will."

"I understand." And he did, clearly. He had been there when Božanović butchered men before. It was a lesson about responsibility and reliability. If you wanted in, then reliable you must be. If not, then he would remove you in a way that promoted fear in others. And fear, at least in Božanović's eyes, was a great motivator.

"We will have our time," he added. "Are we almost at capacity?"

"We have fifty-five with a few more to go. We should be good in two, maybe three days. But we'll be there."

Božanović nodded his approval. They would take this group and transport them to Italy by boat, where they would be joined with others who had already been prepared for delivery for the auction blocks in the Middle East and North Africa.

And then the man with the horrifically scarred face smiled. It was genuine, at least by what Tolimir could tell, but he didn't know for what reason.

But Božanović said it all. "I do love my job," he said. With his hands clasped behind the small of his back, Božanović simply walked away.

CHAPTER TEN

It was late in Paris, and the lights rivaled those of Las Vegas, the city that never sleeps.

Gary and Shari remained separated, sitting at opposite ends of the room, reflecting.

The clock read 3:13 a.m.

"Did the Embassy call?" he finally asked.

She hesitated. Then: "No." *You know they didn't.*

"Maybe they'll call in the morning."

"We've already lost a day," she told him. "We—the girls—have three days left before they're gone."

Gary turned away. His 'we'll find them' comment had finally run its course by growing stale and hollow, the words no longer having any meaning or weight behind them, the once hopeful tone now gone.

"I'm going to bed," she said unemotionally. Gary said nothing in return as she stood and went to the bedroom. Her steps were slow, like the walk of a woman making her way toward the gallows. In less than twelve hours she had aged exponentially, her once copper tone now pale and waxy, her cheeks sallow. Dark rings formed around eyes that were red and rheumy.

She sat on the edge of the bed, the lights of the room off as Paris sparkled through the glass door of the patio. She stared at nothing specific, as everything became detached.

The American Embassy had not called to placate them, or to inform them that they had done everything within the scope of their political power to assure that everything was being done to find their children. Had not called to tell them that they had flexed their muscles to the fullest capacity to get local law enforcement to 'step it up.'

Their efforts, she knew, were as listless as the crawl of a snail. There was no cavalry.

She closed her eyes, her mind searching for the hope that had dwindled to the glow of an ember.

Suddenly her eyes snapped to the size of communion wafers.

She turned on the lamp, grabbed her purse, and dumped the contents onto the bedcover. Lip balm, emery boards, loose change—everything littered the bed. Then she spread the items about with quick sweeps of her hand and divided everything up.

And there it was.

A business card, which had been handed to her by Pope Pius XIII after she had assisted in his rescue, alongside the Vatican Knights several years ago. Pius had given her the card as an exclusive invitation to contact him via liaisons at the Vatican, as a token of his gratitude and a lifelong hand toward friendship. When Pius XIII eventually succumbed to cancer, the mantle of power was eventually handed to Bonasero Vessucci, now Pius XIV, who had orchestrated his predecessor's rescue along with Shari's stalwart support, when he had served as the Vatican's secretary of state. Though they had grown close, she had never contacted the Vatican for one reason: Kimball Hayden.

The man she had been falling in love with while she was married to another.

She tilted the card, knowing that the number was not a direct line to the papal chamber but to a switchboard liaison, who would monitor incoming calls and cull those of nonimportance and disregard them. Those judged with validity would be sent forward.

She tried to smooth out the card, which had formed deep creases. The card itself was essentially nondescript, with nothing but numerical characters on its face side—no names, no addresses. Just numbers that were delicately styled in cursive.

An ember of hope began to shimmer and glow, the spark inside her resuscitating to a flame of renewed vigor.

She immediately grabbed the phone, checked the number once again, and dialed.

The phone rang six times before it was answered.

The person on the other end spoke in Italian, the voice fresh despite the early morning hour.

"Do you speak English?" she asked him.

"I do."

"My name is Shari Cohen," she told him. "And I need to get a message to Pope Pius. *Shari...Cohen.*"

The man on the other end did not question her validity or comment on the unusual time of the call. He simply acted accordingly to his post, taking the message in earnest, reading it back to confirm its accuracy, and writing down her contact number. "The message will be forwarded to the proper authority," he stated.

"Authority? No-no-no, you don't understand. I need Bonasero Vessucci to contact me as soon as possible! Please! I'm a good friend of his—*a particularly good friend!* So please, I beg you since time is of the essence here! Please let him know that *Shari...Cohen* is trying to contact him! That's *Shari*—"

The liaison cut her off. "Yes, Signora, I have your name. I assure you that the message will be forwarded to the proper authority," he said, and then he hung up.

The sound after the disconnect droned, as she allowed the phone to hang close to her ear for a long moment. *Is there no one who will help me?* She then laid the fancy French receiver onto its cradle, as her eyes and soul once again became disconnected by hopelessness. She shut off the lamp. In the darkness, as she sat silhouetted against the backdrop of Paris shining through the glass doors that led to the patio, as the hand of the clock loudly ticked off seconds that seemed eternal, she waited.

CHAPTER ELEVEN

The bare bulb hanging from the ceiling glowed feebly.

The grungy walls.

The closed-in space.

The spartan surroundings of two cots—one for her sister, one for herself.

And nothing more.

Stephanie woke to a world caught within a cataract fog. Everything appeared hazy. And when she tried to raise her head from the pillow, she found it impossible. The pain was so crippling that it caused darkness to close in from the edges of her eyesight, nearly causing her to blackout.

The bulb above her cast an aura of light that was barely strong enough to tell her that she was not alone.

A man—a blur, really—with his head and face distorted in a funhouse mirror sort of way, spoke in a voice that sounded distant and hollow.

He then leaned forward and downward. And despite her hazy vision, as if she was looking through a veil, she could see that his horribly maimed face appeared something less than human. The scar, the downturned eye, the edge of an upturned lip—made him look as if he was pieced together in a horrific way.

And then she felt the painful jab of a needle in her forearm.

The man slowly turned his head back and forth in study. "She should fetch a high price, yes?"

"No doubt. She is a classic beauty."

There was a second person in the room, the phantom voice sounding equally distant, as he stood somewhere beyond her periphery of vision.

"And she's to stay that way. If anyone tries to sample the goods, then they will answer to me. Is that understood?"

"Clearly."

"A taken woman is worth far less on the market." The man stood upright, his features undulating—the raw effects of the sedation beginning to take hold. "And that goes for this one too." He pointed to her sister lying on the adjacent bunk.

And then they were gone, a door slamming, which was then followed by the sound of a deadbolt locking.

Her eyes shifted ceilingward as spreading coldness coursed through her veins. The sedative was working hard to pinch out the last of the overhead light, as purple darkness began to spread inward from the edges of her vision. The illumination of the bulb began to dim to a pinprick, the light becoming a flickering mote.

And then it was gone.

As darkness poured over her, she questioned who this man—this malformed creature—was.

Was it the Devil?

As the thought faded, as a quick chill traced up her spine in a final shiver, the darkness consumed her.

Vatican City
The Papal Chamber

Warm morning light spread across St. Peter's Square, as people began to mill about. The semi-circle design of the Colonnades in the piazza and the Egyptian obelisk, which stood in the center of the *ovato tondo*, served as marquee focal points, as Bernini statues dotted the plaza. The Basilica stood completely majestic in its entirety with its structure breathtaking. And though Vatican City was the smallest country in the world at roughly the size of an eighteen-hole golf course, in Pius's mind it was the most beautiful and the most striking.

When he awoke, he cleansed himself, adorned his papal aprons, and blessed the new day with prayer. His bed-chamber was spacious with scarlet drapery that was scalloped with gold fringes. The floor was covered with veined marble, and ornamental furniture bore the images of cherubs and angels.

Just as he was about to head for the papal office, there was a knock at his door.

It was a bishop from the Holy See. In his hand were three memos. After he handed Pius the messages, the pope kindly thanked the man and lightly closed the door after him. The first memo was regarding a skirmish in the Philippines with a Catholic church coming under the trespasses and vandalism of roving gangs in the south. They were becoming increasingly hostile toward Christians, as radical Muslims were beginning to take root there. It would be a subject to address at a future session with his contemporaries, should hostilities continue in that region.

The second was a memorandum communicating that a cardinal serving in Northern Africa had grown quite ill. Pius would send his blessings.

But it was the third memo that caused a breath to hitch in his chest.

It was from Shari Cohen, the message received more than five hours ago. The old man took the letter and sat on the edge of the papal bed, reading and re-reading the page until the urgency of its content finally settled. Her children had fallen prey to a human trafficking ring in France. And now she was imploring the pontiff for aid that only he could provide.

She was calling upon the Vatican Knights.

Pope Pius XIV, Bonasero Vessucci, held the assistance of the Knights to three criteria: To protect the sovereignty of the Church, to protect the interests of the Church, and to defend the welfare of its citizenry.

Shari would normally come under the third criterion; however, she was a woman of the Jewish faith, which barred her from that particular article. Nevertheless, she had been instrumental in securing Pope Pius XIII from the United States, after rogue American forces had taken him hostage under the guise of a terrorist faction. Without her, the former pope would have died, the woman nearly sacrificing her life and the life of her family to see that he was secured.

Yet the criteria were set, the protocols unyielding. For Vessucci, who acted as the head of the Society of Seven, a clandestine group of cardinals who decided whether or not a situation met the criteria to move the Knights into battle, he would have to lobby hard for their support, since Shari met none of the above.

He stood and went to the phone. Then, after dialing an extension and receiving an answer, he issued a single command: "Tell the Order to meet in the Lower Chamber."

Nothing more was said as he laid the phone down.

CHAPTER TWELVE

The Society of Seven was a secretive sect made up of the pope, the Vatican's secretary of state, and five of the pope's most trusted cardinals. They were gathered around an oval table made of veined marble with legs shaped like Roman columns for study support. The surrounding walls were made of castle stone, the rock gray, with ancient tortures continuing to serve as reminders of a time when electricity was not even a consideration in the minds of men. The ceiling was high and domed, now with recessed lighting. And in the center of the room's floor set in mosaic tiles was the symbol of the Vatican Knights, a Silver Cross Pattée positioned against a powder-blue background with two lions holding up a heraldic shield.

Pope Pius sat at the head of the table with three cardinals sitting to his left, and three to his right.

The debate on whether or not to send the Vatican Knights to Paris had met with opposition among the conservatives in the council, for the simple fact that it did not meet with any of the written criteria of the Vatican's bylaws for engagement.

"There is such a thing as exigent circumstances," Pius stated. "Yes. I understand that her situation does not meet with the sovereignty, interests, or the welfare of citizenry guidelines. But let's not forget that Shari Cohen placed her life and the lives of her family on the line when she aided the Knights in finding Amerigo, Pius XIII, all those years ago when he was taken by a rogue military force in the United States." He leaned forward and clasped his hands together in an attitude of prayer. In a voice that was soft and paternal, he said, "All I'm saying, all I'm proposing, by using exigent circumstances as my groundwork for Vatican support, is that we allow aid to Shari Cohen due to the fact that she has aided the Church in the past."

Cardinal Sambini, a stalwart conservative, believed that any divergence from the written rule was the beginning of the end of stability. If one could justify changing protocol for any reason, then it could be understood that more rules would be changed until the original set of guidelines evolved into something completely unfamiliar. "The easiest thing to do," he said, "is to justify any action, no matter what that action may be—right, wrong, or indifferent. You're laying the groundwork of your argument under the justification of 'exigent circumstances.' But, Your Holiness, once we begin to manipulate the protocols of what governs our judgments as to when to send in the Knights, then there is a breakdown of order within our group. Each one of us is throwing in a reason why we should act accordingly to something that is not set as one of the three criteria: the sovereignty and interests of the Church, and the welfare of its citizenry."

"And your opposition is a strong one, no doubt. But Shari Cohen was made an Honorary Knight, in spirit, by my predecessor. If this is the case, would you not agree that she is now a part of the citizenry?"

Cardinal Gardenzio raised a halting hand. He was tall and thin with somewhat of a scholarly look to him, a learned man who should have been teaching from behind a podium rather than preaching from behind a pulpit. Behind his glasses were emerald-colored eyes that sparked with immeasurable intelligence. Gardenzio, however, like Sambini, was steeped in the political aspect of maintaining strict accordance to the written word or protocol. "I, with all due respect, Your Holiness, concur with the good Cardinal Sambini. I agree that Ms. Cohen's efforts in saving Pope Pius's life years ago deserve merit. However, setting personal emotion aside, let us not forget that we are a Church, first and foremost. We send the Knights into conflict because one, if not all, of the criteria, are met. In this case, none are met. Let us not forget that Ms. Cohen is a woman of Jewish faith. And a person of Jewish faith does not believe that Jesus Christ was the son of God."

"That didn't matter to Shari Cohen at the time she saved the pontiff's life," Pius countered. "She looked upon the pope as a man, a person, and a human being, without denomination. And if you want to use the Church as the foundation of your stance, are we not all the children of God?"

"We are," he answered. "But my stance is purely set within the guidelines of political protocol. My point being, her religious affiliation disallows her citizenry, *regardless* of whether she was made an Honorary Member of the Vatican Knights. It is what it is. The protocols, as they now stand, are what they are. And under the current set of rules, she does not qualify."

Sambini added to this thread. "Besides, you stated yourself that there is a more pressing issue brewing in the Philippines. A church and its members are being harassed by an insurrection of Muslims with very radical viewpoints. It seems to me that the Vatican Knights are needed there, to mandate peace between the groups if possible. What is happening to Shari Cohen is unfortunate, but the need for the Knights is clearly spelled out. Per the criteria, the precedence is that they should be readied to act if the citizenry in the Philippines is threatened any further."

"We have the resources to spread the Vatican Knights out if need be. We can handle both situations."

"Of course, you are the pontiff," stated Gardenzio. "You have the right to overrule us."

Bonasero Vessucci, Pope Pius XIV, waved him off. "If I was to do that, then there would be no point in the Society of Seven. I would simply make the call. And at this table, by the end of the day, it's the majority rule. Arguments are proposed to maintain a balance, so that rules, as you adamantly made your points, don't evolve to the point where certain demands no longer have any weight to them by becoming suggestions, rather than the written law. It is for the good of the Church in the end. But please keep in mind that we are also compassionate people who believe that God is too big for one religion and that He has many faces but only one voice. And as compassionate people, I use 'exigent circumstances' as my point of argument. We're talking about the woman who risked her life to save Amerigo's life when he served upon the papal throne. More importantly, we're talking about two children who are terribly frightened and have no idea what lies before them."

He sighed and appeared somewhat dejected as his face took on a hang-dog look. In his mind he believed his stance was too weak, his audience lost. Then: "There are four other cardinals sitting at this table who have said nothing, but no doubt each one carries an opinion. I cannot deny that the good cardinals Sambini and Gardenzio proposed strong arguments. They did. So, when we vote, I must ask all of you to vote accordingly to what you believe to bear more strength: that the laws can and should be amended under exigent circumstances, or that we continue with the strict observance of the current criteria."

The pontiff stood. "I propose a *yea* for the mobilization of the Vatican Knights to aid in the matter of Shari Cohen."

Cardinal Sambini stood. "I vote *nay*."

Cardinal Gardenzio stood. "*Nay*."

And one by one the cardinals stood to proffer their votes.

In the end, as the cardinals spoke their preferences based on the amendment of 'exigent circumstances' or to keep to the strict adherence of current law, 'exigent circumstances' were upheld by a majority rule. Anyone who would serve the Church in the capacity to better its welfare would now benefit from Vatican aid.

The amendment had been passed.

And Shari would once again be in league with the Vatican Knights.

"Good Cardinal Sambini, would you be so kind as to notify Kimball Hayden and have him report to my chamber immediately? And contact the archdiocese at la rue Barbet-de-Jouy in the 7th arrondissement and have them send the archbishop to Shari Cohen. Time is becoming critical, and we need to amass the teams quickly."

"Of course, Your Holiness."

Pius held his hand out so that the cardinals could kiss the Fisherman's Ring as they passed him by.

When Bonasero Vessucci stood alone in the chamber, he examined the ring by holding his hand in front of him and splaying his fingers wide. The ring was simple in its design yet magical in its symbolism; the authority it wielded within its forged metal was certainly all-powerful within the Vatican and beyond. But as much power as it granted him, he no less felt impotent. His powers to help Shari Cohen beyond prayer were limited. The only *true* power, he considered, rested within one man.

It began and ended with Kimball Hayden.

CHAPTER THIRTEEN

Inside the Papal Chamber
The Vatican

Pope Pius was sitting behind his desk when the knock came at his door. "Yes."

The ornamental door was opened by a security member dressed in a scarlet sports coat, gray slacks, and a black tie. In his ear was a communication bud. "Your Holiness, Kimball Hayden is here to see you, as requested."

"Allow him in, please."

A moment after the security member left, Kimball entered the room and closed the door behind him. "Morning, Bonasero."

Through the years they had become good, if not the best of friends. During the first US war with Iraq, while Kimball served clandestinely under the Joint Chiefs of Staff and for some of the political incumbents that turned a blind eye toward his deeds as a political assassin, Kimball had ventured deep into enemy territory, far enough until his position was compromised by two shepherd boys. In a judgment nurtured by a sense of duty, he killed them.

It had also become the turning point in his life, the very moment he pulled the trigger.

Some people called it an epiphany.

Kimball Hayden called it agony.

In White House circles, he was known as a man who worked with the cold fortitude of a machine—a man with no conscience. And in truth, he was proud of that image and the way it stroked his ego, killing with impunity so that his legend would grow.

But the night after he buried those boys, he lay between the two mounds of desert earth looking skyward, as the stars sparkled with pinprick lights. With a hand on each mound, on each grave, his heart truly asked for forgiveness—not from God, but from the boys who lay beneath the dirt.

He never received an answer. Not from the boys. Not from God. The only sounds he heard throughout the night were the whispers of a desert wind.

By the following morning, when the sky was already white with heat, his outlook as to who and what he was had been completely different from who he wanted to be.

The legend of what he had become no longer mattered to him. So, he absconded from service and was believed to have been killed during the commission of performing his duty by the JCOS, and he was therefore given a memorial with posthumous honors. But the only thing that was buried on that day in Arlington was the legend of what he had become.

In the days to follow under the hot Iraqi sun, Kimball made his way north to safer havens. He eventually wound up in Italy. In a small bar, while watching the Iraqi war finally getting fully underway, a small man wearing a cleric's collar and a genuinely warm smile took the seat opposite him.

At first, Kimball was taken aback and felt territorial since he had claimed the booth as his own and wanted to be alone with his drink. But the man was infectiously kind and warm, almost paternal in the way he conducted himself.

He informed Kimball that he, and they—whoever 'they' were— were watching him. And that he would be welcome into their fold with open arms, as long as he could provide the Church with certain services, specifically his very particular skill set, which would save lives rather than take them away. Kimball recalled that he was stunned by the fact that they—whoever 'they' were—knew every aspect about him, that he was not the nasty little political secret he thought himself to be in Washington, D.C.

And in return for his services, they would give him the one thing he wanted most in life.

They would give him salvation.

By the conclusion of his drink in that tiny bar in Italy, by the time Kimball could feel the inexplicable warmth of camaraderie crawling through him, a friendship as strong as any brotherhood had been created.

But through the years, it had become so much more. It had become a tandem team of a father and his son.

Kimball took a seat made of fine leather before the pontiff's desk.

Pius leaned forward and placed his elbows like wings over the desktop. "How are you, my dear friend?"

"Very good, Bonasero. You're looking good as usual."

Bonasero Vessucci waved a dismissive hand in a friendly gesture. *Stop brown-nosing me. You're not making any points.*

Kimball knew the gesture and the meaning behind it and could almost read the man's thoughts. He laughed.

"It's been a while," the pontiff finally said. "I've been busy. But that's no excuse for not calling upon you for an invite as a friend. I should have."

"You have more important issues to consider than me, Bonasero."

The pontiff's face steadily darkened, which Kimball recognized to be concerns of the most serious nature.

"What's the matter?" he asked him.

The pope fell back into his seat, a winged-backed chair that framed him. "Normally I would call you to the lower chamber where the Society of Seven would propose to you a mission. But there are matters that you and I need to discuss openly—things I did not want to air before the eyes and ears of the assembly."

"Sounds serious."

"Kimball, I need you for a mission. But I cannot call upon you if you're going to be emotionally compromised."

"Emotionally compromised? Have you ever known me to be emotionally compromised on any mission?" He was somewhat insulted by the pope's suggestion.

"Once," he quickly returned. "Just once."

"What are you talking about?"

"I'm talking about Shari Cohen," he said.

Those words struck Kimball hard, like a hammer blow to the solar plexus. Immediately he could feel himself deflate in his chair, the warrior somehow sensing himself growing smaller and more diminutive in size. Though he thought of her often, he never thought that her name would ever be spoken by another again. Over the years she had remained a steady staple of his thoughts, an image he often fed upon to get him through the day. Sometimes she would be his first thought in the morning when he awoke and the last thought at night when he went to bed.

She was also a *very* married woman.

"You brought me up here to talk about Shari Cohen?"

"Kimball…she's in trouble and she needs our help. She needs *your* help."

His interest suddenly piqued. "What's the matter?"

Pius reached across his desktop and grabbed the memo. "She has personally requested that you help her find her children," he said.

Kimball's lips mouthed the word 'children,' as his face surrendered a questioning look.

"We believe they were abducted by a human trafficking ring, while the family was vacationing in Paris."

Kimball remembered the children well. He'd even held them in his embrace after he'd rescued the family from a team of assassins one night in D.C. when he and Shari were getting too close to the truth as to who really kidnapped the pope.

"They're now fourteen and sixteen," Bonasero added.

Have they grown that much since I lost saw them? Has it been that long since I last saw Shari?

"Kimball, this is dire, and we need to act quickly. There is an apparent timeframe in which to find them before the window of opportunity closes. I have asked our liaison in Paris to contact them as soon as possible. I've also requested that the *Servizio Informazione del Vaticano* get involved as well." The SIV was the Vatican's intelligence agency, which rivaled the best agencies in the world, including Mossad and the CIA.

Kimball shot to his feet. "I'll assemble a team immediately."

"Kimball, please. Sit down." The pope waved the large man back to a sitting position. "Though she has requested you, I have to question your ability to lead properly in this situation. I cannot afford you to be emotionally compromised. What I'm trying to say is that I know you care for her more than you should."

Kimball could not deny it. "I can do this. If nothing else, I will do this with the passion for what I am assigned to do."

"I would like to think that you go into every mission with passion."

"You know what I mean."

"Exactly. And that is why I'm pressing this particular issue… Kimball, she's a married woman. And I know it can be difficult to suppress certain emotions, especially when tensions get high, which they surely will be."

"I'm not going to lie to you, Bonasero. That'll be a path I'll have to cross later. But right now, the optimum thing is to find those kids before it's too late. The more time I sit here is more time wasted. I need to assemble my team."

"Kimball, should this fail—"

"It won't, Bonasero. I promise you."

"If I allow you to lead the team, then I must ask you to act accordingly, in the eyes of God. Suppress your emotions in a way that will not destroy your chances of finding the salvation you seek."

Kimball stood, looked at his close friend, and nodded. "I can't do that," he told him. "And I've known you too long to lie to you. With or without your blessing, Bonasero, I have to—I need to undertake this mission."

Kimball could have sworn that he had seen a shadow fall over Bonasero's face, one of overwhelming sadness. "Then I shall pray for you," he said solemnly.

"That's all I ask."

After Kimball left the pontiff's chamber, an odd quiet fell over Bonasero like a pall. He had always seen Kimball as his surrogate son, in constant need of direction—someone he needed to show the way, by giving him a moral compass to guide him. But Kimball continued to skirt the 'Light of Loving Spirits' by continuously making unhealthy decisions along the way. And a man, no matter how many times he's been shown the way to the Righteous Path, had to eventually take its course. But for whatever reason and despite all the judicial guidance of pious men, Kimball Hayden always found a way to get lost.

Bonasero Vessucci began to mouth words that could be heard only between him and his God, and he prayed for Kimball as he had never prayed before.

CHAPTER FOURTEEN

The Hotel de La Motte Picquet on the Rue Cler
Paris, France

Shari Cohen and her husband had been on speakerphone with Larry Johnston, FBI's Director of Field Operations in D.C., on two occasions. He assured them that he and others, especially from the American Embassy in Paris, had been in constant contact with their law enforcement constituencies and were following up on leads. What those were, however, were never expounded upon. He also informed them that their lines were tapped in case someone did attempt to contact them regarding a price demand. But no such call was received.

Shari was becoming more detached, the woman feeling absolutely gutted.

She had not heard from Beauchamp, or as Johnston had stated, from Embassy sources. Worse, she felt completely abandoned by Pope Pius XIV. Despite becoming good friends during their shared alliance, while collaborating on the rescue of Pius XIII, the new pope appeared to have cast her aside, without so much as a consideration or even sending an apology for her situation.

She was tired and clearly fatigued, as she stood in the bathroom looking at her image in the mirror. Her skin was becoming cold and gray looking, the dark rings that circled her eyes even grayer.

Gary was also slipping into his area of remorse as well. The man was becoming just as distant and cold as she was, his behavior equally listless. They had lost their children as though they had been taken by some manner of death. They saw no difference.

Shari peeled away from the mirror, headed to the main suite, grabbed her purse, her jacket, and made for the door.

"Where are you going?" he asked.

"Out," she said. "I can't stay here anymore. Not when my babies are out there…somewhere. Wondering where their mother and father are." Her voice cracked.

"And where will you go?"

"Anywhere… Back to where they took our babies. At least that's a start."

"Everyone says to stay here and to wait for a phone call." Gary sounded so flat and even as he spoke in monotone, he sounded like a man who had lost all hope.

"If you want to wait for a phone call that's never going to come, then you can stay here."

As she was about to open the door, a knock sounded.

When she opened it, she saw a man standing there carrying a briefcase. His hair was gray and conservatively cut. His smile was warm. And the eyes behind his Lennon-like glasses were clear and bright and full of genuine compassion. But when she looked at the man's collar, she noted it was the clerical band of a Catholic priest. When she saw the insignia on the pocket of the cleric's shirt, that of the Silver Cross Pattée set against a powder-blue background with two lions holding up a heraldic shield, she knew what it was.

It was the symbol of the Vatican Knights.

Shari barked a loud cry and fell to her knees, sobbing and shedding tears in the ultimate release. The archbishop quickly went to her aid as did her husband, neither realizing why she had fallen. But Shari knew who this man was and why he was here, as she traced a fingertip over the symbol of this man's shirt, feeling the fine stitching like Braille beneath her touch and the wonderful message it brought with it.

The Vatican had said 'Yes.'

Her hope had been rekindled.

So, she wept.

"Madame, are you all right?"

She reached out and pulled the priest into an embrace, which caught him awkwardly off guard. "I'm fine," she told him as she got to her feet. "I'm so, so fine." And for the first time in more than a day, she smiled, showing even rows of perfectly placed teeth. "You're from the Vatican, yes?"

Gary's ears perked up. *What?!*

"I am, Madame. I am Archbishop Rousseau, from the rue Barbet-de-Jouy in the 7th arrondissement. I have been asked to serve as an emissary from the Vatican. Apparently, you have friends in extremely high places."

"Are you talking about Pope Pius?"

He smiled and nodded. "I am here at his request."

She escorted him to the nearest couch, where he laid his briefcase on the coffee table in front of it and took a seat. "A memo was received through the members of the Holy See with your name on it, a name we have all come to recognize and revere."

Her smile faded. "But?"

"There are no 'buts,' Madame Cohen. It is my absolute honor to be sitting by your side."

"So why are you here?" asked Gary.

"I'm here in response to your wife's request for Vatican aid," he said simply.

"And the answer would be?"

"That your request has been approved. The Vatican Knights are on their way as we speak. You no longer have to feel alone in this," he told them. "You have the complete support of the Vatican, who will now see you through this crisis until the end."

Shari looked euphoric as hope blossomed. Gary felt the same, but with prudence. Of course, they were finally getting what they needed, what they wanted. But the sidebar issue was that the unit's team leader had allowed his affections for Gary's wife to grow unchecked. And though nothing had happened from that relationship, he couldn't quite help that creeping sense of insecurity, which he now had to set aside for the good of his children. "And who, if I may ask, is heading up this task force?"

Archbishop Rousseau opened his briefcase. Inside were a notebook-thin laptop and some loose papers. Grabbing an index card, he read from it. "His name is…Hayden. Kimball Hayden."

Shari closed her eyes as a preamble of a smile began to surface along the corner of her lips. Gary wasn't sure if it was the happy beginnings of an underlying eagerness to see someone, or if the smile was one of brimming confidence, knowing that the job would be done correctly.

Or perhaps it was a combination of both, he considered.

She opened her eyes. "You do know that time is critical in such matters as this, right? We have less than seventy-two hours."

Archbishop Rousseau reached out and patted her arm gently. "And that is why we need to get working right away," he told her. He reached into his case, removed the laptop, and booted it up. "Now," he began, "it'll be a few hours before the Vatican Knights arrive in Paris. In the meantime, we will be working in collusion with the *Servizio Informazione del Vaticano,* the American Embassy, and the Direction Centrale de la Police Judiciaire to expedite matters." He began to type into the computer. "So far, the SIV has determined that the American Embassy has forwarded its concerns to the leading inspectors at the DCPJ on three occasions, but the replies are always the same—those efforts are ongoing. But nothing is explained as to what those efforts are. At least the Embassy is doing its part.

"I also understand that the Vatican, most notably the secretary of state, will also issue a call to the DCPJ, as well. So nearly everyone is doing their part to help you, Madame." He continued to type on the keyboard. "Now if the DCPJ will only do theirs."

"The names of the lead inspectors are Beauchamp and Reinard," said Gary.

The archbishop nodded. "We know. The SIV is searching the data banks of the DCPJ—shall we say, 'under covert circumstances'—for the electronic dossiers on both men. We've also hacked into their files, looking for correspondence to others. Anything that will alert us as to what they may know about the matter but isn't telling the Embassy."

"Why would they hold back?" asked Gary.

"Sometimes agencies feel that intruding organizations who involve themselves in collaborative matters only create delays, as one group tries to out-muscle the other by having certain practices done their way rather than the way of the originating group. And in this case, the originating group is the DCPJ. If they should have information and do not want to share it, then we'll take it." The archbishop shook his head. "But I'm afraid we have nothing—nothing at all."

Shari looked at her watch. Where time had once crawled at a glacial pace, it now appeared to be moving much too quickly toward zero hour.

And still, they had nothing.

The archbishop continued to type, his fingers dancing over the laptop in the same way a skilled pianist strokes the keys of a piano, quick and furious and without error. After a few minutes, the laptop sounded off with a ping: an incoming message.

"Well," he said. "It appears the SIV got hold of some information from the files of the DCPJ, regarding our Misters Beauchamp and Reinard."

"And?"

He read the short summaries on both before speaking. "I'm afraid there's little on Reinard. But your friend Inspector Beauchamp seems to have somewhat of a questionable history regarding alleged affiliations with people of questionable character. But he was acquitted of any wrongdoing on all accounts and reinstated every time without consequence."

"So now what?" she asked.

"We continue to search." The archbishop leaned away from the laptop. "Madame Cohen, Monsieur Molin, please, I need you to think and think hard. Perhaps these are questions that have already been asked by DCPJ, but is there anything else you can add, something you may have forgotten or missed? Perhaps there was a face in a crowd that didn't belong, or maybe a trailing car that appeared suspicious? In most cases like this, the victim is carefully selected and targeted. There is always a scout, who determines whether the target has familial contacts—if she's a runaway, or if she's alone."

"There were four of them," said Gary. "And they wore ski masks."

"No-no-no," said the archbishop, waving his forefinger. "I'm talking about another. Before the abduction, Monsieur Molin. There is one who may watch over you for days, sometimes weeks, before they actually respond. The scout is the eyes and ears of the operation. There may be one, perhaps two. But there are always scouts who pick and choose from the lot, and then they formulate a plan."

"There was no plan," he said. "This was random."

The archbishop shook his finger once again. "In this business, Monsieur, there is no random. There had to be another."

Gary was beginning to get frustrated. "I'm telling you, there was no—"

"Inside the Louvre!" Shari shouted, and then faced off with Gary with a quick snap of her head. "Remember? By the Mona Lisa"

And then it hit him. "Yes, of course."

She turned to the archbishop. "There was this man inside the Louvre," she told him. "Hard looking and improperly dressed, wearing faded jeans and military boots. He seemed so out of character for one who should be there to admire art. And we could tell that he was disinterested, looking from one painting to the next with cursory glances as if to justify why he was there to begin with."

"That's right. The moment we left the Louvre, we noticed that this guy had followed us from the museum. We thought he was going to rob Shari's purse. Shari and I even made mention of that as we were walking down the street."

"Was he on a cell phone?"

They had to think for a moment.

And then: "Yes!" Shari began to recall the moment with clarity. "During the last hour before we took the bus back, we decided to walk the streets running behind the museum."

"Yeah," Gary agreed, and then followed up her line of thinking. "We honestly pegged this guy for a robber. But he never made his move or came any closer."

"In all likelihood, Monsieur, he was keeping an eye on you until the van rolled into view. That's what a scout does. He communicates. Once the team is in position, then the scout disappears, because his face has been exposed. Once he clears the scene, then the abducting unit takes over. They're skilled practitioners, who have performed this routine enough to get it down to a fine art. The abduction takes less than a few moments—the van is usually gone before anyone can get a good look at it. But in most cases, the van is stolen. I can pretty much guarantee you that it's smoldering in a vacant lot somewhere."

"Smoldering?"

The archbishop nodded. "The vehicles are burned to wipe away all traces of evidence and DNA matter. But..." the archbishop began to type a return message to the SIV, "you have given me the tools that I need to find this man."

"What tools?"

"What time did you see this man inside the Louvre?"

"Around noon. What tools?"

"The Louvre," he returned, "is filled with priceless valuables. And priceless valuables are surrounded by cameras. Cameras record images. Therefore, whoever this man is, we will find him."

Shari fell into Gary's embrace. At least a step had been taken in the right direction.

With a final tap of his fingertip, the archbishop hit the 'SEND' button.

"Now what?" asked Gary.

"The information you've given me is now in the hands of the SIV. They'll identify whoever this guy is."

"And once they do?"

"Then Kimball Hayden will find him."

CHAPTER FIFTEEN

Kimball's Chamber
Vatican City

Kimball summarily alerted his top two lieutenants, Isaiah and Leviticus, to gather three additional Knights for a top-priority mission in Paris, and for everyone to be ready to put on their A-game. There were no queries of curiosity or hesitation on the parts of his lieutenants. They simply acted with the speed and discipline of seasoned warriors.

As Leviticus and Isaiah gathered his team, Kimball stood beside his cot, where a set of combat knives were laid out in neat rows. Kimball reached down and grabbed his favorite, a double-edged KA-BAR, and hefted it to familiarize himself with its balance and weight. It felt good in his hand, especially the way it became an extension of him, especially in moments when the enemy was but an arm's length away. He quickly tested the knife by cutting the air with sweeping curves and delicate arcs, the motions so poetically fluid that anyone who saw him would know that he was one of the best when handling such weaponry.

He then grabbed the KA-BAR's twin and strapped one to each leg. Whatever else they would need would be found inside the vault of the archdiocese in Paris.

And then he closed his eyes, sighed, and tried to calm his heart. It was thrumming rapidly against the wall of his chest. He had been to countless battles and had suffered numerous scars and pains. But the pace of his heart was not driven by the anticipation of the fight, but by the expectation of seeing Shari Cohen once again.

In his mind's eye he could see her clearly—could see the uniformity of her cocoa-colored skin, that of tanned leather. And eyes that shined like newly minted pennies. He noted the point of her widow's peak and the pristine whiteness of her teeth whenever she smiled. He remembered everything.

Calming himself with long pulls of air through his nostrils, and then releasing them with equally long exhales, Kimball could feel a sense of peace wash over him.

After opening his eyes, he went to the mirror and gave himself a critical examination, wondering if she would notice the seams that had deepened over the years. With the points of his fingers, he traced the lines, the tips then gravitating to the crow's feet that flared outward from the edges of his eyes.

The one battle he could never win, the one battle whose advancement he could never slow, was the battle against aging.

He stared at his image long and hard, noting the band of the cleric's collar set against the darkness of the cleric's shirt, then considered if he even had the right to wear such a garment. From the waist up he appeared as a priest. From the waist down, a soldier—the military-styled pants blossoming at the tops of military boots, the attire that of a man caught between two worlds, one of divinity and the other of war.

When he first met Shari, they had grown close while working together when the Pope was kidnapped. But in the end, she had chosen the delicate soul of her husband over Kimball's brutal nature.

…I kill people… It's what I do… It's what I'm good at…

He sighed.

Would she think of him differently? Or would she continue to see him as a man who had an underlying savageness to him when called upon?

But the pontiff's voice was noticeably clear, his message even clearer: *she's a married woman.*

So, make your choice, Kimball: damnation or salvation. You either vie for the affections of a married woman, or you continue to seek the Light of Salvation.

In the end, it's always your choice.

But he was losing himself in self-conflict when he should have been outlining a plan of attack. This wasn't about him or Shari. Nor was it about the way he felt or what he wanted. This was about the children. So, he refocused his thoughts by completely handing himself over to a sense of duty. He became what he had always been, a champion to those who could not protect themselves.

He was an elite soldier.

He was a savior.

He *was* a Vatican Knight.

After rearranging his beret to meet with military specs, Kimball left his room preparing for battle.

CHAPTER SIXTEEN

The *Servizio Informazione del Vaticano,* was the Vatican's intelligence service. It had been created to counter early 19th century efforts to subvert the power of the Vatican. So as a precaution, the Church had seen the need in creating an 'unofficial' security agency to solve problems, by conceiving a system of confidential communication and information gathering. And with the constantly growing threat of extremist and radical groups, the SIV has developed into a major organization that rivaled the likes of Mossad, MI6, and the CIA. With diplomatic ties to more than ninety percent of the world's countries, the SIV had become an agency among the world's elite.

Father Gino Auciello, a Jesuit priest and the assistant director of the SIV co-headed the program, which was based inside a restricted chamber south of the Necropolis. The room was state-of-the-art, with banks of TV screens and monitors, and satellite linkups that allowed aerial visuals to any part of the world.

He was the eyes, ears, and mouthpiece of the agency, who reported directly to the pope whenever red flags and concerns came to light. Today, a mighty banner arose and caught the priest's direct attention. The Jesuit was tall, thin, and wiry, with shock-white hair that was conventionally cut. His face was smooth and lean, his complexion the color of light cocoa. And though he was pious to the core, he was also a scholar from Harvard University, who had graduated from the School of Theology with minors in the sciences of politics and world studies.

At the moment, he was colluding with Archbishop Rousseau from the rue Barbet-de-Jouy in the 7th arrondissement in Paris. The matter at hand was not politically seismic enough to cause a marginal threat to the interests of the Church but rather was because one of their own was in jeopardy.

The message received from Rousseau regarded a person of interest who might have been caught by security cameras within the Louvre. A specific date and time were given. So, Father Auciello manned the keyboard and hacked into the Louvre's system and backup files, appropriating still-images from the given timeframe.

There were hundreds of photos, one taken every three seconds for the period of fifteen minutes, the clean snapshots totaling three hundred.

Once the files were gathered, they were sent to the archbishop for closer examination.

Ping!

Vous avez du courrier! You've got mail!

Archbishop Rousseau quickly downloaded the files and brought up numerous photos in black-and-white, then aligned them in chronological order from left to right. "These are the stills taken from the security cameras by the Mona Lisa, during the timeframe you have given," he said, his fingertip touching the screen. "As you can see, there are many photos from different angles."

Gary and Shari studied the stills.

"Can you zoom in?" asked Shari.

When he did, the photos appeared a little fuzzy. So, he hit the proper keys to bring them into focus. "How's that?"

They spotted themselves and their daughters right away, toward the front of the crowd, standing by Da Vinci's glass-encased painting.

Shari narrowed her eyes. "But I don't see him."

"There are plenty of stills to study." The archbishop patiently scrolled through the images one at a time.

While going through the images, Gary spotted the man and nearly put his finger through the monitor's screen with a harsh stab. "Right there!" he hollered. "That's him!"

The still was that of a hard-looking man with a wild look and a face badly creased with fault lines. He was oblivious of the camera, a good photo. And there were other images that were clear and precise as well.

They gathered more than sixty images from different angles. And with a tap of a button, Archbishop Rousseau sent the photos forward.

Father Auciello brought the images up on the main screen. The man appeared feral, with eyes possessing something savage and wild to them, dark pools that had no shine or polish, no gleam to say that this person was even alive, but rather deadened and numb underneath.

After downloading the photos into a facial recognition program, the system began to ferret through the images to pinpoint certain landmarks on the man's face, to identify him. Photos began to race across the screen with blinding speed; the confirmed landmarks freezing upon certain facial points until a clear image was created. The pieces came together like a puzzle. When all the pinpoints for identification landed with a one-hundred-percent certainty, the identity of the person in question came to light.

It was definitely him: the wild eyes and crazy hair, the deep lines along his face. Beneath the photo ID was the name Tolimir Jancovic, which was subsequently followed by a laundry list of crimes.

Father Auciello fell back in his seat and rubbed a hand across his face a moment, before he unknowingly took the Lord's name in vain, in a whisper that was no louder than a sigh.

This was not what he wanted to see.

CHAPTER SEVENTEEN

The features of Jadran Božanović's face remained passive as he listened to Inspector Beauchamp vent, albeit with an underlying tone that wavered.

"An emissary from the Vatican contacted *le Capitaine* at the Direction Centrale de la Police Judiciaire. My *Capitaine.* Do you have any idea who you spotted at the Louvre? Whose children you took?"

"What I took," said Božanović, "was profit."

"Does the name Shari Cohen ring a bell to you?"

Božanović shrugged. "Should it?"

"Cohen is the person who orchestrated the mission to rescue the pope years ago, when he was abducted in the United States, remember?"

Another shrug. "And you think this should matter to me how?"

Beauchamp's eyes fired off. "My department is all over me on this. They want results."

"And this is what bothers you?"

"I've done nothing on this matter, to give you what you want, which is time."

Božanović said nothing, didn't even move, his eyes set on Beauchamp. But when he spoke, he did so evenly. "So, the Vatican thinks they can flex their muscles because of her crusade years ago. Is that what they think?"

"Apparently so, because in my department it has struck a chord with management. The American Embassy is one thing, but the Vatican is another. When they speak, my people listen. And there's not enough money in the world that would make them cross God."

Božanović smiled. "Are you so sure?"

"Why do you say that?"

The corner of Božanović's scarred lip lifted into a scoffing sneer.

"Everyone can be bought," he told the inspector. "There's a price for everything, and no one—*no one*—is immune to the power of wealth."

"The people I pay off," Beauchamp said, "are running scared."

"So, placate them."

"It's not that easy."

Božanović removed his knife from its sheath and placed it on the table. "Do you know what that is?" he asked Beauchamp. "Do you?"

Beauchamp stared at the blade of the knife, at its mirror finish.

Božanović pointed to the running scar along his face "This is the weapon that did this. It is also the weapon that killed many men thereafter by my hand." He then lifted the knife and toyed with it, the weapon as much a part of him as a biological limb. "You will deal with this matter and see it through," he told Beauchamp flatly.

"How?"

"Provide them with a feast of red herrings. Look for things that are not there. Look at people who you could possibly point an accusing finger at—small-time crooks, thieves, anyone. There is a solution for everything." He turned the knife over in his hand like a skilled artisan. "Find that solution, Inspector."

Beauchamp fell away slowly, the message sent: Give Božanović time or give him your life.

"Besides," said Božanović, as he leaned forward to close the gap between them. "What can the Vatican do?"

CHAPTER EIGHTEEN

The flight to Paris from Rome was a short one, via a jet that was chartered by the Vatican.

There were six Knights in total: Kimball Hayden, Leviticus, Isaiah, Joshua, Samuel, and Jeremiah, monikers taken from the Book of the Old Testament, with the exception of Kimball. He had declined the name of 'Archangel' after bearing a call-sign as a government assassin. It was all about distancing himself from his former life.

When they arrived in Paris they were taken, by a prearranged vehicle driven by a member of the archdiocese, to the Hotel de La Motte Picquet. Instructions regarding the room were given, so Kimball and his team, wearing leather overcoats to hide the weapons that lay underneath, and with clerical collars showing their religious affiliation, stood before a bank of elevators and pressed the 'up' button.

They stood silently, their eyes cast to the numbers as they lit up: six, seven, eight...

On the twelfth floor, the doors opened. The room was to their left.

As they walked down the hallway, people gave them a wide berth. These people wearing the collars of Catholic priests seemed odd and highly different. They walked without acknowledging anyone else around them. Their eyes were distant as they passed others in the hallway.

When they got to the room's door, Kimball appeared to hold back, as if debating whether or not to knock.

So, Leviticus took the initiative and rapped on the door three times.

When the door opened, Shari stood there with her eyes to Kimball and his eyes to hers, both locked. In time, her eyes welled with tears, whereas his sparked with the shine of adoration. And they embraced.

It had been years. But to feel her, to actually take in enough of her scent to rekindle old emotions, set him on a path to choose damnation over salvation. He wanted this woman, despite the cost to his soul.

She pulled back and traced the back of her hand along his cheek. "You look good," she told him.

In his eyes, despite the setback of looking hollowed and aged, she was incredibly beautiful.

Gary joined them and pulled her back, separating them, and then offered his hand. "Thank you for coming," he said. "Thank you for coming to find our girls."

Kimball feigned a smile and took his hand. "Good to see you, Gary." And then, and as much as to Shari as to Gary, he said. "We *will* find them."

Gary closed his eyes to blink back tears.

After being ushered into the room, the archbishop took to his feet and offered the Knights a hand in greeting.

"Time is of the essence," the archbishop told them. "We now have less than three days to find them before they disappear completely from the grid."

"Understood." Kimball took a seat on the couch while keeping Shari within sight from the corner of his eye.

Is she overly glad to see me?

He thought so.

But he remained true for the moment. The welfare of the children was the prime concern.

"So, what have you got?" he asked the archbishop.

"It's not good news," the archbishop said.

This brought dire looks from the parents.

"How so?"

The archbishop positioned the laptop to give Kimball a better view. "I have linked directly with the SIV," he said. "This is something you need to hear from them."

After a few taps on the keyboard, the monitor came to life, with Father Auciello on the other end via Skype. "Kimball," he said in salutation. "You made it."

"How're you doing, Gino?"

The man nodded as if he was doing well, then, "On your journey to Paris, we made certain discoveries regarding the person that shadowed Gary and Shari inside the Louvre."

"And?"

"His name is Tolimir Jancovic," he told him. "He's a reputed member of the Croatian mob, who works in the trade of human trafficking." Tolimir's image came up on the screen. "He has an extensive criminal history—petty stuff with small jail sentences. But he seems to have landed on his feet, working for this man."

Another image came on the screen, that of a man with a scar causing severe facial disfigurement.

"He's a cute one," said Kimball.

"His name is Jadran Božanović. Do you recall the name?"

He did, vaguely.

"Jadran Božanović is a leading member of the Croatian mob," he said. "Now the mob is made up of three families, working as a unit of one, but Božanović is a vicious kingpin. He also has his hand in every vice. But human trafficking is his specialty."

From the corner of his eye, Kimball could see Shari standing with her fists balled to her bosom. And within Gary's embrace.

"Go on."

"Kimball, this man is incredibly vicious," he went on. "His weapon of choice is the knife, reputedly the one that caused his own scar. His tendency is to carve people up. It's a hallmark signature of his."

Even Kimball winced at this.

"The human trafficking business is a thirty-two billion dollar a year trade," he went on. "Most are kids and young adults between the ages of fourteen to twenty-five. Boys and girls both. The thing is that Božanović's Bridge of Bones—"

"—Bridge of Bones?"

"It's a term used when talking about transit corridors of human trafficking," he reported. "In Božanović's case, he has multiple Bridges of Bones that run from Europe to Northern Africa and the Middle East. Right now, the percentage of people transported through these lines stands at nine percent of the worldwide transit system. Božanović maintains seven percent. And it's believed that he wants the entire lot so that he can expand the numbers considerably."

Kimball waited for more. "He wants the whole route to Northern Africa and the Middle East to himself? This Bridge of Bones?"

On the screen, Auciello nodded. "He's slowly taking out his competition," he went on. "In trade circles, he's known as The Surgeon—some even call him The Butcher. But according to our information, it appears that Božanović was a freedom fighter during the Croatian War of Independence. He was captured by a team of

Serbs. The man who sliced up his face ended up being on the other end of the knife after Božanović was rescued. I guess he made such a mess of the Serb that it became his brutality of choice. But he knows that it's a psychological tool that's highly effective. And he uses it against his competition. So far, he's outmuscled his competitors, who are abandoning their Bridges of Bones into his complete control, for fear of retaliation if they don't surrender their routes."

"So Božanović wants an exclusive franchise?"

"That's what we believe. And, Kimball?"

"Yeah."

"Mobs, especially the Croatian mob, are known for brutality and viciousness. But this guy Božanović is all about making statements. Of all the people we have dossiers on he's the craziest of the bunch. Every international agency is after him, especially Interpol. He's been known to brutalize entire families—and I'm talking about mothers, fathers, brothers, sisters, children, even their pets—just to make a point."

"So, he's a man without a conscience," Kimball commented.

"Incredibly certifiable."

"Where do I find him?"

"Nobody knows."

"Then what about this other guy—Tolimir?"

"Again, these guys are underground. They're most likely transient to keep from getting caught. But then we've got this." The screen went black for a moment, and another series of photos came up. They were stills of Tolimir getting into a vehicle. "See this?" asked Auciello.

"Yeah."

"We ran Tolimir's facial landmarks into the mainframe system of security cams that are situated at intersections of every main street, avenue, and boulevard around the time of the incident. These photos were taken less than a block away, seventy-six seconds after the abduction of the children. This was the side street Tolimir detoured onto, moments before the capture."

Everyone leaned toward the monitor to get a better view. The still was of Tolimir opening the back door of a sedan. In the next shot, the door was closed, with the sedan angling off into traffic. The following shots were images of the driver and his passenger.

"Can you zoom in on that?" asked Kimball. "Then polish it up."

Auciello did. The still image loomed large, the photo of the driver clear, even through the windshield of his vehicle.

Stunned gasps escaped Gary and Shari.

"My God," said Shari. "That's Beauchamp! He's the one heading up the investigation!"

"Really," said Kimball, as if this was a mild surprise. "I assume that Beauchamp is a man on record, given that he works for the DCPJ?"

"He's the one you need to start with," stated Auciello. "The address for the DCPJ—"

"Oh, no," said Kimball, raising a halting hand. "I want his home address."

"You want his home address?"

Kimball nodded. "This is not going to be a professional call, Gino. In fact, I plan to make this very personal."

"Kimball—"

"His home, Gino."

Auciello hesitated. And then he gave Kimball exactly what he wanted.

CHAPTER NINETEEN

That evening, Jadran Božanović sat alone in his room eating a bowl of mash and gruel, thinking about what Beauchamp had said about concerns coming directly from the Vatican. He could always grease enough palms with Euros within the DCPJ to stave off the worries voiced by the principals of the American Embassy. But the Vatican was something different, a powerhouse that could never be persuaded to join in his venture, even through considerable donations. But perhaps they could be effectively deterred by the threat of retaliation, should they get too close. Either way, it was not a road he wanted to go down.

He continued to spoon food into his mouth, as if it was an involuntary act, his eyes looking out into space as he ate, thinking.

Beauchamp was limited; he knew that since the calls had been coming in from the Vatican. Whoever this Shari Cohen was, she certainly had friends in high places. Normally he would stay away from products with powerful ties or allies with considerable connections. But he had grown cocky and arrogant, pulling and taking people at will, despite their pedigrees. He believed he was untouchable and too powerful to contradict.

He realized he was wrong. He sat there telling himself that he had learned a valuable lesson: that he would be more cautious in the future. No matter the beauty of the product or the high potential for profit, he would choose his future goods more wisely.

His eyes shifted to the clock on the wall.

It was getting late, and the sun was setting.

He would move his goods in a little more than two days, to a port in Italy where he would group his French cache of products with those found in Italy. From there he would take his Bridge of Bones to the Middle East, where there was a market for everything: boys, girls, and adults, people who would never have any will of their own.

The wall clock sounded louder than normal, the time ticking off with every stroke of the second hand.

...Tick...Tick...Tick...

And then it occurred to him that he would have to move quicker than he wanted to ensure that the goods got to their destination. He did not want a follow-up to the *Aleksandra* debacle. So, he decided to err on the side of caution and move his departure up by one day. Of course, he would lose some profit, since the number of products abducted and loaded would be smaller, which soured him deeply. But in the long run, he would own every transit route, every Bridge of Bones, that ran from Europe to North Africa and the Middle East.

He would be king.

The clock continued to tick steadily.

...Tick...Tick...Tick...

So much so that it grated on his nerves.

...Tick...Tick...Tick...

With uncontained rage, he lifted the heavy bowl and tossed it with supreme accuracy, hitting the clock and smashing it.

Gruel and juices cascaded slowly down along the wall.

But at least it was quiet.

CHAPTER TWENTY

Under the advice of Father Auciello, Gary and Shari were checked out of the Hotel de La Motte Picquet and moved into a small apartment that was completely under the sponsorship of the Church.

The residence was small and tight, with the furniture in a French motif. The wall hangings were markedly avant-garde. And the color schemes of the walls were soft and muted to lend an air of serenity. But no matter how delicate the hues were or how much they tried to lend to a peaceful setting, tensions remained critically high now that the room had been converted to the nerve center of all activity.

Monitors tied directly to the SIV were situated throughout the area, as two Jesuit priests manned the consoles.

The Vatican Knights were breaking armaments down then piecing them back together, making sure the weapons were fully functional and without defects.

And Kimball, who was oblivious that he had been under keen observation from the corner of Shari's eye, was unknowingly offering her a profile view of his powerful jawline and aquiline nose while typing away at the PC's keyboard.

When she first saw him standing in the doorway of the hotel suite, she felt her heart skip a beat inside her chest. Other than a few lines on his face that had deepened over time, he remained the same. And then she took inventory of the wide breadth of his shoulders and the deep shine of his cerulean blue eyes. And yes, the way he walked with confidence did not escape her, either.

She closed her eyes.

And she remembered the past.

He had come to her in the middle of the night when assassins quietly invaded her home. They were trying to kill her because she was getting too close to the truth about who had kidnapped the pope. She'd begun to point an accusing finger at those sitting upon Capitol

Hill. In the rarest form of a fighter with a particular set of skills that Shari believed that no man could ever possess, he took out her assassins with brutal efficiency. He was quick and fluid with balanced choreography to his poetically indescribable movements. And in the end, as these killers lay dead by his feet, as his eyes had connected with hers from across the room. She had looked upon Kimball Hayden from that point on as her savior.

She then recalled his scent whenever she stood close, that compelling aroma so unique that it drew her to him with the pull of unexplainable desire. She then looked deeply into his eyes and beyond the starkness of their bright blue colors only to see the true darkness underneath. Here was a man who had murdered women and children, his conscience constantly warring between good and evil, as the burdens of guilt weighed heavily on his shoulders—if not also in the depths of his soul. Salvation, that star-point glitter of hope, always seemed to be something beyond the scope of his grasp.

As she got to know Kimball and got over the hump of what he used to be, she realized that he was like a little boy, lost in a grown-up world.

And she had loved him.

When her relationship with Gary had been strained and the passion between them had appeared to have run its course, she began to gravitate toward Kimball. And in her heart, she knew that Kimball had felt for her as well. Perhaps he even loved her. But in the end, when Pope Pius was rescued, she saw Kimball as a man of brutality and Gary a man of gentle spirit. She had returned to her husband, knowing that he was what she had wanted all along.

Kimball would remain a lost soul.

And for years, her conscience had been in a constant feud with itself, believing that she had left Kimball out in the cold.

Yet here he was—again, her savior. He was a man capable of extreme violence, and he was coming to the call once again.

She looked out the window and at the Notre Dame Cathedral. The day was moving steadily along, as late afternoon shadows from the cathedral's towers were beginning to lengthen along the grounds of the plaza. And because little progress had been made, she tried to temper her patience, since every moment of inert response time was a moment closer to never seeing her daughters again.

She closed her eyes, trying to suppress her emotions.

But the act was completely ineffective, as her mind's voice continued to narrate the disturbing facts of human trafficking with the cold fortitude of a machine. The echoing measure of her tone had no emotion, as it recited in detail the facts that more than 2.5 million people were in forced labor at any given time, with 1.2 million children trafficked every year. Forty-three percent of those were forced for commercial sexual exploitation, of which ninety-eight percent were female. And thirty-two percent of those victims were utilized for economic reasons, of which fifty-six percent were women. More than 170 countries were affected by human trafficking—either as a source, as a transit route (a Bridge of Bones), or as a destination. The United States was ranked among the latter.

These were the cold, hard details. But they were facts drilled into her head as lead negotiator for the FBI's Hostage Rescue Team because it was a necessity to know them. She never thought that she would ever become a part of those statistics.

As the voice faded, she then filled her lungs with a slow pull of air through her nostrils, held it for a long moment, then released it with an equally long sigh. It did nothing to alleviate the stress.

The only way she knew to get rid of the tension was to be a body in constant motion.

In less than ten strides, she was across the room and looking over Kimball's shoulder.

"What are you doing?" she asked.

He didn't turn to acknowledge her. Instead, he tapped the tip of his forefinger against the monitor's screen. "This is the architectural arrangement of Beauchamp's residence from the outside," he said. "I'm sizing it up for entry and escape routes and committing to memory the design of its exterior."

"Kimball."

"Yeah."

"When you go on the hunt, when you go looking for Beauchamp, I'm coming with you."

His finger slowly fell away from the screen. "You know I can't allow that."

"You will allow that," she returned. "You know I'm field capable."

"I know you are. But that's not the point."

"Then what is?"

He hesitated a moment before speaking. "If you go into a situation emotionally compromised, then you could end up compromising the entire mission. And you know as well as I do that focusing entirely on the task at hand is essential."

"Kimball, I spent my entire career 'focusing on the task at hand.' And right now, my focus is entirely on saving my children."

"Shari—" he allowed his words to trail off, as he fell back into his seat. "I don't want you getting hurt."

"Getting hurt, Kimball, is a risk we accept when doing *our* job," she told him. She then rounded the couch until she was in direct eye contact with him. She pulled his hand close and tightened her grip over his. "I know you don't want me to get hurt. I don't want to get hurt, either. But I need to be out there looking for my babies, who are at this moment very scared and very confused. They're probably wondering where their mother is—why she's not coming for them. And I want my face to be the first thing they see when that door opens and I'm standing there waiting to bring them home." Her voice began to crack. "Can you understand that, Kimball? Can you?"

"You don't understand—"

"Then tell me."

"You're good at what you do, Shari. You really are. But you're not a skilled field operative like we are." *And I don't want to lose you.*

"You know I have the skills."

There was no denying that she was practiced in her field. But this was different. Jadran Božanović was a lethal competitor with a large crew to back him up.

His features softened. "Shari, my skills and the skills of the Vatican Knights may not be enough on this one."

"You know what I can do. You know my performance capabilities in the field. I would never compromise the mission by putting my children at risk. You know this."

He looked at her for the longest moment because she had proven herself to be a huge asset in the past. Without her assistance, they would have failed. "If I remember correctly, I believe your weapon of choice is what—the Glock?"

"Your memory's quite good."

Welcome to the team.

Everyone had been given their assignments.

For the moment, Shari was to stay behind with Joshua and work exclusively with the SIV in creating a psychological profile on Jadran Božanović. If Kimball was going to do battle, then he wanted to know the enemy better than he knew himself, predicting Božanović's every move if possible.

Gary would serve as an asset as well, given his background with the CIA, where his duties had included breaking through high-end firewalls and hacking into databases of appropriate information from insurgent countries. At the moment, Gary was pulling up the interior architectural layout of Beauchamp's residence. On the screen were the floor plans and the exit and entryways, everything Kimball needed to commit to memory to move about the structure with a sense of familiarity.

"Once we move on this, there'll be no slowing down," said Kimball. In his hand, he was sizing up his KA-BAR—the flat-black blade wickedly sharp and keen—a moment before he slid the knife neatly into its sheath. "We get in, get what we need, and move to the next target. I don't think I need to tell anyone inside this room that time is limited, right?" Then to Shari: "I want to know everything there is to know about Božanović. Especially his patterns and what he's most likely to do in the future. Once I find out the details from Beauchamp, Gary, I want you to zero in on the target site, by hacking into any available cameras. Big Brother is everywhere. Can you do that?"

"Two things: if I have the coordinates and if there're cameras posted at the scene," Gary replied.

"Good. You're my eyes and ears on this operation." He turned to Shari, and when he did, he could not help that feeling of guardianship over her. Her face in some places was swollen and bruised, flaws against the most beautiful flesh he had ever seen. To lose her would be devastating. But knowing that he had been the one to endorse her membership to the front lines would crush him beyond any care for redemption, should she be mortally wounded. "After you get what I need about Božanović, so that I know what I'm up against, and after I get what I need from Beauchamp, I'll contact you."

"And what if Beauchamp doesn't cooperate?"

"Trust me," he said, patting his sheath. "He'll have no choice."

CHAPTER TWENTY-ONE

Inspector Beauchamp was beginning to feel the pressure from his superiors, most notably from his *Capitaine,* even after giving the man a substantial amount of Euros to help slow the pace of the investigation down to a glacial crawl. At first, the answer was understood without inquiry, as the money was being passed from one hand to the next: *I will turn a blind eye for three days, but no more.* And then *le Capitaine* had tucked the money in his shirt pocket and sealed the deal with a quick wink of his eye.

But the Vatican's secretary of state was applying pressure to the ranking staff of the DCPJ, causing people like *le Capitaine* to reflect on his past deeds enough to make him wonder whether he had surrendered his soul to darkness. Suddenly finding religion, *le Capitaine* returned every Euro to Beauchamp, hoping in part that this would redeem him in the eyes of God.

Beauchamp didn't think so, knowing the moment his commanding officer had accepted the first Euro and then turned an eye toward indifference, was the day he had damned himself. And nobody, not even *le Capitaine,* was exempt from the rules of humanity.

It was simply too late for them all.

As he sat inside one of France's most eloquent restaurants, dining on high-end cuisine and a bottle of wine that was priced in the four-digit range, Beauchamp felt his world closing in. Sooner or later as the investigation by the Vatican continued to evolve, the truth that he had been one of Božanović's key acolytes would eventually come to the surface. And in the end, he would become a pariah, bringing others down with him and cleansing a department that was rich with corruption.

Unlike *le Capitaine,* he knew that salvation could not be bought…or at least bought *back*.

After he finished his meal and paid the bill, he went to get his car from the valet and drove home. Paris had always been a beautiful city, he thought. The lights, the reputation of love and romance, the poetic sound of its language, everything in his life had been perfect. He had money and lots of expensive toys due to his association with Jadran Božanović.

But was it worth it? he asked himself.

And then: *How many lives have I destroyed to make my life what it is today?*

He sighed. And then he thought about running. But Božanović had a reach that was extensively long. And the last thing Beauchamp wanted to become was one of Božanović's *statements*, to become an artwork that only the Croat could create.

When he drove up to his house located in a twenty-four-carat neighborhood outside of Paris proper, he rolled his vehicle into a three-car garage. The other two spots were taken up by cars no less than $80,000 each in American dollars, both sleek and luxurious.

From the attached garage he went into the kitchen and flipped on the lights. The room was large and well-equipped, with a grill-top stove and a range hood that was sheathed with strips of minted copper. The countertops were of veined marble, the edges beveled. And the refrigerator was a stainless-steel unit built directly into the wall, with the surrounding cabinets fashioned by the most luxurious wood.

After tossing the keys on the countertop, he went to the refrigerator and grabbed himself a beer. He then went to the TV room, grabbed the remote, and tried to click on the 70" TV. It would not turn on.

"Now what?" he mumbled, slapping the remote.

From the darkness came a voice: "I took out the batteries."

Beauchamp wheeled around with his hand going to his holster, his fingertips grazing the stock of his firearm when the lights suddenly turned on. A man was standing next to him, pressing a knife to his throat. Beauchamp's reaching hand immediately froze in position.

"Put your hand down," the man told him in English.

Beauchamp did as he was instructed by inching his hand cautiously down by his side. After the intruder grabbed Beauchamp's firearm, he stepped back and returned the knife to its sheath.

Beauchamp looked around, confused. Sitting in a recliner at the opposite end of the room was a large man wearing a cleric's shirt, Roman Catholic collar, military boots, and a beret. Other men were positioned around the room as well, each man wearing the same uniform that was half pious and half military.

For a considerably long moment, Beauchamp's eyes locked with those of the man in the seat, in macho posturing until his will finally gave under the man's gaze. His shoulders then slumped with the crookedness of an Indian's bow in defeat. "You're from the Vatican?"

The man in the chair remained silent and unmoving.

"Is this how the Church does things? By breaking into a man's home and then threatening him with violence?"

"You needed to be disarmed so that no one would get hurt. But if you want to see my brand of violence, I'd be glad to demonstrate it for you."

Beauchamp looked at the man next to him, with the knife. Then at all the rest. These men were not priests, he considered, not by a long shot. They had the seasoned look of skilled soldiers. "Who are you people?"

The man in the chair stood to his full height and made his way toward Beauchamp, who fell back a couple of paces to the much larger man, whose shirt stretched to capacity against a well-manicured physique. The priest's eyes seemed to carry the spark of unbridled anger; a flash Beauchamp had seen many times before in the eyes of Jadran Božanović. These were the eyes of a killer.

The priest stood before Beauchamp the same way a man would look down upon a boy, the height advantage going to the intruder. With an edge to his tone, the man said, "Sit."

Beauchamp immediately complied, taking a seat on a couch made of the finest leather.

The priest began to walk around the room tracing his fingertips along the surfaces of the furniture and decorative precious metals, over the high-end fabrics that covered the contours of expensive statues. "Tell me," he said. "How does a man like you, who earns a fair salary as an inspector, own such luxuries that only a king can only afford? Hmm? Did you get all this by selling away the lives of innocent people? Maybe turning a blind eye every time a kid got kidnapped off the streets of Paris?" His fingers glanced over the frame of an expensive painting, something with a purchase price in the mid-five figures.

Beauchamp pumped his chest out in false bravado. "What do you people want?"

The intruder rushed forward until he was so close to Beauchamp that he could guess what the man had eaten for dinner. "Answer my question," he said with forced repose. "How does a man...like you...who earns a fair salary as an inspector...own luxuries that only a king can afford?"

Beauchamp swallowed, the sour lump in his throat starting to bite with discomfort.

Kimball fell back, stood straight, and removed a photo from his shirt pocket. It was a still of Tolimir. He then proposed it face-first for Beauchamp's study. "Tolimir... Where do I find him?"

Beauchamp narrowed his eyes to feign his study of the photo. "I've never seen that man—"

Kimball shot his hand out and grabbed Beauchamp by the trachea, causing the man to choke and gag. Beauchamp reached up and tried to pull Kimball's hand away, but the grip was much too powerful.

"Tell me what I want to know, Beauchamp. Or I'll rip your throat out. So, help me God, I'll rip it out by the roots."

Beauchamp nodded, though his face was the color of deep cherry.

When Kimball let him go, the inspector fell forward, his lungs wheezing with a sound similar to the scraping of fingers across a blackboard, harsh and grating to the ears.

Kimball leaned forward and placed his hands on his kneecaps. "Let's get one thing straight, Beauchamp. You're not one of my favorite people. So, you're going to give me what I want. Is that clear to you?"

Beauchamp looked at him.

"Now answer my question. Where can I find this man Tolimir?"

Between gasps: "If I tell you...then he'll kill me."

"Tolimir?"

"If not him...then another."

"You're talking about Jadran Božanović, aren't you?"

Beauchamp's eyes detonated when Kimball spoke the Croat's name.

"Give me Božanović, and I'll make your worries go away."

"I can't. No one knows where he is. The man's always transient. Never stays in one place."

"But I can get to him through Tolimir, correct?" Kimball asked.

"I don't know... Maybe."

"Then give me Tolimir, and I'll force the issue with him." Kimball could see that Beauchamp was leaning toward the side of caution. By surrendering Tolimir, Kimball knew that Božanović would view this as a violation that could compromise his operation, thereby meriting the use of his knife against Beauchamp. But Kimball didn't care as he leaned into him.

"Understand this," he continued. "You were instrumental in the kidnapping of two children I hold very dear to my heart. Two children I have held in my arms when they were young. Two children you have condemned to a life of living hell, because of your willingness to turn your head away." Kimball gnashed his teeth and grabbed Beauchamp by the lapels of his jacket, the fabric bleeding through his clenched fingers. He pulled the inspector into close counsel. "Give me Božanović."

"I can't."

"Yes... You will."

Beauchamp's face suddenly took on the looseness of a rubber mask. He was terrified of Kimball almost as much as he was terrified of Božanović. "Please. They'll kill me."

"Where is he?"

Beauchamp shook his head: *no.*

"All right." Kimball lifted Beauchamp by the lapels and half-carried, half-dragged him across the room, through the adjoining room, and out to the balcony that overlooked the pool area. "By the way, did I tell you how much I admired your house?" The light of the pool was on, and the water was a crystal blue that shown beautifully against the landscaped grounds.

The inspector began to choke and gag, his collar becoming too tight, as Kimball twisted it until Beauchamp's face went scarlet.

"Tell me something," he said, pointing to the blanket of grass directly below. "Who's your gardener? I've got to say that he does a nice job on lawn maintenance."

Beauchamp grabbed Kimball's wrist and tried to pry it away.

"How does he get the grass so...nice?"

"Ahhggg!"

"What was that?"

"Ahhggg!"

Kimball looked over the side in admiration if not in consideration.

"Really sweet," he said. Then: "How far up from the ground do you think this balcony is?"

Beauchamp's eyes widened. "Ahhggg!"

"Ten feet maybe? Certainly not much higher than that."

"Ahhggg!"

"Are you going to give me Tolimir?"

Beauchamp shook his head.

Fine! Kimball hoisted the man up and over the railing, sending Beauchamp to the surface below with the inspector's arms pin-wheeling.

Beauchamp hit the grass hard, the impact knocking the wind out of him. Before he was able to focus, Kimball was standing over him as a hulking mass, impossibly tall.

Kimball reached down, grabbed Beauchamp by the collar, and lifted him to an upright position. The Knight's face maintained a no-nonsense look. "Tolimir."

"You don't understand. They'll kill—"

Kimball was beginning to lose patience. "Give me Tolimir!"

Beauchamp said nothing.

Fine. Kimball lifted Beauchamp to his feet and guided him to the pool area. As soon as they reached the pool's edge, Kimball tossed Beauchamp over the side with his hand still clutching the inspector's jacket. "Your life is immaterial to me," he told the inspector, and then he shoved Beauchamp beneath the surface. The inspector's hands flailed madly and splashed water everywhere.

"Kimball." Isaiah moved closer. "We're not about this. This is not what we do. There are rules of engagement."

Kimball turned on him as Beauchamp continued to struggle beneath his grip. "This is what *I* do," he said firmly. "In a perfect world, Isaiah, rules are great, as long as everyone is complying. But as soon as someone decides to go against them, then rules need to be adjusted to put those who stray from the values back in line."

"Kimball—"

"We are running out of time," he emphasized. "We're talking about the lives of two children here."

He then allowed Beauchamp's head above the surface, the inspector wheezing in a lungful of air. "I can do this all night," he told him. "Or until you're lying at the bottom of this pool. I don't care which. It's your choice... Where's Tolimir?"

When Beauchamp refused to answer, Kimball pushed him under once again. "You'll be the first man to die by baptism, Beauchamp. I guarantee it. Now give him up."

When Beauchamp finally waved his hands in surrender, Kimball lifted him out of the pool and sat him down against a lounge chair for the man to catch his breath. After a moment, Kimball allowed him to speak without coercion.

"There is this place on Les Halles, a small bar that's nondescript and does not advertise its location. It is a simple door that leads into a bar area that serves as a front for money laundering. It's a dummy business under the ownership name of someone who does not exist."

"And this is where I'll find Tolimir?"

He nodded. "Every night he's there counting money taken from the proceeds of current auctions."

Current auctions. Kimball had to bite back some stinging words.

"Where is this place?"

Beauchamp shifted; the man was obviously uncomfortable. "It's a white building set between two smaller stores, one is a bakery and the other a milliner's shop."

Leviticus knew exactly where the shops were.

Kimball reached out, grabbed Beauchamp by the collar of his jacket, and lifted him to his feet.

"So, what now?" asked the inspector.

"I'm going to see if you're telling me the truth."

"I am."

"I hope so. Because if you're not, then I'll be back to finish off what I started." He ushered Beauchamp roughly into the house, sat him down in front of one of two decorative columns that led into the dining area, and secured his hands behind the pillar with his handcuffs.

"What are you doing?" Beauchamp asked. "I gave you what you wanted."

"I wouldn't believe a word out of your mouth until I know otherwise." Then to Isaiah: "Disable the phone systems. I want this house completely shut off."

"Aye."

"And as for you," he said to Beauchamp, his words so soft it was as if he was mouthing them, "you deserve everything you get." He stood and looked down at the inspector with a look that could only be considered as disdain.

"When you see that I am telling the truth, priest, then you'll come back and undo these cuffs, yes?"

"Somebody will be back," he told him. "But it won't be me."

"Then who?"

An artist.

CHAPTER TWENTY-TWO

"*Up! Ustani!*" Up! Get up!

The voice was loud and demanding, the tone curt. Too many hands seemed to reach out through the fog and grab the girls, then hoist them forcefully to their feet.

"*Rekao sam premjestiti!*" I said move!

Both of the girls were groggy, their hands held in front of them as if to feel their way along as they moved. Often, they were shoved from behind as an incentive to move faster. The girls stumbled and fell, then were violently lifted to their feet, as the world around them appeared different.

Nothing made sense as they tried to register what was happening to them. Their surroundings seemed to move at a sluggish pace because their veins were lit up with a mind-numbing sedative. The colors were heightened, and the movements of their surroundings were slow and awkward, to the point where it appeared as if they were a part of some Wonderlandian landscape, where nothing seemed genuine, and the timing was unrealistic.

They had been ushered into a room with people mostly their age, with a few being younger, some a little older. Mostly women were grouped with a small number of males spotted throughout the chamber. Under the feeble glow of the lighting, everyone appeared ghostly and translucent, their skin appearing as pale and wan as the underbelly of a fish. Gray half-moons circled eyes that were red and rheumy from the constant shedding of tears and from imploring pleas that went unheard; their pitiful wails of suffering sounded off like a soft wind passing through the eaves of an old house.

The stench of human waste was strong, especially that of uric acid.

When Stephanie was shoved to the floor, she fell onto someone who was lying prone, her sister then falling on top of her. Limbs and body parts moved beneath them, around them, everyone writhing with a living-dead slowness to their motions.

Stephanie then sat up as much as her mind and body would allow, and tried to focus, with her sister lying next to her. All around her, a sea of people seemed to blend into kaleidoscopic designs and colors like a bad acid trip. At the other end of the room, two men stood by the door speaking Croatian, a language she did not understand.

If she had, then she would have understood that the plans for their transit to the Middle East had been moved up a day, which was why they were being gathered like cattle.

Time was running out.

CHAPTER TWENTY-THREE

For the past two hours, while Kimball and company were concentrating their efforts on finding Beauchamp, Shari Cohen brought up as much data as she possibly could regarding Jadran Božanović. Her forte as a specialist with the FBI was to develop enough of a psychological profile that would enable her to prognosticate a subject's future actions, based on past events, thereby preparing a counter-reaction that would give her the overall advantage.

From what she was reading on Božanović, he was an extremely learned individual who had been schooled by the finest institutions that money could buy. He could speak four languages fluently, English being one of them, as he could converse in Arabic and the known dialects of Northern Africa.

And there was more, a profile coming to fruition.

At the beginning of the civil war and on the day of his seventeenth birthday, his high-end life had come to a crashing halt, and the privileges of wealth had all but evaporated. His family was gone, the members executed in front of a luxurious estate that the Serbs razed by fire. And Jadran was left alone in a world that had gone from grandeur to abject poverty within a blink of an eye.

Within months he found his way into an insurgent group and fought by way of courage and anger, his emotions becoming twisted by hateful revenge.

One day his unit had been ambushed and captured, only for a secondary unit to come in and save the proverbial day. It was here that he had become horribly disfigured. And it was here that Jadran Božanović had found his emotional release, by cutting and slicing his opponents until their skins resembled savaged flesh.

Being learned, he did not go without seeing the impact the event had had on those around him—those within his circle and those

101

outside it. Word of mouth had spread about a boy who was on the cusp of becoming a man, and that this boy-man was marking his territory with the sliced-up bodies of his enemies. There were no reprieves. There was no mercy. To challenge Jadran Božanović guaranteed a most hideous death.

It was the first message of many—and one that always worked to his advantage, to the point where he thought he had become so legendary over time that he could move mountains. People feared him. The mob loved him. And Božanović had grown to be a man who was untouchable in certain circles, which included political, judicial, and members from many departments of law. The only ones willing to act against him were those who sat upon the thrones of international courts.

But even they weren't beyond Božanović's reach.

She scrolled down to the next page.

One month after the siege of the *Aleksandra*, Colonel John Majors of an international task force, the man who headed the raid, was found dead in his flat in London. The murder had all the earmarks of a Jadran Božanović slaughter: the man's torso having been flayed of flesh with the strips hanging purposely over the shower rod in a macabre display. There were no trace elements, no DNA, nothing that would tie him to the murder, other than the obscenity of the scene.

And this is what scared her the most.

Because on a prior siege that was headed by a member of Interpol, eight months before the siege of the *Aleksandra,* the commander had been found tied to the four corner posts of his bed in Lyon, France, with the flesh of his torso peeled away with such surgical precision that the anatomy of muscle fiber was showcased, as it would have been on a cadaver in a medical study. There was hardly a nick against the muscle bands. And this, too, took place about a month after a failed attempt by Interpol forces to capture Božanović in Spain. Although there was no trace evidence, the area always sanitized, it bore all the hallmarks of the Croatian's artistic quality.

The images on the screen were gruesome. The man's face was untouched, as his eyes stared ceilingward. The sheets were spotted and stained, the color of blood drying to the shade of burgundy. He had the look and stare of a man who had been deeply surprised by his mortality.

Next page.

Božanović's statistical kills were listed: eight known kills and a probable seventeen more. Names and faces were given, as well as the locations of the kills, which were global.

Apparently, Božanović would traipse across the world to exact revenge on those who bested or challenged him on any level, just to make a point. It was to let others know that the planet wasn't big enough for them to hide.

On the surface, Jadran Božanović was a man who had the psychology that retribution was everything. And the 'revenge paradox' did not apply to him, which is when a person takes revenge out on another and feels worse about it instead of better. Božanović seemed to revel in the glory of his kills, keeping his anger alive. The history of his actions was a testament to this by showing a sadistic, if not serial, disposition of someone who relished the dark side of reciprocity.

In other words, Jadran Božanović knew no boundaries, and he would travel the world to make a kill, to calm the beast inside. And once the kill was made, only then would he feel justifiably whole.

On a scratch pad beside her, Shari continued to make notes.

"Ms. Cohen, your husband would like to know if you would like something to eat."

She looked up at Joshua—at the fresh-scrubbed look of his face. He had marginal good looks and emerald-green eyes that sparkled with youth. And if she were to hazard a guess about his age, she would have said no more than twenty if that. She then wiped the fatigue and itch from her eyes with her thumb and forefinger. She had not rested since the kidnapping of her children. "Can I ask you something, Joshua?"

"Yes, ma'am."

"Is Joshua your real name? Or is it a moniker?"

"It's a moniker, ma'am." When he spoke, he did so with an accent that was either British or Australian, she could never tell the difference.

"Please," she told him. "Call me Shari. You make me feel old when you call me ma'am."

"Yes, ma'am."

She wanted to roll her eyes. *It's Shari!*

"So, what's your real name, Joshua?"

"It's Thomas, ma'am. Or Tommy."

She sized him up. He was no Kimball or Leviticus in size, but more like Isaiah, with that wiry range that gave him incredible speed and agility. "OK, Joshua. Tell me. How did you become a Vatican Knight?" She knew the Knights were recruited as orphans, children with no familial ties or any real future other than what they made for themselves in the streets.

"In London, ma'am—"

It's Shari!

"—I was seven or eight when I tried to pick the pocket of this man in Hyde Park. I wasn't particularly good at it, since he chased me down and caught me within two strides. But that's when I saw his collar." He pointed to his own cleric's collar. "I remember him walking me to the nearest bench and sitting me down, and for the longest time, we just sat there looking into each other's eyes. Even at seven or eight, I could remember seeing this sadness about him. But I thought it was for what I did. But the sadness never went away—not even after he took me in and gave me direction."

"You're talking about Kimball, aren't you?"

He nodded. "He saved me. I don't know where I'd be today if it wasn't for him."

"Are you happy?"

"Very."

It's amazing how Kimball can bring happiness to so many others but not to himself, she thought.

She smiled becomingly. "Tell Gary that I *am* hungry. I know he mentioned someplace close to the cathedral, where he could pick something up for us."

Joshua tipped the corner of his beret. "I'll tell him, ma'am."

It's Shari!

For the better part of his marriage with Shari, Gary Molin, his last name different because Shari opted to keep hers, was a househusband who raised his children at home by choice, leaving his CIA admin position to do so.

As a specialist, he was tasked with wending his way through firewalls, intercepting data and restrictive information from insurgent and allied countries, the information gathered crucial to American sovereignty.

In the other room, where a console station had been set up, Gary was typing and hacking his way to any port or ISP that might have had information on times Beauchamp contacted Tolimir or Božanović online.

So far, the inspector had hidden his tracks well.

"She's hungry, Mr. Molin." It was Joshua.

Gary gave a few quick taps on the keypad, and one final bang on a button like a pianist trying to hit a final note. "Very good," he said. He stood up and stretched, his arms reaching skyward. "What about you, Joshua? You want something? My treat."

"No, sir, but I do appreciate the offer."

"Tell her I'll be back in about an hour. If there's a problem, she has my cell."

"I think we'll be fine, sir."

But they wouldn't be fine.

In fact, it would be the last time Gary would see Joshua alive again.

CHAPTER TWENTY-FOUR

The streets surrounding Les Halles were dark and considered a blind spot regarding the lack of surveillance cameras on every corner. And that was because the area was a festering eyesore that pooled with strange and moving shadows the moment the sun went down.

Outlines of those who felt most comfortable in the shadows stayed beyond the fringe of feeble lighting. The only thing that gave away their position was when the ends of their cigarettes flared whenever they took a drag.

Sometimes they only come out at night, thought Kimball.

There were five in total, as they took to the streets wearing long coats to cover up their weaponry with the exception of Kimball, who was going in dry. They walked in silence, and their footfalls made no noise.

When they came upon their destination, there was a doorway situated between the entryways of the bakery and the millinery, just as Beauchamp had claimed. But there were no signs or significant mentions as to what the door was for or to where it would lead. It was completely nondescript.

"You think Beauchamp was telling us the truth?" asked Kimball.

"I don't see why not," returned Leviticus. "There *is* a door here, where he said it would be. And it has to lead somewhere, right?"

Kimball nodded. "All right, then. Circle up."

Everyone huddled together as Kimball quarterbacked his unit. "Leviticus and Isaiah will stay close to the door and watch those who come in and out. Samuel and Jeremiah will man the opposite corners of the room and maintain a 360-degree view. I want eyes everywhere, people because they'll be watching us just as hard as we'll be watching them."

"And what about you?" asked Isaiah.

"I'm going to do what I came to do," he told him. "I'm going to find Tolimir."

"And if he's not here?"

"Then I'll use my diplomatic skills to find out exactly where he is."

Everyone knew what that meant when it came to Kimball Hayden. His diplomacy came by the way of fists.

The door, a piecing together of metal sheets that were riveted together like a fire door, opened easily. And as soon as they stepped inside, the noise level immediately zeroed out to cold silence, as everyone looked upon them with more than just a critical eye.

The place was dingy, with the surrounding walls peeling curls of off-white paint to show the gray concrete underneath. The floor was so aged that the varnish had worn off to expose wood that was becoming warped and splintered. To their left, along the entire length of the wall, was a bar with a mirror backing so dusty their images were vague figures. Tables and chairs spotted the area with the notion that the establishment only wanted to cater to a few, with an occupancy maximum set at twenty. And to the right, which caught Kimball's eye, was a thin staircase that led to a second floor. Along the entire wall of the second tier that overlooked the bar area was a two-way mirror. There was no doubt in Kimball's mind that this was where Tolimir was—the man perhaps even looking down on them as they stood there.

The moment Kimball stepped forward; it was a cue for everyone else to fan out. Isaiah and Leviticus took an empty table by the door. Jeremiah took a post at one end of the bar, and Samuel stood next to the stairwell, close to a Croat who stood guard, the man keeping an eye on the Knight with a sidelong glance.

As far as Kimball could see, there were nine people, including the bartender, that were situated throughout the room, the men appearing capable of extreme violence.

When he crossed the room, his footfalls echoed off the walls, the acoustics poor, until he came upon the bar. When he swiped his finger across the bar top, the tip came away dust-laden. He showed it to the bartender.

The bartender shrugged: *So.*

Kimball lowered his hand, smiled, and then he leaned forward until his elbows and forearms rested along the top of the bar's surface.

In Croatian, the bartender said: "Something I can do for you, Father?"

However, Kimball didn't speak the language. "Speak English?"

The bartender nodded. "You are American." This was not a question, but a statement made with passable English.

"I am."

"Something that you…and your friends," he eyed the Knights suspiciously, "want?"

"As a matter of fact," Kimball said graciously, "we do."

"And what would that be?"

"We're looking for someone," he said. "Maybe a couple of someones."

The bartender suddenly spoke Croatian and said something humorous since everyone lit up with laughter, except for the Vatican Knights.

Kimball's smile never wavered as he returned to a seat between Isaiah and Leviticus, removed his jacket to expose his sheer size, folded it over the empty seat's backing, and then returned to the bar with his grin still intact. "I like that jacket," he told the bartender. "I don't want to get it dirty."

The bartender's eyes slowly flared as he assessed the wide breadth of Kimball's shoulders and the thickness of his arms. He also would have noted the exceedingly tight shirt which showed off Kimball's musculature beneath the fabric.

Kimball pointed to his Roman collar. "Don't let this fool you," he said evenly, the smile still there.

"What do you want?"

Kimball fell back from the bar and took note of the faces that had grown suddenly tense.

It was here that the bartender saw the large man's dress of military boots and pants. From the waist up he was piously dressed, from the waist down—not so. Kimball saw the man suddenly grasp that they were not priests.

"I'm here," began Kimball, "in good faith. We all are."

"Then you want a drink?"

"No."

The bartender shrugged: *Then what?*

"I want Tolimir Jancovic."

The sound of chair legs scraping against the floor echoed throughout the room, telling Kimball that people were beginning to posture themselves for a fight.

Kimball sighed and raised his hands in supplication. "Please, I'm not looking for trouble," he said. "I'm not. But I do want to speak with Tolimir Jancovic."

The bartender nodded and waved him off. "No such person here. Never heard of him. Now you go."

Kimball lowered his hands and looked to the mirror running along the second tier. He pointed. "Is that where he is?"

"You go. No such person here."

Kimball leaned forward and looked the bartender straight in the eyes. "Come here," he said, beckoning the bartender with a flex of his fingers. "Come on. I won't hurt you."

"I said go. No such person—"

Kimball lashed out with amazing quickness, grabbing the man by the throat and choking him until he turned a shade of candy-apple red. When a patron stood and began to advance toward Kimball, Jeremiah reached out and grabbed the man by the shoulder, stopping him. The man turned aggressively on the Vatican Knight and leveled a right cross. In a swift movement, the Knight raised his left arm, easily deflected the blow, and came up with the flat blade of his right hand and caught the man in the throat. The Croat's eyes widened as he gasped for air, and then he went to his knees, hard. And then he fell to the floor gagging.

Jeremiah gave Kimball a mock salute. "You're good to go. No worries here."

Kimball stared down the rest of the Croatians, who were willing to risk their welfare. "I just want to see Tolimir... Just to talk. A negotiation."

"And what would a priest want to negotiate about?" This came from a man sitting in the center of the room with two others. His eyes were dark and calculating, and his face held the features of someone who was not impressed with Jeremiah's skills.

"That's for me and Tolimir Jancovic to discuss."

"Just you?"

He nodded. "Just me."

The Croat waited a long moment before giving the posted sentinel standing at the base of the stairway a signal to go to the second tier. The guard nodded in acknowledgment and began to mount the steps.

"Now release my man," said the Croat.

Kimball did, the bartender staggering backward until he was

pressing himself against the mirror wall with his hands to his throat.

"Who are you?" asked the man. "It's apparent that you are no priest. None of you are."

"That's for me to discuss with Tolimir."

The guard disappeared behind the door, closed it, and after what seemed like an eternity opened the door and called Kimball forward with a beckoning wave.

"First, we must check you for weapons," said the Croat, standing.

"I have no problem with that," Kimball returned, raising his arms ceilingward for a pat-down.

The Croatian glared harshly, as he neared the much larger man. "Do not make a stupid move."

"I just want to talk to Tolimir. No problems."

The Croatian patted Kimball down thoroughly, the procedure one of violation as the man searched every inch of his body, including a methodical inspection of the groin, which caused Kimball to wince with moments of discomfort. "Stop being a dick," he finally said. "I have *nothing* on me."

The Croat gave a smug grin and gestured his arm toward the staircase. "You may now go," he said.

Kimball would remember the man's face.

Taking the steps, he knew that he was being watched through the two-way pane of the mirror. The guard at the top of the stairway fell back to give Kimball entrance, allowing him to step inside the room. The door closed softly behind them, the snicker of the bolt locking. Besides Tolimir, there were four other men in the room. Two flanked Tolimir's desk with each one carrying a bolo machete, the weapons themselves a psychological deterrent. One stood by the door. And another, a man as sizeable as Kimball, stood by the mirror overlooking the room below, maintaining a keen watch over the rest of the Knights.

Sitting behind his desk with his hands tented, Tolimir bounced his fingers thoughtfully against his chin, as he appraised Kimball for a long moment, staring at the Roman Catholic collar around his neck. On his desk were three small TV monitors showing the activity of the floor below, the screens revealing the people who walked in with this man were wearing cleric's collars as well. He continued to bounce his fingers against his chin as his eyes ventured from Kimball to the TV monitors, and then from the TV monitors back to Kimball. After a long period of examination, he asked, "Who are you and what do you people want? And why do you come here dressed as priests?"

"We're not priests," Kimball said. "We're emissaries from the Church."

"When you say 'Church,' do you mean the Vatican?"

Kimball hesitated at this, and then said, "Yes."

"And I was told that you wanted to negotiate a deal. Is this true?"

"It is."

"What could the Vatican possibly want from me?"

"First of all, I know who you are and what you do."

Tolimir smiled at this as he un-tented his fingers and let his arms fall by his sides in mock crucifixion. "I am but a lowly businessman operating a bar in Les Halles. My profits are minimal. But I get by."

Others in the room snickered and chortled.

Kimball, on the other hand, didn't find humor with Tolimir at all.

"You are nothing, but the lowest form of life on Earth," he told the Croatian.

Tolimir's smile faded to a grim line as he hunkered over his desk and set his elbows and forearms on the desktop. "You dare to speak that way to me? Do you know who I am?"

"I just told you I did."

"No. I mean, do you *really* know?"

"I know you peddle children for profit. You're deep into human trafficking, and this dive is nothing more than a front to launder money—perhaps one of many for Jadran Božanović."

Tolimir's eyes sparked at this. He then fell back into his seat, tented his fingers, and once again began to bounce them off his chin in thought. "Then you are a very stupid man," he finally said, "to come in here and tell me my business and to talk to me in the manner that you do. Did you really think I was planning to negotiate with you on any level? I don't care who you're an emissary for."

"I don't just act as an emissary for the Church. I also head up a very special team of people."

"You mean those down below?"

Kimball's face shifted with a nervous tic. This was not going well.

"I'm curious," said Tolimir. "What exactly is it that you wanted to negotiate?"

"Several hours ago, you headed a team to kidnap two children on the streets behind the Louvre. You remember the moment?"

The muscles in the back of Tolimir's jaw worked. "I remember nothing. But go on."

"We want the children back."

"Just like that? You want me to hand them over? I don't hear anything as to how I'm supposed to benefit from this…negotiation."

"The benefit…is that you live."

Tolimir narrowed his eyes at this. "Excuse me?"

"You heard me."

Tolimir then spoke to his team in Croatian, driving intense laughter from them. "You are in no position to bargain or negotiate any terms, especially with me." And then: "How did you find me?"

One word: "Beauchamp." Kimball had no qualms about sealing the man's fate.

Tolimir nodded. "Beauchamp." He stood. "Well, at least the man sent you right into the devil's playpen, yes? In the next few moments, you will be dead by the hands of my people." He pointed to the two men holding the machetes. "Your fate was dictated the moment you stepped inside that door. There will be no discussions, no debates, *and* no negotiations."

"Božanović might think otherwise."

The Croat laughed. "You are nothing to him," he said. "You're nothing but a fly in Božanović's ointment. He will simply be told of this, and he will let it pass without as much as a fleeting thought."

"Božanović knows that the Vatican is looking into this matter. He might want to know on this one. I need to get close to him—"

Tolimir nodded. "No. The only way to get close to Jadran Božanović is if he wants you to. And I know that he does not care to hear what you or the Church has to say."

"That's very disturbing then."

"What is?"

"That you're not allowing me the privilege to meet the man I want to throttle."

Tolimir questioningly arched the corner of an eyebrow. "Is this what you call American humor? Do you think you're funny?"

"I want those children," he told him with no uncertainty. "And if I have to rip out your intestines so that you'll tell me where Božanović is, where the children are, I *will* do so."

Tolimir shook his head. "You, American, are not so funny. But you *are* stupid. Look around you. I have four soldiers who can kill you within a heartbeat."

Tolimir was right. His team was rugged and armed. And the quarters were too tight for Kimball to apply his skills adequately. In the end, he realized that Tolimir was right. He *was* stupid for allowing his raw emotions to dictate his ability to negotiate terms. The moment he stepped inside the room, he automatically hated these people for who they were and what they did. And because of that, he could not restrain his inability to negotiate on an objective level. Kimball was being Kimball. And then it dawned on him that he just might have sealed the fate of the children by his unwillingness to play nice.

"Now, American, you will die. And so will your—"

With rage quickly bubbling to the surface, Kimball reacted the only way he knew how.

With a Kimball Hayden-style of diplomacy.

CHAPTER TWENTY-FIVE

Everything on the ground floor was quiet as Isaiah and Leviticus kept careful watch over Jeremiah and Samuel. And Jeremiah and Samuel kept a vigilant eye on everyone else inside the barroom. None of the Croats moved. And no one allowed their steely gazes to drift, either.

"This is a first for me," Leviticus whispered to Isaiah.

"Delicate situation."

Leviticus cast his eyes upward to the second-tier mirror. "You think he's all right up there?"

"He can take care of himself."

"Yeah, well, I hope so. I hate sitting blind as to what's going on up there."

"Don't worry about Kimball," said Isaiah. "He knows what he's doing."

"You think he's making any progress with Tolimir?"

"One could only hope."

Despite Jeremiah and Samuel, who were dispersed inside the room, Leviticus and Isaiah had become the focal points for the Croats. Isaiah could almost feel the heat of their intense glares.

He eased back in his chair, feeling his muscles tighten. Kimball's time upstairs was stretching uncomfortably long. *Leviticus is right*, he thought. Like him, Isaiah hated sitting blind as to what was going on behind closed doors. "How much longer should we give him?"

Leviticus gave off a slight shrug. "I don't know… I guess Kimball will let us know if diplomacy fails."

"How's he going to do that from behind closed doors?"

They immediately got their answer.

Kimball lashed out with his leg, a strong thrust, and hit the large man directly on the small of his back, sending him airborne through the mirrored pane. The crescendo of the mirrored glass breaking was alarm enough to those below, as the big man cart-wheeled through space in fast revolutions and landed hard on a table, crushing it beneath his weight and setting off plumes of dust. The man didn't move, as dust motes lingered around him like a slow-moving fog.

The opponent standing by the door quickly reacted with a flailing of arms and legs in a synchronized display of martial arts. He hammered the points of his fingers on each hand directly at Kimball—left, right, left, right—his arms working like pistons as they drove the Vatican Knight back against the wall. And then he lashed out with a roundhouse kick, his foot hitting Kimball squarely on the temple, knocking him off balance.

This guy is good.

The martial artist jumped in the air again. But this time he spun in a full circle, so he would come across with a kick that would completely disable Kimball with a crushing blow to the skull.

But the Knight was quick. He countered by catching the man's leg and holding him aloft. For a period of a single heartbeat, he allowed their eyes to meet. Then: "Have a nice flight." He pitched the much smaller man through the opening where the mirrored glass used to be, the man barking out a cry a moment before he hit the ground below.

Kimball quickly pivoted toward Tolimir, who was now standing behind his chair, using the high back segment as a poor substitute for a shield. His once-dominant look of cockiness had been replaced with a fusion of raw terror and uncertainty. In ten seconds, Kimball had managed to take out two of his best.

Tolimir gave sidelong glances to the two men flanking him—first looking to his left, then to his right, and then straight at Kimball. Both men had their bolo machetes ready.

"You think that chair's going to protect you?" asked Kimball.

"No. But my men will."

When Tolimir uttered something in Croatian, the men advanced toward Kimball with their machetes held high.

When the large man came crashing through the mirrored pane and collapsed the table he fell upon, everyone down below knew that diplomacy had failed.

The Croatians didn't hesitate, knowing all along that this would be the result.

Leviticus and Isaiah quickly got to their feet, flipped back the panels of their long coats, grabbed their firearms, and tipped the table onto its side, hunkering behind it.

Jeremiah immediately vaulted over the bar, as a volley of bullets stitched along the wood veneer a moment after the leap.

Samuel was completely exposed by the open stairwell, as he attempted to take refuge behind one of the empty tables, planning to flip it as Isaiah and Leviticus had done with theirs. But as he went for his Glock, a bullet caught him in the shoulder, causing the flesh to pare back and form a blooming rose petal of pulp and gore. As the impact of the strike knocked him back, more bullets found their marks, striking his arms, legs, and abdomen with eruptions of blood arcing through the air. His eyes rolled in his sockets with dizzying effect until he fell to the floor, hard, his blood fanning out beneath him in an obscene halo.

Behind the bar, the bartender went after Jeremiah with a machete that had been stocked on a shelf. As Jeremiah got to his feet, and with the bartender nearly on top of him, bullets crashed around them and summarily took out the mirror. The Knight kicked out his foot and caught the man in the chest, sending him crashing to the floor. The bartender lost his grip on the machete, and it skated out of his reach. When he tried to stand up, Jeremiah had his pistol out and struck the man over the head, rendering him unconscious. Though now free to support Isaiah and Leviticus, furious gunfire continued to strike and splinter the bar, forcing him to lay low.

Isaiah and Leviticus were under the same hail of gunfire, as bullets struck their makeshift tabletop shield, its surface becoming further decimated with every impact, as wood fell away in splinters.

"We're getting slaughtered!" said Isaiah. "This table isn't going to hold for much longer!"

When a bullet finally pierced through and missed them by inches, Leviticus reached around with his gun-hand and fired off a succession of shots.

The Croats fell back and tried to hide behind whatever obstacle protected at the moment. When Leviticus's magazine fell empty, he quickly seated another and began the fight all over again. "Go!" he yelled.

Isaiah took advantage of Leviticus's cover of gunfire. He angled his way toward the bar with his gun-hand raised and looking for targets.

A Croat poorly hidden behind an upturned table saw Isaiah, attempted to raise his firearm, but fell short when a bullet hole magically appeared at the center of his forehead. Isaiah had hit his mark.

Leviticus slipped in his third and final magazine, racked the weapon, and then angled to his right as the Croats were distracted by Isaiah's movements.

They were flanking the enemy.

As Leviticus moved, holding his weapon in a cup-and-saucer grip, with one hand supporting the shooting hand from underneath, he crossed the floor until he had targets in view and fired off several rounds.

Bullets punched holes into shoulders, arms, and legs—wounding shots that caused a couple of the Croats to cry out in pain.

Two more were down and a third was dead.

That left five healthy souls as Leviticus and Isaiah continued to fire, mostly missing their marks as the shots skipped off the floor and into distant walls. In return, the Croats shot off their weapons in random, with haphazard rounds hitting all points of the room with hopes that one or more would find their marks of a Vatican Knight.

None did, as the air filled with the smell of gunpowder.

"Jeremiah, go!" It was a launch code from Isaiah saying that the enemies' attention was no longer concentrated on the bar. So, Jeremiah stood and fired, pinning the Croats down as Isaiah and Leviticus continued to maneuver about the room for promising angles.

Volleys and hails of gunfire continued to erupt, smoke rising.

And then there was the awkward sound of multiple dry clicks, as everyone exhausted their ammunition. In the heat of battle, no one ever pulls the trigger just once.

Five Croats stood looking at their weapons questioningly, then looked at the Vatican Knights, who were doing the same with theirs, and then everyone holstered their firearms. Silently, the Croats began to divide and spread across the room, each man removing a knife from his sheath.

From behind the bar, Jeremiah cautiously made his way across the room, joining Isaiah and Leviticus.

"The bad thing about Glocks," said the Croat who had frisked Kimball, "is that they eventually run out of ammo. But this," he held his blade up to display the combat knife that was wickedly keen and whose metal shined with a mirror polish, "never fails to disappoint me."

In unison, the Croats raised their knives.

Having no choice, the Vatican Knights did the same.

The two men with the bolo machetes advanced on Kimball, as the sound of bullets strafing across wood and concrete carried on down below.

The Croat to his right attacked first, bringing the sharpened edge of his machete down at an angled arc, cutting the air as Kimball fell back, just enough to miss its cutting sweep. The man then came up and across, forcing Kimball to fall back beyond its reach again, finding himself up against the wall.

The second machete wielder was on his comrade's heels, waiting to get in a lick.

Then came a blow that caught Kimball across his upper chest, the blade cutting deep above the pectoral region. Wincing in pain, Kimball feigned to his left, causing the wielder to shift in balance, and then the Knight got low to the ground and swung his leg across and knocked the man off his feet and to the floor. As the second machete wielder watched his teammate go to the ground, Kimball came across with a series of elbow strikes—left, right, left, right, left, right—the lightning-fast flurries breaking the bones of the man's face until it had somewhat of an asymmetrical look to it. And then the attacker fell to the floor, with his hand unknowingly extended as if to pass off the mantle of the machete before he landed. Kimball grabbed it just as the first wielder got to his feet.

The men were now squaring off with each other. Each carrying a machete as they cautiously circled one another looking for an opportunity to strike.

And then the Croat lashed out with a jab that was easily deflected by Kimball, the two metals striking, which caused a spark to alight, dwindle, and die.

After pointing the tip of his weapon at Kimball, he said, "Now you will die, priest."

Kimball said nothing. He simply waited for the man to make his move.

And he did.

The wielder jabbed and swept his machete across and down, with fluid motions and unpredictable speed, which drove Kimball back as he continuously warded off blows with stunted motions, because of the injury to his upper chest. Sparks flared in midair at the strike of the blades, the Knight losing ground. And he could see Tolimir smiling in his mind's eye, as the man hid behind his chair, watching the Vatican Knight in a losing effort.

Another blow from the machete wielder caught Kimball on the left shoulder, the graze ripping the fabric of his shirt.

Then Kimball thought of the children again. Not just Shari's, but all those who were being forced to live out horrendous lives because of a man such as this, a person who was so vile and without any moral compass. Then in a scream of savage anger, as laces of red stitching raced across the whites of his eyes, Kimball's rage knew no boundaries.

Suddenly his motions became electric, his actions swift and coordinated as he fought through the pain. His arm, his hand, everything about him moved with blinding speed, almost too fast for the human eye to register.

The wielder's eyes widened with surprise at his sudden conversion to fighting at a much higher level. The man was now on the defensive, as Kimball fought with savagery.

The machete's blade coursed through the air with whipping speed, as Kimball struck blow after blow, the metals striking and sparks flying. And then Kimball kicked his leg out and caught his attacker in his midriff, sending the man hard against the wall. After shaking his head as if to clear away cobwebs, the machete wielder attacked Kimball with his attack hand raised and the blade glinting. Kimball reached up, grabbed the attacker's wrist, and proceeded to dance around the room with him in a drunken tango.

The assailant then brought a knee up and connected with Kimball's groin, striking a hard blow that forced Kimball to release his grip and retreat a few staggering steps, his face going scarlet. Then he went to the ground on a bent knee.

The moment Kimball went to his knee, his attacker brought the machete over in a downward rush. In quick response, Kimball deflected the blade and brought his bolo across in a horizontal sweep, gashing the man's stomach. Then he punched the tip home and drove it clean through the attacker's gut.

The Croat appeared stunned by this sudden transience of slipping between life and death. His eyes widened with shocked disbelief. He then dropped the weapon to the floor, fell to his knees, and as the light of his eyes faded, the Croat slumped forward like a flower slowly wilting until his forehead rested against the floor.

And that was how he died, in a kneeling position.

Laboring to his feet and wincing as he did so, Kimball turned to see a panel closing flush against the wall behind the desk, the seams of the passageway barely visible to the naked eye.

Tolimir was gone.

There were five against three, as the Croats slowly advanced with the points of their knives leveled at the Vatican Knights.

When they went into a spread formation, so did Leviticus, Isaiah, and Jeremiah.

The five men spread across in a semi-circle, closing the gap and entering the kill zone—the area of combat with the most potential of affecting a fatal blow.

And then the teams converged, knives and blades swinging, cutting and slashing the air in arcs and sweeps and thrusting jabs.

Isaiah took on the two uniting from the left, Leviticus the two from the right, and Jeremiah the one in the center.

With motions that were both elegant and graceful, Isaiah easily warded off the blows from the Croats, who struck at him simultaneously. Knives clashed in a series of strikes and metallic clangs, one against two, the blows furiously paced, as the Croats battled Isaiah in a showdown that appeared choreographed. The blades struck repeatedly as sparks ignited, flourished, and died.

Arms moved in synchronized concert until their motions became a blur of attacking and defending.

Leviticus was in the same mode of defensive maneuvers, fighting off two Croats with a single blade by artfully deflecting their blows. They struck, they jabbed, they came across in killing arcs and horizontal sweeps, as the Knight warded off the blows with superior countermeasures.

Jeremiah had no problem with his attacker, the man wielding the knife with no more skill than that of a first-time user. In a quick assault, Jeremiah turned aside the blow of his attacker's knife with a simple flick of his blade, went to a knee, and came across with a horizontal slash that cut deeply into his attacker's legs above both knees. He sent the man crashing to the floor in pain.

Jeremiah quickly grabbed the assailant's knife and segued beside Isaiah to battle against the two Croatian fighters. Arms flailed with blinding speed as the Knights fought side by side and drove the Croats back with their far superior skill set.

Isaiah then found an opening and brought his blade across, finding the mark of the Croat's arm, where the bicep met the shoulder. The knife sliced easily through flesh and tendon, separating the muscle and rendering the arm useless. The Croat screamed as white-hot agony shot through his system with the venomous bite of acid, then he fell away from the fight.

Isaiah then joined Leviticus, who was losing marginal ground against his attackers. He worked his way beside Leviticus, intercepting blows, taking the strikes onto himself.

Their arms and hands moved in blurs, driving their opponents backward. And then Leviticus launched a series of jabs that pierced his attacker's lower abdomen with five quick stabs—*jab, jab, jab, jab, jab*—all non-lethal blows that crippled the man and sent him to the floor in a fetal position.

Another had fallen out of the battle.

After seeing that they were outnumbered and out-skilled, the remaining two Croats retreated to the door.

When Jeremiah was about to go after them, Leviticus grabbed his arm. "Let them go," he said. "We have more important issues to deal with."

As soon as that statement left his lips, he looked at the hole where the mirror used to be on the second level.

It was much too quiet up there for his comfort.

CHAPTER TWENTY-SIX

Tolimir Jancovic was a man of quiet communication, saying only what needed to be said to get his point across. As a child growing up during the war-torn battlefields of Croatia, during the era of 'ethnic cleansing,' he had seen the atrocities that emphasized the word 'genocide.' Like Božanović, he had seen his family killed with no thought from the executioners, as if they had swatted flies with the club of a rolled-up newspaper. Their bodies were left in the streets for the mangy curs to eat.

And in the ensuing months, as he avoided detection from opposing forces, Tolimir Jancovic hid in the skeletal remains of razed buildings and ruins, the smell of death all around him, until Božanović and his forces found him cowering behind the ruined beams of what used to be a mosque.

In the subsequent months, he had fought beside Božanović but found himself to be a poor soldier and an elite coward. When firefights were waged, Tolimir found himself falling back without a single shot having been fired from his weapon; always taking to cover until the volley was over.

But Božanović was not swayed or disappointed in Tolimir's actions since a Croat was a Croat. And he kept with the Arabic proverb: the enemy of my enemy is my friend.

And so, they remained friends and talked of war stories and reminding each other that they had so much in common—such as how they lost their families, how they had survived one of the most atrocious times in human history, and how they survived its aftermath.

When Božanović started as a foot soldier with the mob, Tolimir stood by his side, as his aide, and he became Božanović's voice. His eyes and ears in places that Božanović could not be, which extended his range through representation.

As Božanović began his operation as a trafficker and began to seize Bridges of Bones away from his competitors, Tolimir would stay at base camp sitting upon Božanović's throne in proxy, relishing the fact that everyone feared him as much as they feared Božanović.

During his commander's absences, Tolimir would rule with God-like authority, deciding who lived or died by his command, whenever he saw fit the circumstances to promote their needs, which Božanović normally supported because of the agendas he was assigned to always seemed to pan out profit-wise.

In time, as the wealth began to accumulate when the need to launder money became paramount, fictitious and satellite businesses with bogus owners were created to clean up money trails obtained through the auctions of living persons.

The bar was one such satellite station—his station, which had been compromised.

After escaping through the panel in the wall and down the wrought-iron fire escape, Tolimir rummaged for his keys, found them, and hit the panic button on his car, a Citroën.

Just as he opened the door to his vehicle, a rectangular beam of light washed over the parking lot, as a doorway on the building's second level opened. Standing silhouetted against the backdrop of light and looking down at Tolimir from the space that used to be his office, was the priest who was not a priest.

Kimball easily managed to open the panel in the wall, which allowed access to a wrought-iron fire escape that led to an adjoining parking lot in the back.

Tolimir was running across the pavement toward a row of cars, his footfalls echoing off the surrounding buildings. When he reached his Citroën, he opened the car door, looked up at Kimball, and then jumped inside, the engine soon starting.

Kimball raced back to one of the attackers lying on the floor, reached inside the assailant's pocket, grabbed a set of keys, and quickly gave chase.

His only ticket of ever finding out where the children were was getting away.

Leviticus and Isaiah quickly climbed the stairway to the next level, taking two steps at a time. Jeremiah stood sentinel next to the body of Samuel and watched over the disabled Croatians, who crawled along the floor in crippling pain.

When the Knights reached the second level, they immediately saw bodies and a pool of blood spreading across the floor. One man was still alive, but barely, his face smashed into an asymmetrical shape, while the other lay dead in a kneeling position.

Opposite the room, a doorway was open.

Leviticus raced to the opening, and saw Kimball down below, running for a vehicle and using the panic button on the key ring to find the right one.

"Kimball!"

But the Knight didn't answer as he got into a sedan, started the engine, and raced away as tires squealed to grip the surface.

Leviticus could only stare: *Where are you going?*

CHAPTER TWENTY-SEVEN

Tolimir got behind the steering wheel of the Citroën, inserted the key in the ignition, revved the engine, and backed out of the spot, the tires spinning. He then shifted into DRIVE. As soon as the vehicle found traction, the car fishtailed and veered wildly to the left, clipped the bumper of a parked car, and damaged the front fender of the Citroën. After righting himself, he gave a cursory glance to the rearview mirror and saw the large man descending the wrought-iron staircase to the parking lot.

Tolimir pressed hard on the accelerator, the Citroën weaving as it began to pick up speed.

Fifty.

Sixty.

The front end started to rattle in protest, the steel of the fender coughing up sparks whenever it hit the pavement during a turn or struck a dip.

Sixty-five.

Sixty-six.

Suddenly the sedan was in view and closing in on the Citroën, its high beams flashing. Within moments it had tailgated the Citroën to the point where the headlights could no longer be seen in the rearview mirror.

And then the strike—solid and hard, the sound of metal collapsing, as the Citroën pitched forward and settled, the car's rear end lifting from the impact.

Tolimir quickly veering back and forth across the road, refusing his attacker any leeway to come up on the side. And then the priest struck him, hard, the Citroën's rear bumper buckling as Tolimir swerved out of position and fishtailed until he corrected the vehicle on the pavement.

The priest-warrior tried to pass Tolimir on the left and forced his sedan along the Citroën's side, the impact crushing the door and side panel. As Tolimir swerved to the right in a struggle to gain control, he was able to maneuver back into the center lane where he struck the priest's sedan again. The cars hit and bumped one another, the sedan weaving erratically a moment before it corrected itself. It fell behind and then sped up as the streetlights went by in a blur.

The priest affected a movement to the right, toward the shoulder, and then turned sharply to the left when Tolimir countered. The man stepped on the accelerator, bringing the vehicles side by side.

The sedan kept pace, inches away from the Citroën, the cars sometimes touching, teasing, caressing. And then the priest rammed him, the sedan's right front bumper locking beneath the well of the Citroën's lowered fender, pulling and tugging, the Citroën drawing to the left under the sedan's control.

The vehicles swerved to the left, and then to the right, fighting from one side of the road to the other, with Tolimir trying to pull free and his attacker trying to keep possession.

A lamppost loomed ahead, the silver of its post reflecting from the cast of the headlights as it came closer. The priest turned hard to the right, forcing Tolimir onto the shoulder, in line with the pole, the silver of its reflection more prominent in the direct light.

The vehicles tugged, pulled, the pole getting closer, the Citroën trying to pull away.

Can't.

Fifty feet away.

Tolimir tugged hard to the right, the vehicle moved little.

Thirty feet and closing.

The course to the pole was now a straight line.

Twenty feet away.

The silver of the pole was blindingly bright in their headlights.

It was now ten feet away.

Tolimir slammed on the brakes and pulled hard to the right, the forward momentum of the sedan tearing the fender free and carrying it to the left of the pole, while the Citroën skinned it to the right, sending countless numbers of sparks swarming into the night.

The sedan pulled along Tolimir again, the sides touching, teasing.

A game.

Then hard-core hitting. Bumping. The screaming of metal.

Metal collapsing like sheets of aluminum.

Sparks spiraled, danced, and died.

His life, Tolimir thought, *is going to be a finale of twisted metal and ruined flesh on the streets of Paris.*

And then a tire on the sedan blew, a sharp piece of ruined fender catching the tread and slicing it open, causing the vehicle to swerve wildly before it slowed to a crawl.

The Citroën sped away.

Kimball slapped the steering wheel repeatedly with the heel of his hand, screaming nonsensical words at the top of his lungs. Catching Tolimir was paramount. Without him, they would never find Božanović or the children.

As his car slowed and Tolimir's sped ahead, the sedan's front end labored as it limped along with a flat tire.

Tolimir would soon be out of view and forever lost.

The image of the sedan was falling behind in the rearview mirror, the driver's side front end lowered to the ground in obvious damage.

Given the opportunity to escape, Tolimir grabbed his cellphone and dialed a quick-call number.

"Yeah." It was Božanović.

"Jadran, the castle on Les Halles has been compromised."

"By whom?"

Tolimir looked into the rearview mirror. The one working lamp of the sedan was growing smaller as he widened the gap between them. "A priest," he said. "He said he was an emissary from the Vatican, who wanted to negotiate the release of the American woman's children."

"How did he know where to find you?"

"He said Beauchamp informed them."

There was silence on the other end. And Tolimir knew that Božanović was stewing. "No problem," he finally said. "There is to be no negotiation. Take the priest, Tolimir, and make an example of him to the Vatican that they are not welcome to invite themselves into my affairs."

"You don't understand, Jadran. This man took out four of my men in forty seconds. He fights like no one I have ever seen before. And he was oddly dressed. Piously from the waist up, all wearing collars, but dressed like Special Forces from the waist down, like the military."

"And where is this priest?"

"When I left Les Halles, he was following me in a sedan."

"You're on the road?"

Though Božanović could not see him, Tolimir nodded. "His vehicle is damaged," he said. He looked into the rearview mirror. The single light of the sedan had now grown to the size of a mote. "He's falling far behind. There's nothing he can do."

"Did you tell him about the children?"

"Of course not."

"Does he know where they are?"

"He knows nothing."

"He knows you—knows what you look like and knows what you do."

Tolimir's heart skipped a beat inside his chest. "Jadran, please, I did nothing to compromise the organization."

"I know you didn't."

"It was Beauchamp."

"I know that, too. And Beauchamp will be taken care of."

Then imploringly: "Please…"

"It's all right, Tolimir. You did what you had to do. And the Les Halles team?"

"Gone."

"All of them?"

"This priest did not come alone," he added. "He came with others. And the last I checked, they were taking everyone down left and right."

"Are you sure?"

"While the priest was engaged, I checked the monitors on my desk before escaping out the back. Our team below was assuredly on the losing end. So, I left."

There was a moment of silence before Božanović finally spoke. "Are you safe from the rest?"

"Yes."

"Are you sure these priests are not giving chase as well?"

Tolimir didn't think about that, now wondering whether the priest was somehow directing the balance of his team forward to catch up.

He pressed down on the accelerator, the car hitching and laboring over the pavement. "I'm clear," he told him.

But Božanović didn't pick up the confidence in his voice.

At base camp, Božanović closed his eyes with the phone to his ear. Les Halles had been compromised, which meant that an international team under the influence of the Vatican was getting close.

They knew Tolimir and where to find him, which could lead to future hunts. And since Tolimir was a coward at heart, should he be caught, it wouldn't take much for intelligence to extract damaging testimony that could cripple the Bridge of Bones operations.

"Do you think you can make it to base camp?" he asked.

"The car's damaged. But I think I can."

"What are you driving?"

"The Citroën."

Božanović motioned for the computer tech sitting beside him to bring up the image of the Citroën on screen. After a few taps of the buttons on the keyboard, a two-dimensional display of the vehicle surfaced on the computer's screen. Above it was a box that stated: ACCESS CODE REQUIRED.

Božanović took over and typed in a seven-digit code, the numbers showing up in the box as a series of asterisks.

And then the box read: CODE ACCEPTED. WEAPONRY ENGAGED.

"You have been a good friend," he told Tolimir. "And we shared good times, yes?"

"We have."

"But I'm afraid that you have become a liability."

"That's not true, Jadran."

For the first time, Božanović almost felt a pang of grief when he heard the obvious pain in Tolimir's voice from the few words spoken.

"I'm sorry, Tolimir."

"Please, Jadran, let me come in and explain."

Božanović let his finger hover above the ENTER button.

"Jadran, please—"

"Goodbye, my friend." He hit the button.

Tolimir heard a click coming from somewhere beneath the hood of the car—a snap, really—as licks of flame surged through the vents of the dashboard and were then followed by an explosion. The car leaped upward nearly two stories before twisting over and crashing onto its roof.

Tolimir never knew what hit him.

Božanović, hearing what sounded like the beginning of an explosion before the phone went dead, knew that his friend was no more.

He hung up and started to call his Damage Control team.

CHAPTER TWENTY-EIGHT

Even from a distance, Kimball could see the fireball lighting up the night sky, the fiery sphere blooming a moment before settling as a canopy of black smoke.

As the car limped along, he continued to coax it by willing it to move faster, the vehicle now riding on its rim.

When he arrived at the scene, there were several cars situated around the flaming vehicle. It was the Citroën.

When he got out of the sedan, he could feel the heat of the flames against his skin, the warmth tolerable. But as he neared the vehicle the flames intensified. He raised a hand in front of his face to shield himself from the growing temperature.

And then that's when he saw Tolimir.

The man was crawling through the window space, his body aflame. And he had no legs from the mid-thigh down, the ends ragged with trails of burning flesh. As he crawled toward Kimball with his flaming hand reaching out to him imploringly, Kimball ran through the wall of heat reaching out a hand to the man. But the fire pushed Kimball back and the intense flames singed the hairs on the back of his hand.

Tolimir was wide-eyed. Yet he didn't seem to have any recognition as to what was happening to him, didn't seem to feel the effects of the flames as they burned and blackened his flesh.

Kimball reached out his hand, braving the heat, with his pain becoming heightened.

And for a moment their eyes connected. Tolimir's were surrounded by blackness, the skin charred and flaking, stark white against black. But there was nothing behind them. At least nothing with a cognizant mind. It was a mind that moved by the mechanics of self-preservation, the brain knowing just enough to get away.

The man was lost, as the flesh surrounding his lips burned and peeled away, giving him a sardonic grin like a human skull. And then his hand fell to the pavement, slowly, his entire body now aflame as the air became filled with the stench of burning flesh.

It was an indescribable moment for Kimball if not surreal.

No one, not even an animal like Tolimir, deserved to die like this.

Somewhere beyond Kimball's circle, someone screamed. And then there were many calls for someone to help this man who lay dead in the street, all in French, as the car continued to burn down to its skeletal frame.

Kimball fell to his backside and stared at the vehicle. The flames mesmerized him, his eyes hypnotically entranced, while someone beside him was reminding him that he was a priest and that he should do something. All Kimball did, however, was to reach up and trace a finger along his Roman Catholic collar, now smudged with soot, a moment before allowing his hand to slowly fall to his lap.

When the voices eventually faded to echoing whispers in his mind, he closed his eyes and thought of Shari.

How do I tell a mother that her only hope of ever finding her children just went up in flames?

How?

In the background, the consuming fires of the vehicle crackled.

CHAPTER TWENTY-NINE

When Božanović called to mobilize his DC unit, there was an obvious edge to his voice. When the person answered the line on the other end, Božanović didn't even call him by name. "I need a complete sanitization," he told him. "I need you to send someone to Beauchamp before he ends up bringing down whatever assets we have inside the DCPJ. And I want a Tier-One unit dispatched immediately to the Hotel de La Motte Picquet to take out the compromise. I want the father, dead! I want anyone else who's with them, dead! But I want the mother brought to me! Is that clear?"

When it was, he snapped the phone shut.

His teams were on the move.

Beauchamp's Residence

Beauchamp felt the incredible need to release his bladder. For the last hour and a half, he had been handcuffed to a decorative Roman column. And for that last hour and a half, he had tried his best to free himself. But the clasps were secured and double-locked, so any attempt at escaping was all but impossible.

Somewhere in the house, a clock was ticking. Probably the Howard Miller grandfather clock in the hallway, he thought.

But there was another sound, like the measured footfalls of someone walking across the tiled floor as well.

"Hello?"

The footsteps stopped a moment.

Silence.

"Someone there?"

The footsteps started up again as they homed in on his position, the steps getting louder with every footfall.

Inspector Reinard moved out of the shadows and into the blue light that was cast through the windows and across the floor from a full moon. His hands were in his pants pockets as he stood over Beauchamp.

"Thank God," said Beauchamp.

"What are you doing?"

"What am I doing? I'm living a dream. That's what I'm doing. I'm handcuffed to the post!"

"I see that. But how did you get that way?"

"I was getting kinky with myself. Now undo the cuffs," Beauchamp said.

Reinard stood unmoving as he looked down on Beauchamp.

"What the hell are you waiting for? Undo the cuffs."

"I'm afraid I can't do that," Reinard said.

"What? Why the hell not?"

"Less resistance if I keep you this way," he answered. "It just makes my job so much easier."

"What the hell are you talking about?"

Reinard took a few steps closer, took his hands out of his pockets, and got to a knee beside Beauchamp. "You broke the cardinal rule," he said evenly.

Beauchamp's eyes flared. He knew exactly what Reinard was talking about. "Look," he said. "I didn't have a choice."

"We all have choices. You just decided to make the wrong one." He leaned in. "The choice you made, Monsieur Beauchamp, compromised one of Božanović's laundering facilities. More so, Tolimir is dead as a result of your loose lips."

"They were going to kill me," he lied. "They had a knife to my throat, saying that if I didn't talk, then they would end my life."

Reinard nodded as if he understood the man's predicament. "You want to know something?" he asked rhetorically. "I always found you to be…what's the word?" His eyes drifted upward as if the answer was printed on the ceiling. "Arrogant," Reinard finally said, looking back at him. "I always found you annoyingly…arrogant. So, I'm not surprised that it has come to this. You always boasted. But when it came right down to standing tall at a moment you needed to, you fell short by popping off at the mouth, didn't you?"

Beauchamp's lips moved in mute protest.

"Yeah. I thought so," said Reinard. He then reached into his pocket, grabbed a pair of tight-fitting gloves, and tugged them on, his fingers flexing until the gloves were securely fit.

"What are you going to do?" asked Beauchamp, his voice riddled with tension. He then began to wrestle with the handcuffs, a futile attempt that was driven by self-preservation. "You're my partner, for God's sake!"

"And in a few minutes, I'll be your ex-partner."

Reinard reached a gloved hand behind him, lifted the tail of his sports coat, and removed a knife that had been parked in a sheath behind the small of his back. He held it up to display, to show Beauchamp the finer points of its craftsmanship, such as the keen edge and razor-sharp point. "Not the best knife, where knives are concerned, but still a magnificent tool. Don't you agree?"

"Please..."

"You did this to yourself," Reinard told him. "You knew the rules and you accepted to play by them at all costs. Now the cost, in your case, is that Božanović wants your hide. And I'm not talking figuratively, either. You know how he is about making statements and the power behind them."

Beauchamp's bladder finally let go.

But Reinard ignored the sudden stench of uric acid. Instead, he twirled the knife in his hand—back and forth, back and forth—with malicious amusement.

"I'm not as good as Božanović about this kind of stuff," said Reinard. "But you know what they say about how practice makes perfect, right?"

Beauchamp started to scream, causing Reinard to clamp a hand over his mouth.

"Shh-shh-shh-shh," he said. "Let's not go disturbing the neighbors now."

Tears began to stream down Beauchamp's face.

"I'll tell you what? How about if I cut your throat first, put you out of your misery, and then cut you up the way Božanović wants me to? I'll tell him you were alive throughout the entire ordeal. I'll lie to him, how about that? What he doesn't know won't hurt him, right? And, of course, you won't be around to tell him differently."

Beauchamp shook his head. He didn't want anything to happen to him at any level.

"No? No. You don't like that idea?"

Beauchamp shook his head vehemently. *No-no-no! It's not that! I don't want you to do anything to me at all!*

"Well, if you don't like my proposal…"

Beauchamp's voice was muffled beneath the gloved hand. He wanted to implore Reinard with his best oratory efforts and make a case to live. But Reinard disallowed that by pressing his hand so hard against Beauchamp's jawbone, he thought the man was going to push it right through the back of his skull.

Please!

"I'm sorry, partner. But rules are rules. And if I don't follow through with this, then it'll be my turn at the end of someone else's blade. You know that."

Beauchamp blinked back the tears and closed his eyes.

He waited.

Then Reinard brought the blade to his partner.

CHAPTER THIRTY

Božanović's Tier-One unit asked the concierge at the desk of the Hotel de La Motte Picquet, in a not so friendly manner, as to the whereabouts of the Americans. The concierge who, like everyone else in the hotel since the kidnapping, was much talked about and hardly a maintained secret, knew exactly who they were talking about. He had told them of the comings and goings of the archbishop from the rue Barbet-de-Jouy in the 7th arrondissement. And that they had checked out with the archbishop, who had offered them residence.

The unit leader then gave specific mention to the concierge that he was not to speak to anyone about their visit, about the questions asked, or the insightful answers he gave them. In other words, they never existed. If the concierge decided otherwise, then he was told in no uncertain terms that he would wind up at the bottom of the Seine with his throat cut.

As soon as the team left the Hotel de La Motte Picquet, the team leader got on the cell phone and called Božanović.

"They checked out," he said. "The concierge stated that they were held up under the authority of the Vatican at the rue Barbet-de-Jouy. Do you know of this place?"

"Yeah. It's a residential block of houses usually for Vatican dignitaries. Find out which one they're in, and then do what you've been tasked to do."

"Yes, sir."

Božanović hung up.

CHAPTER THIRTY-ONE

The surviving Knights had seized one of the vehicles in the stronghold's parking lot and followed Kimball's route. The van eventually arrived at the scene of Tolimir's misfortune.

In the subsequent moments, Kimball got into the van, his face and clothes dusted with soot. In the rear of the van was the bullet-riddled body of Samuel. His arms had been crossed over his chest in gentle repose.

As the van took the roads smoothly and the city lights passed by in a blur, Kimball had eyes only for Samuel. Slowly, he placed his palm against Samuel's forehead and felt a certain coldness starting to take root. And when he saw the dead Knight's eyes at half-mast and showing nothing but slivers of white, Kimball closed them.

He then fell back until he was sitting against the van's side wall. He traced his fingers against his chest wound, the tips coming away slick with blood.

This mission had been an abysmal failure. Samuel was dead and the one man who could have led him to Božanović was also dead. More so, Božanović's network was more powerful than he could have imagined.

He closed his eyes and listened to the motor of the van as though it was a lullaby, the engine running smooth and even.

As the team leader, he had to lay the blame on himself. His skills of diplomacy were woefully lacking. But the moment he stepped inside the room, he knew Tolimir was not going to be amenable to any level of negotiating. But to get at Tolimir, he'd had to go through the man's team. And time was running critically low. So, he'd had no choice but to take action that would leave Tolimir as the last man standing. And that he achieved. What he didn't count on, however, was Tolimir going up in flames. And with him, the answers as to where Shari's children were being housed.

He sighed.

And then he opened his eyes to look at Samuel.

Like all Knights who had fallen in battle, he would be transported to the Vatican, where services would be held. Then he would be entombed in a place of honor within the necropolis, beneath the Basilica.

Samuel had earned it.

"What do we do?" asked Isaiah. His voice sounded distant, almost like a whisper coming from the depths of a tunnel. "Kimball?"

We do the only thing that's left to us.

"We return to base camp," he finally said. "And go from there."

But the between-the-lines interpretation was that they had run out of options and now had to rely on chance.

And their window was closing.

All Kimball could do to keep himself from punching a hole through the side panel of the van in frustration was to believe that there was a solution to everything.

He had to have faith.

CHAPTER THIRTY-TWO

The Tier-One team arrived at the rue Barbet-de-Jouy less than ten minutes after Božanović called. There were four of them, all elite assassins specifically tasked to terminate all targets of compromise, without leaving behind a measure of trace evidence. They were quick and neat and efficient, a unit of seasoned killers who reacted like a collective of one mind, one soul, one body.

The quarters located at the rue Barbet-de-Jouy was a small tenement with three separate residences attached like brick-row housing. Two of the residences were lights out, both vacant. The one in the middle, however, had lights on.

The four assassins stood in the shadows across the way, watching intently as the team leader scoped the residence with a handheld night-vision monocular.

In the window with the light of the room serving as a backdrop stood the silhouette of a man.

The team leader, a man named Antun, zoomed in by working the joystick to maneuver the lens. The image began to take on clarity until he could tell that it was a man wearing a beret and a cleric's collar, a priest.

He lowered the monocular. "There's one tango in view, but I don't see the parents." He then spoke of a plan of action. "Capeka and Grgur will go to the rear of the tenement to set up a perimeter. Once you get confirmation…" he tapped his lip microphone, "that Mihovil and I have breached the front, then you are to enter, flank out, and take down those we drive to the rear of the house. Božanović wants the woman alive. Is that clear?"

There was a chorus of "yes."

Antun nodded. "Then ready up."

Joshua stood by the window looking out into the night. In the distance, the spires and towers of the Notre Dame Cathedral were spotlighted as the area's marquee architectural feature, a stunning display of lights showcasing a spectacular design.

He then noted the time from the wall clock hanging above the fireplace mantel.

8:31 P.M.

Since he still hadn't heard from Kimball or anyone on the team, concerns were beginning to rise, questions beginning to surface. The Vatican Knights were an elite and efficient group that was quick to respond.

Something's wrong.

He fell back from the window and ventured down the thin hallway. Shari was sitting at her computer, typing, the door to her room slightly ajar to offer him a view.

He grabbed his MP5 off the dresser of a neighboring room, and quietly surveyed the rest of the living area.

The house was empty.

But something continued to nag at him in the same way a dog raises its hackles when sensing great danger.

Something wicked was closing in.

So he raised his weapon.

And he waited.

As Antun and Mihovil were quietly working the front locks to the residence, Capeka and Grgur were in the back, setting up a perimeter. All entrances to the house were now completely covered.

Mihovil was on a knee working the picks cleanly in the lock. Tumblers moved with the faintest of noise, the nearly imperceptible clicks inching them closer to a breach of the residence. With every play of Mihovil's lock picks, Antun ground his feet to the floor and braced himself with his suppressor-tipped weapon pointed forward.

He would kill the priest immediately. And with Mihovil by his side, they would secure the area and drive whoever remained standing into the kill zone of their teammates in the back.

The final click of the lock was the loudest. And with a turn of his hand, the knob turned, too.

141

The breach was made.

With guns readied, they entered the residence.

Antun thought the residence to be much too quiet, which raised a red flag.

They slowly progressed through the rooms, Antun on the left side of the residence, Mihovil on the right, with the points of their weapons raised and their heads turning as if on a swivel.

With the tip of his weapon, Antun pushed the doors wide, the hinges protesting with a marginal squeal, then he led with the point of his weapon ready to strike down the first target.

But all the rooms were empty.

What happened to the priest?

When Antun finally reached the kitchen area at the rear of the house, he found Mihovil sitting at the kitchen table with his chin resting against his chest. The man was unmoving.

What the hell is this?

"Mihovil," he whispered.

The assassin remained unresponsive.

"Mihovil." When Antun reached out and grabbed his companion by the shoulder, Mihovil's head fell to the side and hung at an awkward position. His neck had been broken and he'd been seated at the table.

Now Antun knew he was completely exposed.

When he pivoted to get a 360-degree view of his surroundings, the priest was on top of him and smashed the butt-end of his weapon against Antun's face, crushing the blade of his nose flat. As the Croat fell back, his finger engaged the trigger, the silent bursts stitching up along the wall and across the ceiling, causing plaster to rain down.

The moment Antun hit the floor; the back door was kicked in.

And all hell broke loose.

Bullets strafed across the kitchen, the impacts splintering the wood of the cabinets and smashing ceramic cups and plates, pieces flying everywhere. Glass shattered and the faucet handle was completely blown off its mounting, sending a steady stream of water ceilingward.

The priest quickly ducked out of view and into the hallway, the bullets following the course of his wake.

Capeka gave pursuit while Grgur helped Antun to his feet, his face bloodied.

When Capeka turned the corner, the hallway was empty, so caution prevailed as he took tentative steps and lowered his lip mic. "Antun? Antun?"

Antun lowered his mic. His mind was still cloudy. "Yeah."

"He's gone," he whispered.

"He's not gone. He's here…somewhere." He then pushed Grgur in the direction of the hallway to press upon him the point that he needed to help Capeka with his search for the priest. "Find him. And find the woman. If you find anyone else…you know what to do."

"Aye."

Capeka and Grgur sidled up to one another; their weapons leveled, and they began to move along the corridor.

Antun shook his head until the blurred vision cleared. He looked down at Mihovil, who sat there in a too-loose position with his limbs flaccid by his sides, then Antun took to the opposite side of the residence.

They were closing in.

Shari heard the multiple muted firings of bullets in the kitchen, and immediately recognized the fact that the residence had been compromised. She opened the drawer of her desk, grabbed her Glock, shut off the light, and took a Weaver stance in the back of the room, where the shadows were darkest.

She looked out the window.

Two stories up.

But at least it was a route.

Where are you, Joshua?

Her door began to slide open, the light of the hallway pushing back the shadows of the room until her cover was gone.

So, she leveled the Glock and began to pull the trigger.

Grgur used the tip of his weapon to nudge a door open at the end of the hallway. The room was dark. But the hall's light washed through the shadows and lit up the woman. The Croat immediately tried to center the point of his weapon to the target, but a bullet pierced his

143

forehead and punched a hole through the back of his skull, pulp, and gore splashing the back wall and parts of Capeka, who fell backward out of the line of fire.

For a seemingly long and impossible moment, Grgur stood there, as if his brain was trying to catch up and register that he was dead. Then his legs and knees began to buckle, and then the rest gave way, the man finally falling to the floor.

That whore-of-a-bitch is armed!

Capeka lowered his lip mic. "Antun, I found the woman. She's armed. And Grgur has been terminated. I repeat: Grgur has been terminated."

Antun was infuriated. Božanović would not be pleased since the entire operation had turned into something well beyond a sanitation project. Bodies were lying around. The residence was shot up. And trace evidence would most likely be found and linked to their squad.

"We have two minutes to accomplish the means," he told him. "Use the flash."

"Copy that."

Capeka reached into the pocket of his bulletproof tactical vest and pulled out a pipe approximately the size of a tube of toothpaste. In Croatian, he yelled something out to Shari, something she wouldn't understand, which was subsequently followed by the tube rolling along the room's floor.

Shari's eyes widened when she recognized the flashbang and tried to duck away. But it was too late, the bang going off with a flash of blinding light as the accompanying concussive wave knocked her to the floor. Suddenly her world became a collection of double and triple images. Nothing appeared centered and everything seemed to move with a life of its own. The world became animated in an odd sort of way. Her desk and chair rippled and waved, going from a double image to four images. And her landscape had gone from vivid colors to black and white.

As the internal stars began to clear and the images began to turn back to normalcy, she looked up to see the Croat standing over her. His mouth was moving, but she could hear nothing. Then with the slowness of a bad dream, and for which there was nothing she could do to counter his action, the Croat raised the end of his weapon and brought it down.

Lights out.

Joshua heard the flashbang and realized that the Croats were approaching Shari.

With his weapon raised at eye level, the Knight used the scope as his primary surveillance tool. He moved silently from a recess in the living area and ventured back to the hallway. At the corner of the wall, where the room met the hallway, Joshua removed a mirror from his pocket. He curved the neck to which it was attached and angled the instrument so that he could view the length of the hallway from his position around the bend.

There was a body on the floor, a boneless heap. Blood was spattered on the wall. Other than that, the hall was vacant. After returning the mirror to its pocket, Joshua raised his weapon to eye level and began to maneuver down the hallway.

But someone had come up from behind.

The Vatican Knight quickly swung around with his weapon to draw a bead. But the man deflected the gun off target, as a volley of shots from Joshua's weapon went off in quick succession, the bullets drilling holes in the walls and floor in a series of cacophonous staccato bursts.

...tat...tat...tat...tat...tat...tat...tat...

The glass of picture frames and the pictures inside them were decimated. The molding along the walls and ceiling were pulverized. And the once immaculate floorboards of the finest wood splintered into dangerous-looking shards.

As the intruder brought his weapon up, Joshua kicked it aside, the weapon now sliding across the floor, the man's hands now grabbing Joshua's firearm, with each man trying to wrench it free from the other's grasp. In an awkward ballet, they moved about the room trying to gain control of the MP5. The men twisted and turned, each one grunting with their efforts to maintain control. And then Joshua came up with a series of knee strikes to the man's thigh and groin, connecting. The Croat released his hold and went down to a knee.

Just as Joshua brought his weapon around, the point of a knife punched through the front of his vest. Another man had come up from behind him to run his blade through.

Viscous strands of blood seeped out from between Joshua's lips, and his eyes widened with the stark reality that the pain was a simple prelude to his life ending. Then, he fell to one knee and then to the other, with a hand reaching imploringly outward toward something only he could see. The man behind him withdrew the knife from his back, stepped around, and wiped the blade clean against Joshua's shirt. With a shove from his foot, the man knocked Joshua to the floor, where he lay unmoving.

Antun was breathing heavily, his face a mess, his groin in worse shape. And he nodded his appreciation to Capeka. As good a soldier as Antun was, he had been easily bested by the priest lying dead before them. "You have the woman?" he uttered. The pain was evident in his voice.

"I do."

"And what about the rest?"

"There is no one else," he said. "It was just the woman and the priest."

Antun tried to straighten up. But the pain had yet to subside, making it, for the moment, impossible to do so. "We need to move," he finally said.

"What about the bodies?"

"There's no time to sanitize the unit. We need to go."

Capeka quickly picked up Shari in a fireman's carry, and along with Antun, who moved with a marginal limp, they exited the residence.

CHAPTER THIRTY-THREE

Gary drove by the moment a man laid Shari down in the rear of a van and slid the door shut. He had gotten a good view, which drew the attention and scowl of the man's partner. But it was dark inside Gary's vehicle, so the Croats could not identify him, as he continued to a stand of trees about a kilometer down the road, where he shut off his headlights and parked.

From his position, he could see the windows of the residence lit.

Where is Joshua?

But he knew the answer since Joshua would never have allowed a hostile faction to take Shari without a fight.

He began to rake a hand nervously through his hair.

Now what?

As the van pulled out of its spot, Gary watched it go in a direction that was opposite of where he was parked.

Immediately shifting into reverse and keeping his lights off, Gary put the car into DRIVE and followed the van.

The food was getting cold beside him.

CHAPTER THIRTY-FOUR

By the time the Vatican Knights arrived at the rue Barbet-de-Jouy, it was apparent that the residence had been breached by hostiles, the apartment in chaos.

Kimball was the first to set foot inside, with Isaiah, Leviticus, and Jeremiah taking up the rear.

Bullet holes were everywhere. Vases and ceramics and wall hangings lay shattered upon a wooden floor that was splintered and severely damaged. The walls were riddled with punctures. The elaborate moldings were destroyed. Tufts of stuffing bled through the fabric of couches and chairs that had been penetrated by gunshots.

Kimball raised a fist and then pointed for Jeremiah and Isaiah to take the opposite hallway. Leviticus was to follow Kimball. And since their firearms had run dry, each man carried his knife in a tight-knuckled grip, ready to strike and slash.

Kimball and Leviticus moved silently through the room with their footfalls nonexistent as far as noise went. And then they took the curve of the hallway where they found Joshua lying on the floor. Next to him lay the body of a Croatian. Their blood was beginning to pool and mingle along the tile.

Kimball remained at the ready-state as he stared at Joshua, reminding himself that the entire operation had become a complete disaster, with one failure coming right after another. And Joshua was just another testament to this. Kimball then went to a knee and placed a hand over the young man's heart, remembering when Joshua had been trying to find his way.

Years ago, when Kimball was in Hyde Park, in London, listening to a political incumbent standing upon the podium and voicing his strategies to garner the support and backing of the people, he suddenly felt the tickle of small hands trying to lift his wallet. In a nimble motion, he reached out and grabbed the child by the forearm after taking two strides. It was here that Kimball looked deeply into the young boy's eyes and saw so many things. He saw fear and abandonment and the anger of being left alone. And he also saw the boy's need for help—a silent plea deep within him that confirmed how badly he wanted to be rescued.

So, for a long time, they sat on a bench, looking into each other's eyes, both learning from the other without speaking a single word.

Kimball had seen the child's need to be rescued, just as the boy had seen the man's very same need.

Then after an hour, with the incumbent gone from the podium, Kimball stood and offered the boy his hand. And the boy took it. His small hand was eclipsed by the larger one, and Kimball had walked with him in silence, knowing what he had to do.

He had taken the child to a strange land filled with colonnades and an Egyptian obelisk, a land of holiness, where the shadows of a church fell upon you to bless your soul with an extraordinarily peaceful feeling.

It was a magical place.

Yet the boy could see in the man's eyes that he had yet to be blessed by this magic, that his soul was in constant turmoil, and that the shadow of the church had yet to set upon him this power of almighty peace.

And as the boy grew to be a man, he would often find himself standing within the shadow of St. Peter's, praying for the man who had become his savior, and for God to provide him with the salvation he so deeply needed.

Years later, as the boy learned the ways of the Vatican Knights, becoming schooled and learned, as he became skilled with the weaponry of martial arts and tutored in the philosophies of good and kind men, he always saw the pain in his savior's eyes.

I want to help you.

Kimball never forgot that look, the one that told him that Joshua would stand beside him within the shadow of the church until its magic finally found its way to the core of Kimball's soul.

But Kimball never stood beside Joshua within the shadow of the Church.

Nor had he been there when Joshua went down by the hand of their enemy.

It all came down to the end when he realized that not only had he failed himself, but he'd also failed the boy.

Kimball could feel an uncontainable rage birthing, something with a very ugly head that was beginning to crown. And with all the control he could muster, he closed his eyes and clamped his teeth until the muscles in the back of his jaw went firm.

When a marginal calm began to work over him like a mild narcotic, he opened his eyes and moved forward, stepping over the bodies.

He and Leviticus checked all the rooms along the corridor, finding them empty.

When Isaiah and Jeremiah rounded the corner of the same hallway, Isaiah said, "It's clear. There's a tango downed in the kitchen, as well."

Kimball sheathed his knife, as did the rest of the Knights.

"Shari's gone," he said evenly. "And so is Gary."

Kimball went to the kitchen, which was beginning to flood from the broken faucet. He checked the Croatian for ID, while Isaiah checked the man lying on the floor of the hallway. Neither possessed credentials. No surprise there. And then he spoke to Leviticus with obvious weight to his tone: "Contact the SIV," he told him. "Tell them to send a unit to pick up Joshua and Samuel."

"And what are we going to do about Shari and Gary?" asked Isaiah.

"We'll find them." But Kimball sounded completely defeated, and everyone knew it. He was leaving out one crucial matter: with 360 degrees of direction, he didn't know which way to turn.

Kimball had finally run out of options.

The remnants of the flashbang lay on the floor along with Shari's Glock, which nestled against the baseboard of the wall. No doubt a battle had taken place here with Shari ending up on the losing side.

Her cell phone was on the desk beside the computer; the screen had gone black because of dormancy. A nearby scratchpad had the words 'reciprocity,' 'serial,' and 'sadistic' written on it. Apparently, she was developing Božanović's psychological profile when she had been interrupted.

When Kimball moved the mouse, the computer screen illuminated with her last download. They were the dossiers of the last two commanders who had compromised two of Božanović's operations. One was from Interpol, the other from a London-based force. Both men were found dead in their residences with their flesh peeled and stripped away, the macabre display was the signature handiwork of Jadran Božanović—even though Božanović could never be tied to either killing. But all the hallmarks were there.

And both men had died within a period of four to five weeks after the compromise.

Kimball looked at Shari's notes again.

Reciprocity. Serial. Sadistic.

These were the three ingredients that made up a madman.

Kimball fell into the seat and sighed.

Shari was gone. And so was Gary. What had begun as a solvable endeavor had now turned into a complete and colossal disaster. Not only had they lost the chance of acquiring the whereabouts of the targets, but Shari and Gary had gone missing, as well.

He closed his eyes.

Just as he had failed Joshua, he now felt that he had failed Shari.

Perhaps Pope Pius was right, he considered. Maybe he was too emotionally compromised. Acting out, instead of thinking things through—pushing and shoving his way to get a quick answer, since time was a critical factor.

Not only had he lost Shari in his efforts, but he also lost the right to make a family whole.

He opened his eyes, looked at her cell phone, picked it up, and turned it over in his hand numerous times to study it.

"Kimball." It was Leviticus.

"Yeah."

"We need to get moving."

Get moving? To where?

"A unit has arrived. And a sanitation effort is underway." After a long moment of silence, he said, "Kimball?"

Kimball ignored him as he cocked his head to one side, then left it there while looking at the phone, as if it was something alien. *Everyone has one,* he thought, *including Gary.* He then went through the phone's menu until he came to the CONTACT section, and went through the set of choices, eventually coming to Gary's number.

He immediately stood up and went through the items on the

151

desktop, moving everything aside and lifting papers, books, and journals. And then he checked the drawers and all the shelves in the room.

Gary's phone was missing.

"Kimball?"

After waving off Leviticus to stifle him, Kimball called Father Auciello at the SIV. Since the number was not recognized on their caller ID, he was forced to initiate a series of specified codes and numbers and keywords.

Once he was patched through to Auciello, Kimball's words could hardly be understood because he was talking so fast.

"Kimball, slow down," Auciello said on the other end.

"I have a phone number," he told him. "I need you to geolocate its position if you can."

"Give me the number."

Kimball did. "How long will this take?"

"It's going to be a bit."

"How long is a bit?

"Five, maybe ten minutes."

"Good." Kimball let the phone fall by his side as he directed a command to Leviticus. "Get the team to the armory and gear up," he told him. "You've got five minutes."

"You have something?"

"It's not a lock," he said. "But yeah, I've got something. It may be nothing or it may be everything. But I want the team ready, nevertheless. If this pans out, then we're going to war."

After Leviticus left the room, Kimball was kept on HOLD for another six minutes until Auciello finally returned.

"We got something," he said.

Kimball placed the phone tightly to his ear. "Yeah. What?"

"It's active and it's moving west. You want me to dispatch you through?"

"No. That's the last thing I want to do. If he has the phone and it rings, the kidnappers will disable it should they find it. Let the signal ride out to its final destination."

"The signal," Auciello said. "It's stopped."

"Where at?"

"He's at Les Vedettes de Paris, docks just west of the Eiffel Tower."

"That's not too far."

"This will only serve you if he has the phone."

"If not, then someone else has to be, right, since it's on the move? And that someone is going to tell me where he got it from."

"Be careful, Kimball. You've seen firsthand what Jadran Božanović is capable of doing, even when he's not there. You've seen the wake he's left behind."

"Yeah, well, now he's going to see what I'm capable of doing. And he's going to see firsthand the wake I'm about to leave behind."

"*Kimball—*"

Kimball didn't want to listen anymore and hung up.

He then exited the residence, revving himself up emotionally. With or without the support of the Church, he knew he was going to cut a wide path of destruction right through Božanović's operation until he cornered the Croatian himself.

He was not about to be denied.

Not this time.

Not ever.

This was for Joshua.

And he wasn't about to fail him again.

CHAPTER THIRTY-FIVE

The van had pulled up to Les Vedettes de Paris docks, where the riverboats were tied up along the Seine. In the mix was a 190-foot Hokulani yacht with an aluminum superstructure. It had a sleek and shimmering exterior and a twin-screw propulsion system. The yacht sported three decks with the top two being luxury suites and rooms, the bottom the engineering and propulsion areas, with a 1200-square-foot salon at the level's center. Of the riverboats docked here, this particular one was unique, in that it did not cater to tourists. This was a privately owned ship.

When the rear of the van door opened, a Croat jumped down and, with the help of another, he removed Shari from the vehicle.

From his vantage point approximately 250 feet away, Gary sat in his Renault with his mind spinning as to what action to take. Quietly, he exited the vehicle and watched the two men carry the trunk up the loading ramp.

Gary then reached for his phone. But it was completely useless since the only contact number he had was Shari's. There was no way he could contact Kimball or any member of his team. And he didn't dare try to call the DCPJ, fearing that his call might alert someone who would then contact Božanović. Such a call would only place his entire family in further jeopardy.

So that his phone wouldn't chime due to an incoming call, Gary tossed it into the vehicle and began to make his way toward the yacht without so much as a plan in mind, hoping that someone would be wise enough to realize that his phone was a beacon.

For now, he had no other choice but to wing it.

"That looks bad, Kimball." Leviticus peeled back the fabric of his shirt to reveal the angry red lips of his wound, just above the left pectoral. "Take a whack from a knife, did you?"

He nodded. "From a machete."

Leviticus winced at this as if he had been the one who took the slicing blow. "Well, it did a number," he told him. "It's a deep laceration that's going to need some serious work. It looks like the muscle's torn almost to the point of complete severance. Can you navigate your left arm over your head?"

Kimball didn't even try. "No."

"How about rotating it?"

"I can move it some."

"It's not what I'm asking. Can you rota—"

"I can move it, Leviticus. I'll be fine."

"You won't be fine, Kimball if you go into battle compromised."

"I don't see where we have any other choice. Do you?"

He didn't. Kimball was right. The only choice they had was no choice at all. "I can stitch it up to stem the bleeding. But it won't be a good job by any means."

"I don't care if you put a band-aid on it. Just get me ready."

It took all of five minutes to close the wound, a superficial job at best. When Leviticus tied off the last stitch, Kimball tried to maneuver his arm, wincing as the pain suddenly became electric.

"You have no strength in that arm, do you?"

"I've got some."

"You know what I mean, Kimball."

"I'll be fine, Leviticus. So, stop henpecking me to death and help me with my gear."

In an armory just west of the residence, they equipped themselves with domed helmets, with a formation of gadgetry marching up one side and down the other, an assemblage of night-vision goggles and thermal ware. Their ensembles were entirely 'Robocop' with specially designed composite shin and forearm guards.

Just as Leviticus was aiding Kimball with his bulletproof vest, they received word from the archbishop that a call was coming in from Father Auciello at the SIV.

"Patch it through," Kimball told him.

"Kimball."

"Yeah, Gino. Go ahead."

"The signal is completely stationary."

155

"Where at?"

"Same place. At the docks."

Kimball nodded. "We're about to move on this," he told him. "ETA will be about fifteen minutes."

"Good enough. And Kimball?"

"Yeah."

"I'm sorry about Samuel and Joshua. I just heard."

"Yeah. Me too. But no one is going to be sorrier than Božanović once he gets a load of me. You take care, Gino. Out."

The communication was severed.

And the Knights were on the move.

CHAPTER THIRTY-SIX

Gary quietly made his way on board.

The deck had a top-quality varnish to it—the woodwork glazed to a fine polish. And the rails and brass trimming had all the glimmer and shine expected of a thirty-nine-million-dollar yacht.

As he moved cautiously down the deck, the ship barely moved under his feet.

And then he heard voices speaking in Croatian. He could identify the difficult twists and curls of pronunciation, even though he didn't speak the language.

When he had heard enough, he pressed on, not knowing what his next move would be. The man was driven to move along by the instinct to save his wife and his children, his courage born of a father's willingness to make his family whole without thinking of the dangers or consequences involved.

As he stood on the deck, he took a glance down a stairwell that led to the lower level. The lid of the trunk was open, the trunk itself empty. They had taken Shari somewhere deep inside the boat.

Then there was tapping against Gary's shoulder. When he turned, he saw two Croats standing there with suppressed Uzis in their hands. They had snuck up behind him, which told Gary that he had been surveyed the moment he boarded.

With a grin of malice from the man on the right and speaking words Gary could not understand, he raised his weapon and brought it across, catching Gary square in the temple and sending him into darkness.

By the time Shari came to, Jadran Božanović was sitting in a swivel chair with a stemmed glass of liqueur in his hand. As her eyes began to focus, she recognized the man immediately, her sight tracing the

157

diagonal track of his scar.

"Ms. Cohen," he said, his English perfect. "I'm impressed with your mother's instinct to seek out your children, no matter the cost. I applaud you."

"Where're my babies?" she stated with venom.

"They're fine. For now." He took a sip, pulled the glass back. "Would you like to see them?"

Her heart skipped a beat in her chest. She couldn't answer.

"I'll take that as a yes, then." He reached over and tapped the intercom button on the phone. "Bring them in." Then to Shari, he said, "You have two minutes."

He had pre-planned this meeting, Shari considered. Her children were already at the door waiting for their mother to wake.

When they saw each other, the world seemed to hitch and stagnate, then it stopped as nothing seemed to move at all, including the air around her, which seemed to hang inside the room like a heavy pall.

When she raised her arms, the world was suddenly in motion as her children raced across the room and fell into her embrace. Hugs and kisses were shared, with Shari tracing the back of her palm over the washed-out faces of her daughters, feeling the sharp edges of their cheekbones from slight weight loss, and seeing the once dazzling color of their eyes diminished to a dimmer hue. They were breaking down by the inches.

Two minutes later Božanović was true to his word.

Two Croats entered the room and wrenched her children away, the girls screaming nonsensical words at the top of their lungs. When Shari tried to get to her feet to act as a champion, one of the Croats kicked her forcefully to the floor.

And like that, the children were gone, leaving Shari on the ground in a fetal position, sobbing.

"Get up," he finally said.

She ignored him.

"I said...*get...up*."

She slowly complied by getting into a sitting position. "You bastard."

He scoffed at this. "Is that the best you can do? Call me a bastard? You don't think I've been called worse?"

She could tell that he was relishing the moment. "Please release my children."

"Your children," he said, taking another sip of liqueur, "will grow up to be whores. And you—" He cut himself off when she broke. "And you," he continued, "although a little too aged to fetch top Euro, will still bring in a good amount as a laborer."

Her head snapped up. *What?*

"You should have left well enough alone," he said. "If you had, then you wouldn't be here right now... And neither would your husband."

"Gary..."

"Is that his name?"

She got to her feet, feeling dizzy as her world continued to waver like a drunk-buzz.

"There's nothing you can do," he told her. "There's nothing that anyone can do. Not the Embassy. Not the Vatican. Not even the police. There is...no one." The corners of his lips curled into a grin of wicked delight. He looked as if he thought there was nothing better than to break a person down mentally.

He threw the carrot out before the horse. "Would you like to see your girls again?"

"Please."

"Then tell me about these priests...these men...who attacked my establishment tonight."

Kimball.

"I don't know what you're talking about."

"Of course, you do. They took out an *entire* team. Most of them severely injured, with some of them salvageable and some not so. But these priests, so I'm told, fight like no other, especially this one man— big, noticeably big. Do you know him?"

"No."

"You lie, yes?"

"I don't know him."

"Would you know him better if I threatened the lives of your children?"

"Please don't."

"This isn't a rhetorical question. Would you know him better if I threatened the lives of your children?"

"I don't know him!"

Frustrated, Božanović hit the intercom button once again. "Bring in the youngest," he said.

159

Terry was shoved into the room, the young lady putting up more than just a fight, her legs kicking wildly as she tried to wrestle her way out of the man's hold.

Božanović removed the knife from his sheath and used it as a pointer. "Put her here," he said, pointing to the area in front of his feet. The moment she was thrust upon the floor, Božanović grabbed her by the hair, jerked her head back to expose the openness of her throat, and placed the edge of the blade across her flesh. "I would strongly suggest that you remain still."

Terry didn't move.

In the background, Shari was screaming, as the Croatian enforcer kept her at bay.

"If you don't shut up," Božanović told her, "I will kill her."

Shari, her face stained with the tracks of tears, became silent.

"That's much better," he said. "Now I want you to tell me all…about…the priests."

Having no choice, Shari spoke in earnest.

CHAPTER THIRTY-SEVEN

The Vatican Knights were traveling in a cube van procured by the archdiocese; the vehicle itself was black to blend with the cover of darkness.

It moved westbound toward the docks, with Jeremiah at the wheel. In the rear sat what was left of the team—Kimball and his two lieutenants, Leviticus and Isaiah. They were four in total. A number that was insubstantial when going up against Božanović and his seasoned unit.

They would be outmanned, outgunned, and without a doubt, overrun by forces trained to take no one alive.

The van took the bumps in the road easily, the ride smooth, as Kimball sat back with his eyes focused on the opposite wall, on a point only he could see. His eyes were narrowed and intense, his mind going a million miles per second with thoughts and insights, of plans and strategies. The man was pitting the pros against the cons until a good and viable approach against Božanović eventually favored his team.

They had been here before, in the Philippines and South America, in Eastern Bloc countries, and places of insurgent uprisings with the Vatican Knights always outmanned but a group that always rose to the occasion.

This time was different. He had already lost a third of his team, and they had yet to lay eyes on Božanović.

Kimball wiped a hand over his face as if to erase away the tension of his appearance, his eyes once again returning to razor sharpness.

He thought about Joshua, remembering the youthful face of a child in need. And he could recall that face maturing, as the evolution of the boy's jawline became sharper and stronger, the intelligence in his eyes then hungering for the knowledge of the philosophies. And he could see that appetite of learning fashion the boy into a man of goodwill and strength that went well beyond the power of his body.

Kimball mourned for him just like he mourned for Samuel, who was one of Bonasero Vessucci's discoveries, long before Bonasero had become Pope Pius XIV. Samuel and Joshua grew together as brothers of faith, believing that they could make a difference in the world by protecting those who could not protect themselves.

And now they were gone. The two would be buried within the crypts beneath the Basilica in homage for their services to the Church.

Kimball's teeth clamped so tightly that the muscles in the back of his jaw worked continuously. Losing a third of his team before complete engagement with the enemy was unacceptable.

"Are you all right?" The question came from Leviticus, who'd been observing Kimball along the way.

"Yeah, I'm fine," he lied. *Just...fine.*

From the van's front cabin, Jeremiah called back through the chained window. "We're approaching our destination," he said. "ETA is two minutes."

Everyone immediately responded by putting down their face shields, and they did a last-minute examination of their MP5s.

When the van pulled to a stop, the rear doors opened, and the Knights stepped out into the shadows. Approximately 80 meters away stood Les Vedettes de Paris docks.

To their left was Gary Molin's car, a Renault.

It was empty.

Shari Cohen had told Božanović everything he wanted to know, what he needed to know. She told him about Kimball and his team of Vatican Knights. She told him their purpose of coming to Paris was to help look for the children *he* stole. She told of the unbelievable skill sets they possessed, and in the end, once the smoke settled, Božanović's unit would lay dead at the feet of the Knights, which caused the Croat to scoff with the arrogance of his disposition.

Because there was one major problem: Nobody knew where they were.

When she gave all that was to give, when she had spoken until her voice went dry, Božanović stood and released Shari's daughter to her, allowing mother and child to embrace.

For a long moment, he watched them and saw the indescribable

162

love between mother and daughter, then wondered if he would have grown to be someone different if such a mother's love was there to comfort him. But that opportunity had been taken away from him on the day he watched his mother executed in the streets of Vukovar all those years ago.

After casting these thoughts aside, he hit the intercom button and told the pilot to 'start the engines,' and that he wanted to be on his way to the English Channel within the half-hour.

If the Vatican Knights *were* out there, he wanted to be gone.

Without saying another word, Jadran Božanović went to check on his team.

Gary was tied to a chair, somewhere on the second deck below the ship's flybridge. His face was bloodied, and one eye was swollen shut. Beneath his chair was a plastic sheet, to keep the blood off the carpet. And standing in front of him was a Croat who boasted meaty fists like hammers. Behind him stood two additional members of the Croat's team, each man armed with a rifle.

"You board this boat, why?" The question was a simple one. But getting through the man's thick accent and then piecing the words together to make sense was difficult for Gary. So, when he gave a response that had nothing to do with what the Croat had asked because he simply misunderstood what was being said, the Croat would then lose control and strike Gary with a flurry of blows, pummeling him to near unconsciousness.

"You will answer my questions, yes? You board this boat, why?"

Gary spit out a wad of blood onto the plastic sheet, trying his best to send the spit onto the carpet, but he missed.

This invited more punches.

At the end of the strikes, Gary was nearly incapable of raising his head, his chin now resting against his chest. Strands of blood ran from between his lips and from his nostrils.

The Croatian fell back a step to examine the American. "I said 'why?'"

"Because he is the father of two of our products," said Božanović, stepping into the salon. "He is the husband of the woman Capeka brought on board. Now the family is whole." Božanović took a few steps forward, hooked a finger beneath Gary's chin, and raised his head. He then turned the head one way, and then the other. "You do nice work, Angulu."

The Croat beamed with praise. "Thank you, Jadran."

"But let me show you how it's really done." He removed his knife from its sheath and held it steady before Gary's face. "There's no closer shave than actually flaying off a man's skin, is there?"

This brought a round of laughter from his teammates.

And Jadran Božanović brought the blade forward.

CHAPTER THIRTY-EIGHT

Through the Renault's window, they could see Gary's cell phone sitting on the seat.

"Why didn't he take it with him?" asked Jeremiah.

Kimball knew exactly why. "Because he's former CIA," he said. "He knew about geolocation tracking. That's why he left it in the car, hoping that we'd follow the footprint. He didn't take it with him, because if he got caught or captured, then the phone would have been destroyed."

Good boy, Gary.

There were six boats docked. Five were riverboats for tourists of the 'City at Night' river runs. The sixth was a yacht, sleek and impressive looking, and much larger than the other boats.

Kimball raised a hand to his helmet and toggled a switch, causing his visor to switch to night-vision mode with the face shield serving as a high-tech lens. He zoomed in to the flybridge.

There were three men. One was the pilot, who was initiating the ship's engines, which in turn caused the twin screws to churn the water behind the stern into a frothy and creamy mix. The other two looked on with submachine guns festooned across their shoulders and backs.

Kimball switched off the night vision. "That's it, boys." Then to Leviticus: "What do you think?"

"Three levels that I can see. The ship's about—what, sixty meters? Say one hundred eighty feet, maybe a little more. And with three decks—that's a whole lot of ship."

"There are three on top, which gives them the vantage point of the high ground. We need to take them out immediately. Then we move to the lower decks, with Leviticus and me moving on the starboard side, and Isaiah and Jeremiah working portside. We move methodically with our heads on a swivel. And keep your mikes open. I want both teams to keep each other apprised of their position and movement at all times. Is that clear?"

When it was, Kimball placed a closed fist over his heart, as did the rest of the Vatican Knights. It was their salute. "Loyalty above all else," he said, "except honor." *Hoo-wah!*

They began to move stealthily toward the boat with their weapons raised at eye level.

CHAPTER THIRTY-NINE

The guards and the pilot standing on the flybridge never knew what hit them, as well-placed bullets found marks on their foreheads, the holes emitting ribbons of smoke as the men went to the bridge's floor, hard. The pilot looked stunned right up to the moment he was struck with two shots to the center of body mass, both to the heart, the double impacts driving his body onto the levers and pushing them forward, causing the propulsion system to max out. The screws were now turning at full throttle, while the ship was still moored.

Once the flybridge was cleared and the vantage point taken away, the teams moved in unison, canvassing the ship from the stern to the bow.

Kimball and Leviticus moved along the starboard side—the right side—with Isaiah and Jeremiah moving parallel to them down the port side.

Two guards were posted before decorative glass doors that lead to the first-level suites. Kimball took careful aim with his red-dot scope, drew a bead, and pulled the trigger, the double spits from his weapon perfect head shots. Matter sprayed against the glass in Jackson Pollock designs. The sliding doors, however, took the rounds with quarter-sized holes in the glass. The windowpanes maintained their stability from the exit shots and refused to shatter, though the bullets had splintered the ornate wood carvings on the inside.

Kimball winced at this, knowing that if the glass didn't hold, then the noise of its explosion would have alerted everyone on board.

Leviticus gave him a knowing stare: *Careful!*

Kimball nodded.

They moved forward, stepping over the bodies, and sliding the doors open.

The first-floor salon was warm and inviting, and highly elaborate in its setting. Couches and chairs were upholstered in leather. The polish and sheen of the bar resonated with the most expensive wood, and a bank of 42" inch TVs were lined side by side to make one huge screen against the far wall.

So, this is what children's souls can buy. Kimball was livid.

From the opposite side, Isaiah and Jeremiah silently entered the room.

Kimball raised his hand and pointed to what appeared to be the rails of a spiral staircase that led to the lower level.

They approached.

And voices speaking in Croatian could be heard. But the tones were distant.

Kimball took point with the mouth of his weapon at eye level. Leviticus followed with Isaiah and Jeremiah pulling up the rear.

The voices were getting louder.

At the bottom of the staircase was a hallway that curved slightly inward from their position toward the bow of the yacht's interior. Kimball motioned with his hand by forming it into a pistol with his thumb raised and the forefinger pointed forward, and the remaining three fingers folded into the palm. With multiple flexes of his thumb, which symbolized a trigger, and pointing to the adjacent side, Isaiah and Jeremiah acknowledged Kimball's signal that he wanted them to flank the Croats from the opposing side with weapons ready to respond.

They hunkered low, making themselves smaller targets, and maneuvering into position.

With a great measure of prudence, they moved along the corridors and closed the gap between themselves and the Croats.

Then there was peaked laughter that was quickly followed by a bloodcurdling scream.

CHAPTER FORTY

The foolish husband had raised his head in time to see the sharpness of Božanović's blade edging its way closer to his flesh. The Croat smiled in malicious amusement as his scar pulled at the corner of his lip and drew it higher in an obscene way.

"Ch-ch-ch-ch," said Božanović, as if to calm the man a moment before the slice. "Like I told your wife, you should have left well enough alone."

As he inched the knife closer, his sneer became more pronounced. This was going to be a moment that he would relish.

Suddenly the men beside him fell, their bodies going to the ground as lifeless heaps—blood fanning out beneath them in near-perfect circles against the floor. Božanović snapped his head up in time to see the Vatican Knights descend the stairway with the tips of their suppressors leading the way.

His men had been downed by perfect kill shots. And Božanović couldn't help but be impressed by the pinpoint accuracy, as he backed away from Gary and closer to the salon's rear door.

"Don't move, Božanović." It was their leader, who leveled his weapon to the point of the Croatian's cold heart.

By Shari's in-depth description, he knew these men to be Vatican Knights, and this one to be Kimball Hayden.

Božanović tilted his head and offered a wanton smile when he saw that each man was wearing a Roman Catholic collar. "So, it's true."

"What's that?" said Kimball.

"Are you the leader?"

"Maybe."

Božanović nodded his head. "You are the one."

"The one what?"

Isaiah and Jeremiah worked their way carefully to Gary and untied

169

him.

"Have you ever heard of what we Croatians call *urbana legenda*?"

"No. Should I have?"

The Croatian's smile broadened. "Every culture has them," he said, backing away with his knife moving in figure eights, a movement of distraction. "American's call them urban legends."

"That's nice. Now stop moving, Božanović. I have some love I want to give you regarding a few people."

But Božanović ignored him. "These *urbana legenda* were once called urban myths. But the word 'myth' usually alleges that the story is false."

"Is this going somewhere?"

"A few years ago, a new *urbana legenda* grew within the circle of people I deal with, the men talking as if this particular *urbana legenda* was more legend than a myth. It speaks of a man who walks from the shadows of the Vatican to help those who cannot help themselves. He is considered to be an angel to some and a demon to others. He is called the priest who is not a priest. Have you heard of such an *urbana legenda*?"

"Again, should I have?"

The Croatian chortled when looking at Kimball and his collar. "No, I guess not," he said. "It is after all—what, a myth?"

"If you don't stop moving, Božanović, I'll put a bullet in each leg if it'll keep you from taking one more step."

But it was too late. The Croat had inched his way to the rear exit and shot a hand out, hitting the light switch by the opening. When the fluorescents winked off, Jeremiah raised his weapon and pulled the trigger, sending forth a volley of shots, the muzzle flashes illuminating the room with staccato bursts of light. Božanović ducked as two bullets tugged and grazed his clothing, near misses, and he rolled through the exit where he quickly gained his feet and disappeared into the shadows.

Jeremiah held back on the trigger as the smell of gunpowder permeated the air. "I went for the legs," he shouted. "But I don't think I hit him." After taking several steps, he hit the switch.

Božanović was nowhere to be seen. And Jeremiah was right in his assumption about missing the man. There wasn't even a trace of blood

170

left in Božanović's wake, no trail to follow.

"Jeremiah, get Gary out of here. Isaiah and Leviticus, you two follow me."

Gary was all but exhausted. Dried blood, bruised lumps, and a swollen eye rendered his face close to something unrecognizable. Sweeping an arm underneath and then above Gary's shoulder, Jeremiah was able to walk him toward their point of entry at the ship's stern. Over his shoulder as he was being led away, Gary called out to Kimball: "Get...Shari. She's here...somewhere."

Kimball acknowledged him, then quickly galvanized into action, with Isaiah and Leviticus close behind.

During the pursuit, Kimball had concluded that the advantage now belonged to Božanović, who knew the ship's layout and was most likely alerting his people to ready for battle.

In a few moments, they would swarm like locusts to a feast.

And before the hour was up, Kimball knew that the entire ship would be nothing more than a den of carnage.

The Vatican Knights pressed on.

The ship's third level had been gutted and remodeled to serve Jadran Božanović's needs.

The walls dividing the numerous salons and suites had been modified into three areas: a large holding cell, an interrogation room, and a specifically designed escape route. The engine room in the stern remained untouched.

Božanović took the spiral staircase to the lowest tier, which ended up in the hallway between the ship's engines and the holding cell. From where he stood, he could feel intense heat coming from the direction of the propulsion room, and he heard the high-pitched whine of the engines running at full throttle.

He looked ceilingward as though he could see all the visual obstacles and look directly into the flybridge three levels up. He wondered why the pilot was keeping the ship's engines throttled at maximum.

The heat was beginning to waft down the corridor and toward the bow.

Footsteps sounded above him, the Knights now in pursuit.

Božanović ran toward the bow, where he came upon a metal hatch leading to the holding cell. To the left and right of that room were two corridors. He took to the right side, running, and bypassed the interrogation room in the same manner, by taking the hallway on the right that led to the specifically designed escape route.

When he reached the final room of the deck, he opened the hatchway door and entered the room.

Božanović smiled. He had planned for every contingency.

Even the Vatican Knights couldn't track him through here.

Kimball and company made their way to the bottom tier, where the heat was building to a high degree. Behind them was the engine room. In front of them was a room flanked by corridors.

"Which way?" asked Isaiah.

"You and Leviticus check the stern and clear it. If Božanović isn't there, then we move forward toward the bow and push him into a corner."

"Copy that."

With weapons raised, Isaiah and Leviticus moved toward the ship's rear, the heat becoming increasingly elevated.

"Something's not right," Isaiah commented. "It shouldn't be this hot."

When they reached the propulsion room moments later, they could feel the heat radiating from the seams around the hatchway. Leviticus reached out and touched the door, which was warm to the touch. Draping his weapon over his shoulder, he then grabbed the wheel and turned it, the hatch opening.

A battery of immense heat greeted them. The engines had been running at full capacity for far too long; they were overheating. Nevertheless, the men canvassed the area by checking every niche and recess, for whatever cubbyhole in which Božanović could possibly hide or through which he could escape.

But they found nothing.

The room was clear.

And then the engines took to an unhealthy whine, the system beginning to labor under its docked position.

They quickly exited the room. If Božanović was on this ship, then he was somewhere toward the bow, where Kimball was keeping surveillance.

The hatchway door leading to the bow appeared odd and incongruous in such a luxurious setting. Whereas everything on the upper levels appeared state-of-the-art and steeped with the most expensive accouterments that money could buy, this doorway seemed old and rustic, like something from an old submarine that had been mothballed.

Kimball raised his weapon and moved forward with great caution, one slow step at a time until he came upon the door's wheel. He gripped the wheel and turned it, the latches pulling away from their sockets and unlocking the door.

With his MP5 aimed forward, he pulled the door open to reveal a room that was as black as pitch. A tidal stench of human waste, vomit, and the smell of urine rolled at him with such an overpowering wave, it knocked him back a few steps.

He then lowered his face shield, clicked on the night-vision mode, and entered a room that was no longer black, but the color of phosphorous green.

As he stepped over the room's threshold, his heart sank to his gut.

Dozens of children and young adults, all cringing and cowering into masses against the walls, remained silent and unmoving, trying to be as invisible as they could possibly be in the setting of darkness.

And Kimball felt for them.

In their faces, in their eyes, even through the darkness and with the aid of the night vision, he could see their hurt and pain, and the need to be rescued. It was the same look he had seen in the eyes of Joshua that one day in Hyde Park.

To his right was a light switch. After shutting off his night-vision system, he flipped the room's switch. The children immediately pressed themselves against other bodies that were already pressed against the wall. It was like roaches scurrying for darkness after having been exposed to the light, but there was nowhere for the children to go.

Kimball stepped further into the room with the mouth of his weapon tilted toward the floor. He looked to his left and then to his right, seeing children sitting in their collective filth—their ages ranging from young teens to young adults. They were tired and scared, and their faces were fish-belly pale. Their bodies shivered as if they were mind-numbingly cold. But the room was exceedingly warm from all the body heat that had gathered—and there were no vents to aid in circulation.

They had given Kimball a wide berth as he walked down the middle of the room, the children parting like the waters of the Red Sea.

And a child, a young girl whose face was wan with gray half-moons circling her eyes, saw the collar he was wearing and got to her feet.

With small steps, and with her hand raised and her fingers extended, she approached the man with courage and caution.

Kimball stood there, waiting.

And when she was upon him, her fingertips reached up and grazed the band of his Roman Catholic collar.

Here was a priest.

In response, Kimball laid his hand on the crown of her head. She then grabbed his hand in hers, brought it to her cheek, and used it to caress her skin, as if it had the softness of velvet.

Other children began to follow her lead, each one wanting to touch this man, the tides of the Red Sea closing in as Kimball became the centerpiece of their attention. Hands grazed and touched him. And Kimball tried to reach out to every child, to touch them all, and to let them know that everything would be all right.

Dozens pressed inward from all sides, from all angles.

Suddenly everyone wanted to touch this savior.

CHAPTER FORTY-ONE

The room was specifically designed for Jadran Božanović, the same way the pyramids had been designed for the pharaohs—with hidden walls and recesses and a few deterrents thrown in for good measure. The room was a maze, with corridors running into other corridors that often led to dead ends. Only Božanović knew the specific route. All others would get lost, which would give him time to escape, while his pursuers were locked in.

Before the first doorway was an intercom system, a small box. He pressed the button so that the message could be broadcasted throughout the entire ship. In Croatian, he said, "The ship has been breached. All hostile elements are in the lower decks. You are to terminate without prejudice. I repeat: You are to terminate without prejudice." And then he released the button.

He knew that Kimball was drawing closer, and he considered the fact that the Vatican Knight thought that he was forcing Božanović into a corner, from which there would be no escape. But Božanović had the benefit of knowing the ship's layout. Fighting on the territory of one's homeland always provided the advantage. So, at least in his mind, the Vatican Knights didn't have a chance.

So Božanović waited.

He wanted to play a game.

Isaiah and Leviticus stood in the doorway of the holding cell and watched the children gravitate toward Kimball as though he was a living oracle offering salvation.

In their assessment, they were amazed.

"Kimball." It was Isaiah.

When the children turned, they saw two men with guns. But they

175

also saw the Roman Catholic collars. So, they went to them as they did to Kimball, wanting to touch these angels. The Vatican Knights were overwhelmed with feelings, as they looked upon faces that hadn't smiled in days or weeks and could see the light of hope once again burning in their eyes.

"Leviticus, get the children to safety."

This was going to be somewhat difficult since some of the children were still sluggish, in a drug-induced haze. More so, they had to deal with Božanović's men.

"I can't do this alone," he said.

"Then wait for Isaiah to return after he and I check the fore. Gary said that Shari was here. It won't take too long. Just keep your mic open and hold the position until we return."

"Kimball."

"Yeah."

"Be careful up there. Shari may be to the fore...but so is Božanović."

Kimball immediately understood the gist of Leviticus's meaning: *Let's hope Božanović didn't use her as artwork simply to make a point.*

"I've got to move," Kimball said with urgency. Then, after giving the gesture to follow, he said, "Isaiah!"

They exited the room through a door at the other end and entered a small hallway. Ten feet away was another hatch. Kimball turned the wheel, opened it, and found the room to be just as black as the holding cell. He entered the room alone. When he did, he could hear something whimpering in the darkness.

It was the sound of a child in need.

The door opened slowly, allowing a shaft of light to stretch across the floor of the small room. When the girl looked up, she saw a massive shadow silhouetted against the backdrop of lighting. He was carrying a weapon.

When she saw the man and the firearm he carried, she curled into a fetal position against the wall and whimpered.

Suddenly the area's overhead light went on, the man's hand still on the switch.

For a moment she stared at the man's face. And she remembered.

He had come to her once before, in the past, to fight bad men who had come to kill her and her family. He had become her champion that night and their victor. And here he was again, her savior, a man who had changed little over the years, with continuing strength in his features and brewing sadness in his eyes.

"Hi, Stephanie," he said. He held his hand out to her. "It's time to go home."

Kimball stepped into the room and flipped the switch to give light to the source of the cry.

The girl was young, and she was beautiful. And he could see the shared features of her mother from the color of her skin to the remarkable color of her eyes. She was scared and terrified, her body language conveying the need and want to be left alone. But when she saw him, when her sight drifted to the whiteness of his collar and then to his face, her fear immediately washed away at that moment of recognition.

Kimball held his hand out to her. "Hi, Stephanie," he said soothingly. "It's time to go home."

But Kimball read the features of her face as the lines of a script. It was obvious to him that she didn't want to leave. Not yet. Which was something he couldn't quite understand. "What's the matter, Steph?"

"My mother and sister," she said, pointing to a place beyond the wall. "The ugly man left them alone in a room several minutes ago. I don't know if they're alive or not."

"His name is Božanović," he informed her. "Did you see him come back this way?"

She shook her head. "No."

Kimball realized that Božanović bypassed all the doors and took the faster, unimpeded routes of the corridor to the ship's bow. "Stay here," he told her.

She lashed out and grabbed his bad arm, causing him to wince in pain. "Don't leave me alone, please."

He gently removed her hand. "You'll be fine," he said gently. "I'm going to get your mother and sister. Once I do that, then Isaiah here will take you all to freedom."

177

"Who?"

Kimball pointed to Isaiah, who was standing in the doorway. She would recognize him as well. They had both been there on that night several years ago—angels in dark clothing.

Kimball then eased her into Isaiah's clutches, went to the hatchway against the far wall, turned the wheel, and opened it. With his weapon leveled and taking prudent steps, Kimball entered the room. Unlike the other rooms, the light was on in this one.

Although it was spartan, it did have a desk, a chair, and an intercom system with little else. Sitting in the corner as huddled masses were Shari and Terry, with Terry mounted on her mother's lap with Shari cradling the girl in comfort.

The instant she saw Kimball, her eyes flashed with the spark of recognition and surprise. "How did you find us?" she asked, standing.

"You can thank Gary for that," he told her.

"Is he all right?"

"He'll be fine," he said, omitting the fact that Gary's face had seen better days.

She walked up to him with Terry by her side, mother and daughter in a tight embrace. Though her eyes were red and raw, Shari couldn't quite hide the endearment behind them from Kimball. Slowly, she reached out to him, pulled him close, and rested her head against his chest. And in return he raised his arms and wrapped them around her, pulling her so close that he could smell her scent and feel a different kind of warmth that only she could exude. It was at this moment that he wanted to kiss and hold her forever, and to be able to look down at Stephanie and Terry and be able to call them his own.

But he knew that could never happen.

Some things in life were just unattainable.

When she finally drew away, he could tell it was with reluctance.

"Stephanie's with Isaiah in the next room. It's time for you two to leave."

"Kimball."

He never took his eyes off her.

"About Božanović," she said. "There's something you need to know about him."

"Yeah, I know. I found your notes on the desk."

"They were incomplete," she told him. "Several months ago, the unit leader of Interpol compromised one of Božanović's deals. Almost four weeks after he was found dead at his residence in Lyon, France. The killing had all the hallmarks of a Božanović slaying, but nothing could be proved. A few months after that, Colonel Majors of the London team raided the *Aleksandra*, one of Božanović's ships that were about to set sail to North Africa. Same thing: One month later he was found dead in his flat in London, presumably by the hand of Božanović. And again, nothing could be proved.

"My point is that Božanović has what is called reciprocity. Jadran Božanović would travel the world to make a kill, to appease some internal conflict that he had been bested. He has to retaliate to feel vindicated once the murder is complete."

Kimball waited, knowing that she was driving toward a particular point.

She suddenly took on a look of shame. "I told him who you were," she told him. "He wanted to know about the people who compromised his establishment in Les Halles. He knew I had some sort of a tie with you and the team."

He grabbed her softly by the triceps area. It was a touch of assurance. "It's all right," he told her warmly. "It doesn't make a difference."

But she continued to justify her betrayal. "He had a knife to my baby's throat."

He looked down at Terry and smiled. She looked so much like Gary, he thought. "You don't have to prove anything to me, Shari. You know I understand."

"Thank you." Then: "There's more."

He offered her a perceptible nod, the slight inclination of his chin telling her to go on.

"He knows who you are and where you come from. Given his personality traits, if he gets away, he may return in a few weeks and cut a path right through the Vatican to get to you. Everyone you care for might be in jeopardy, including Bonasero. Jadran Božanović believes in the power of making statements, especially ones that strike a psychological chord with his enemies."

Kimball looked over her shoulder and toward the direction of the bow. For every passing moment, Božanović was getting away. So, it was time for him to strike a chord of his own with the Croat. "All right," he finally said, "time to get everyone out of here."

He ushered Shari and Terry toward Isaiah. Once they were reunited,

Kimball turned to make haste toward the bow of the ship, which was, at least by Isaiah's concerns, the wrong way.

"Kimball, we need to hook up with Leviticus."

"You and Leviticus take charge," ordered Kimball. "The two of you are more than capable. So, pair up and take point, while Shari manages the children. You can do it."

"You're going after Božanović, aren't you?"

"It's something that has to be done."

"Kimball, we've completed our objectives. The children are safe. We need to get them out of here."

Leviticus stepped forward in support of Isaiah. "He's right, Kimball. Going after Božanović to cut his life short isn't what we're about. We go in as a team, complete the objective, and get out—mission done. Božanović can be somebody else's mess. Right now, the important thing to do is to see that these children get back home."

"I won't disagree with you there, Leviticus. These children need to be home with their families. But there's no way I'm about to let Božanović off this ship."

"The objectives have been met." Isaiah sounded heated, his words tense. "Kimball, the Vatican Knights are not about going beyond mission boundaries. We only take lives as a means of self-defense or in the defense of others. Going after Božanović out of a sense of vendetta is against the protocols of what we do. Let him go."

"Let him go? Are you kidding me? And then what? We just let him go so that he can set up shop somewhere else and take someone else's kid next week? Or maybe ten kids the week after that?"

"If you take him out, Kimball, somebody else will just take his place. This is a war that's not ours to fight. It's not our responsibility."

Kimball shook his head. "That's where you're wrong, Isaiah. A world without Jadran Božanović is still a better place. And making the world a better place *is* what we're about."

"But not like this, Kimball. The Church would never agree with your actions."

Kimball stood motionless for a long moment before reaching up to remove the Roman Catholic collar from around his neck.

"What are you doing?" asked Isaiah.

Kimball stared at the pristine white band. "You're right," he told him. "I will not sully the image of the Church." He put the collar in his pocket. "But I can't let it go, either."

"Kimball, you *have* to let it go. It's always been loyalty above all else, except honor. That's what we live by. That's what *we're* about. There's no honor in vendettas."

"What you're talking about is the law, Isaiah. What I'm talking about is justice. They're two different things."

"They're the same in the eyes of the Church."

"What I'm about to do," he told him, "the Church would never condone. I know this. So, what I'm about to do, I do of my own free will. Maybe it's wrong in the eyes of the pope, and maybe it's wrong in the eyes of God, but I can't stop being me, Isaiah. I kill people. It's what I do... It's what I'm good at."

"Kimball—"

"Just get the children out of here. Make sure they get home safe."

"Are you sure this is the path you want to take?"

Kimball's face didn't betray a single emotion. "I just need you to understand me on this," he told them, "as friends. I need both of you to understand this."

Isaiah pursed his lips and nodded. Then he placed a closed fist over his heart and got to a bent knee. Leviticus did the same. And in unison, they said, "Loyalty above all else, except honor."

"Thank you … Thank you, both." Kimball then disappeared into the rooms beyond and headed for the area of the bow.

CHAPTER FORTY-TWO

Though Gary was severely beaten, he did not prove to be burdensome, either. By the time they reached the second tier, he was capable of moving without assistance, though he continued to show minimal bouts of weakness with missteps and dizziness.

"Are you OK?" Jeremiah asked him.

Gary nodded, his face bloodied and one eye swollen shut. "Yeah." He was warring with himself, the man constantly looking over his shoulder, because he questioned himself about running away from Shari's position when he wanted to run toward it.

"She'll be fine," Jeremiah told him. "Trust in them. They'll find her." And then: "Are you capable of handling a firearm?"

Gary looked at him with a cyclopean stare. "It's been a while. And I only have one good eye."

"That's all you need," Jeremiah said, removing the Glock from his holster. "A trigger finger and one good eye; it's the perfect combination." He handed Gary the weapon. "Božanović's forces are on their way. We've been compromised."

Gary looked at the weapon for a long moment, and then tested its heft.

"Are you up for this?" Jeremiah asked him.

Gary continued to weigh the weapon in his hand, could feel the power it brought. But he knew that he was too weak from a concussion, his world still dizzy. He returned the gun back to Jeremiah. "I can't," he said. "In fact—" Purple rings from at the edges of his eyesight began to close in, causing him to teeter in his stance, the vision from his lone eye squeezing down to a pinpoint of light, but he had enough vision to see Jeremiah lash out and grab him by the forearm to keep him from falling. As soon as Gary's sight righted, Jeremiah released him. "I'm sorry, man. I'm not right." *So, you're going to have to man the front lines all by yourself on this one.*

Jeremiah holstered his weapon. "Understood."

Footsteps sounded from the stairway leading down to their level. So Gary took position alongside him behind the bar.

Three men entered the area carrying weapons, all Croats, bearded and angry looking, their heads moving from left to right, with the points of the barrels leading the way.

When a Croat leaned over to check behind the bar, Jeremiah reached up, grabbed the man by the collar, and yanked him over the side. The Croat's finger responded by pulling the trigger of his weapon, which sent rounds into the bar, smashing bottles and sending liquor everywhere.

As the Croat lay there trying to register the quickness of the Knight's action, Jeremiah came down with the point of his elbow and struck the man at the bridge of his nose, rendering him unconscious.

Gary pulled himself into a tight mass, enfolding his arms around his legs and bringing his knees up into acute angles.

Jeremiah then rolled to his left and away from the bar, catching the remaining men in the open. He pulled the trigger of his MP5, strafing the weapon in a horizontal sweep, the rounds catching a Croat and sending him through a walled pane of tempered glass, the pieces shattering and spreading across the carpet like chips of diamonds. The third soldier ducked beneath the volley and took to hiding behind a stainless-steel table that complemented the couch.

Getting to his feet and moving forward, as the smell of gunpowder and smoke drifted in the air, Jeremiah never relented on his pull until his magazine ran dry. He looked at the Croat. The Croat looked at him. The quiet moment between them passed, as their minds tried to adjust to the sudden pause.

When the Croat got to his feet and attempted to direct his weapon on Jeremiah, the Vatican Knight lashed out with a roundhouse kick and knocked the weapon free of the Croat's hands.

The Croat then grabbed Jeremiah's weapon and tried to wrench it loose from his hold. With a free hand, Jeremiah grabbed the man by the back of his head and forced it down into an oncoming knee and connected. The Croat saw a brief flash of internal light a moment before collapsing to the floor.

"Gary," he whispered. "Are you all right?"

Gary raised his head above the bar. The three Croats were lying across the floor of the salon. The glass was smashed. And bullet holes pocked the woodwork. "Yeah, I'm fine," he said.

"We have to move ... Now."

Gary did move, and quickly, rounding the corner of the bar and joining Jeremiah. As soon as he reached the Vatican Knight his vision swayed.

"Gary?"

Gary nodded as his sight slowly returned. "I'm good."

"You sure?"

"Yeah. I'm sure."

They pressed forward.

They had heard the gunfire on the second level, which caused the children to gather, each finding reassurance in the clutches of another.

Jeremiah was clearing them a path from above.

But they knew he couldn't do it alone.

Leviticus lowered his lip mic. "Jeremiah." All he got over his earbud was static and white noise. "Jeremiah."

"Yeah. Go."

"We heard gunfire."

"Contact with tangos. Three down. We're moving toward the stern and the first level."

"Hold your position," Leviticus told him. "I'm moving up to support your push. Do you copy?"

"Copy that."

Leviticus raised his lip mic and addressed Isaiah and Shari. Without saying a word, he handed Shari his Glock. "You know how to use this. Use it if you have to. Jeremiah and I will clear a path topside. I need you two to keep the children safe at all costs, do you understand? At *all* costs."

She took the firearm.

Leviticus looked at the sea of children that seemed to extend to the end of the ship. This was an evacuation.

Then back to Shari: "At all costs."

He raced down the corridor and up the stairway to join Jeremiah for the final battle to freedom.

CHAPTER FORTY-THREE

The door opened uncontested, as Kimball stepped inside Božanović's maze.

"Welcome, Vatican Knight." Božanović's voice echoed throughout the hull, making it impossible for Kimball to pinpoint his exact location. "You do know that your attempt to bring me down, just like all those attempts before yours, will fail, don't you?"

The man's English was flawless.

Kimball took a step into the first corridor. The hallway was thin; the walls were just wide enough to give his shoulders the necessary breadth to walk through without brushing against the panels.

"Kimball...Hayden," the voice said.

Kimball stopped in his tracks and raised his weapon.

"That's right. The woman told me everything."

"We found the children, Božanović."

Silence.

"And they're going home. Every...single...one of them."

More silence.

Then: "Let me tell you something right now, those children aren't going anywhere. My team will see to that. Besides, there's always more where they came from. There are always more children—always more product."

"Not for you, Božanović. I'm here to make sure that your days in the trade are over. I'm here to dismantle your Bridge of Bones piece by piece, bone by bone. And I'm starting with you."

Božanović laughed at this. His arrogance and confidence knew no boundaries. "Come forward, Knight. Come forward and take me out...if you can."

"Oh, I can," he said, taking careful steps inside the maze.

The corridors ran into other corridors, with those corridors running into dead-end walls. It was literally a maze to which Božanović knew the precise route. And Kimball knew that he had made the wrong choice by entering. Every wall, every hallway, looked the same as any other.

He was lost.

"The thing about you, Vatican Knight, is that you don't even know that you're already a dead man."

Kimball stopped in his tracks. *What?*

"I need to join my team," Božanović called out. "Those children, my products, will be gathered like the cattle that they are and returned to the stall you found them in. Your teammates will die by my hand; this I promise. And they will die in a manner I see fit. And that manner, I'm sure, you know quite well."

"You're underestimating my team," he returned.

"The same way you underestimated me?"

Božanović was right. Kimball had underestimated him. A third of his team had already been eliminated, and he wasn't sure about the rest.

"*Urbana legenda,*" the Croat finally said. "I guess the one they call 'the priest who is not a priest' is a myth after all. I was hoping that the legend would be true and that I was in for more of a fight, more of a challenge. But all I got was you." There was a pause of dead silence, then: "Goodbye, Vatican Knight. Have a good death."

Suddenly the panels began to shift and move, propelled by hidden weights and balances within the walls and ceiling.

In response, Kimball ran down the corridors, the constant reconfigurations of the walls forcing him down pathways until he was eventually guided into one that had dead-end walls at both ends.

There was no way out, no avenue of escape.

He was trapped.

And then the walls began to close in on him.

CHAPTER FORTY-FOUR

It took Leviticus less than three minutes to join up with Jeremiah. Although Gary looked lucid, he also appeared less than completely sound.

"This boat," Leviticus told Jeremiah, "was one of Božanović's launch vehicles. We found sixty-four children down below in a holding cell."

Jeremiah was shocked. They weren't prepared for this. To secure the safety of four targets was one thing. But to provide a safe passageway for an evacuation, in an enclosed and hostile space without the proper strategy, was something else altogether.

Leviticus read into Jeremiah's expression. "We clear a path," he told him. "We protect the citizenry of the Church. And we do this at all costs."

Jeremiah knew exactly what he was saying: they were to make a safe passageway at the cost of their lives or the lives of their captors. The parents of sixty-four children, after all, were out there waiting, and none of them cared how they got their children back, as long as they did.

The Knights knew that the numbers of the enemy had been reduced. But the ship was big. And neither knew how many more opponents were left.

Leviticus addressed Jeremiah: "You take portside. And I'll take starboard. Gary, you follow me."

The three moved forward with great caution.

When they reached the stairway that led to the first and final tier, they halted and listened.

From their position, they could hear only the revving of engines running at maximum thrust in the ship's stern, which was loud enough to mask the sound of any movement above.

Leviticus shook his head. *This is not good.*

He took the lead, scaling the steps with his weapon at eye level and using the scope as his visual guide.

Jeremiah followed, with Gary not too far behind.

Reaching the top and final step, Leviticus removed the stemmed mirror from the pocket of his vest, bent and angled the stalk, then raised the mirrorlike periscope so he could survey the room without proffering his head as a target.

He turned the stalk in his hand so that the mirror would rotate and provide him with a 360° view of the salon. To the west and east of the room stood seven Croats, the teams guarding the glass doors leading to the deck.

He lowered the mirror. "Seven," he said, "all heavily armed."

"And the only way out is between us and them."

"Bingo."

"Now what?"

Leviticus smiled. "As a brave soldier once said, we will fight in the shade."

CHAPTER FORTY-FIVE

The walls were closing in, the power behind their movements promising to make Kimball the pasty mortar between them.

He raised his weapon and fired off a volley of shots, the bullets pinging and denting the metal, but doing little else. "Božanoviiiiiiiiiiiiiiić!"

There was no answer, no response, as the shots continued to echo throughout the chamber with hollow cadence.

Kimball searched high and scanned the ceiling. Nothing. But against the wall's northeast corner was a series of junction boxes of brushed nickel, the three units standing side by side. They were connected by heavy-gauge cables.

As the walls picked up momentum and pressed closer, Kimball raised his weapon, took aim, and pulled the trigger.

Bullets strafed across the wall until they ripped into the boxes, the impacts crippling and destroying the power boards and wiring underneath, casting off a shower of sparks.

The walls began to slow, and then they stopped altogether, confining Kimball to a space that was no larger than a closet.

The panels were about ten feet tall, which was about two feet higher than he could jump.

So, he needed a lift.

He looked at his weapon and at its length. Properly fitted and effectively used, it could provide him an additional two feet of height. He then removed the magazine and the chambered bullet, and wedged the submachine gun in the corner, so the mouth of the barrel was placed securely against the floor with the stock two feet above the ground. It would act as a makeshift stepladder. He tested the weapon's stability, which was not very stable at all. Under his weight, it would probably wobble and give. But he had no other choice, no other option.

It took seven attempts until it finally held his weight without sliding to the floor.

He reached upward toward the upper rim of the wall, his fingers falling short by nearly two feet. The weapon wobbled beneath his weight, but he managed to balance himself until he chose his moment and jumped.

The fingers of his right hand folded over the edge. His left arm, however, was proving useless with his strength almost gone and the pain going hot along his left side.

Beneath him the gun fell flat to the floor, leaving him to hang by one arm.

With all the strength he could muster and using the toe-end of his boots to provide him with scaling support, he was able to mount the wall, and he sat upon its top the same way a rider would sit on a bronco. He viewed his surroundings from his new vantage point. The room was not that large. But the numerous walls and panels made it appear so.

Wincing against the pain and realizing that his weapon was lost to him, he checked for his KA-BAR, patted it, and then shimmied along the wall tops until he came to the opposite side of the room, where he dismounted. In front of him was a door. So, he opened it.

It was another corridor—one that was designed to run along the length of the starboard side for Božanović's exclusive use.

Kimball removed his knife, entered the hallway, and continued his chase.

CHAPTER FORTY-SIX

The engines began to work to the point of overheating, as steam began to rise from the turbine thrusters, the heat causing the copper leads to the connectors to become red-hot. Below the propulsion room, two fuel tanks containing 9200 gallons of fuel were beginning to feel the effects of the heat, the insulated area growing to unimaginable temperatures as the twin screws rotated at top speed for much too long without any reprieve.

Pressures were building and gasses were beginning to escape between the seams of the gaskets and permeated the air.

Momentum for the perfect explosion was gathering.

And no one on board had a clue.

CHAPTER FORTY-SEVEN

Leviticus reached into his bulletproof vest and removed a flashbang. He motioned to Jeremiah to do the same.

"There's a power panel beside the door," he whispered. "The network is behind a glass panel with red and green lights to monitor and pinpoint problem areas. I'm assuming it's an easy-access board that serves the entire ship. So, this is what we're going to do. In unison, we'll toss our flashbangs into the salon, to confuse the opposition long enough to take out the power supply. Once we do, then the advantage is ours to take, the moments the lights go out. We lower our face shields, turn the units to night-vision mode, and take new ground."

"So, we fight in the shade?"

Leviticus nodded. "We fight in the shade."

CHAPTER FORTY-EIGHT

Isaiah and Shari waited down below. The children remained unmoving, afraid that a motion—any motion—would trigger a noise that would invite calamity.

But Shari moved about consoling them with soft whispers, telling them that everything was going to be all right. She examined the range of faces and noted that their flesh was covered with grime and filth as if they had just walked out of a war-torn region.

They looked back at her with saucer-like eyes, all big and wide and full of hope.

It'll be all right.

But there was such a long way to go.

And hope, like anything else, could only carry you so far.

CHAPTER FORTY-NINE

By climbing the wall, Kimball had reopened his wound, the shirt underneath his bulletproof vest becoming wet and sticky with blood.

The corridor was built with a low ceiling, about five feet from the floor, with walls so close that he nearly had to walk sideways to make any advancement down the corridor. It was obvious that this particular hallway was fitted to Božanović's specifics, a hidden pathway designed for his escape when things became heated. But in the end, wherever this corridor led to, Kimball would find Jadran Božanović and he would kill the man.

Kimball maneuvered down the corridor with the point of his KA-BAR held forward. The slightly curved passageway, which rounded alongside the hull of the ship from bow to stern, was lit with a string of overhead lights.

Then he heard it, the closing of a metallic hatchway somewhere toward the stern, an area not too far away.

Kimball now moved with a sense of great urgency and planned to make a statement of his own out of Jadran Božanović. Piece by piece and bone by bone, as promised, he would make his masterpiece with this man's carcass.

If nothing else, Kimball's dark faith was completely unshakable. So, with venom coursing through his veins and with inner darkness with which he'd become all too familiar, Kimball was once again the beast of his past. He was a man with no conscience, no remorse, and he carried himself with the cold fortitude of a machine.

And in his mind—somewhere—he knew he was condemning himself to damnation, from which there would be no return and no salvation. Once he killed Jadran Božanović, there would be no light great enough to cleanse his soul.

But Kimball had conceded to his fate.

And he was good with it.

CHAPTER FIFTY

Leviticus and Jeremiah were ready.

In concert with one another, they pulled the pins of their flashbangs and tossed them to opposite ends of the salon.

Explosions quickly erupted, with a pop of brilliant white light and a concussive wave, the effects numbing the guards in the room, the men staggering around with arms and hands in front of their faces, each trying to get a fix on their surroundings, which had suddenly become upended.

Jeremiah and Leviticus lowered their shields and entered the room from the stairway. With horizontal sweeps of his rifle, Leviticus strafed the control panel with a hail of bullets, smashing the control boards underneath.

Suddenly the lights in the salon went out and the backup system kicked on, the room now steeped with red lighting that was reminiscent of a satanic landscape, dark and gloomy with the surrounding furniture little more than darkened shapes.

Jeremiah crossed quickly to the opposite side of the salon where three of Božanović's foot soldiers were starting to come back to reality, the effects of the blasts beginning to minimize as they turned and directed their weapons at the approaching Knight.

With running momentum, Jeremiah leaped through the air and came down with the hardest punch he could muster, knocking his opponent out. He then turned on the other two, their weapons on the rise, and came across with his leg, knocking away the mouth of the weapon's barrel in one direction, while with his backhand he deflected the aim of the second man, by hitting the point of his weapon into another—a one-two strike in a single move.

Both weapons went off in rapid succession, the salon lighting up in a strobe-light effect from the muzzle flashes. Bullets struck neighboring walls and the ceiling. And Jeremiah went into a series of punches and kicks, the blows alternating from one soldier to the next, each man falling back as Jeremiah dispensed his brand of special techniques by showcasing his skill set.

He came in with a series of straight-on blows, pummeling one soldier in the solar plexus with a blinding flurry of powerful jabs that were so fast that the thrusts could barely be seen with the naked eye. Then with elbow strikes, he came across with his left, and then his right, and hit the man squarely in both temples, sending him unconscious to the floor.

Without skipping a beat and before the second man hit the ground, Jeremiah turned on the third man and drove a flat-footed kick into his stomach. The man doubled over and fell to a knee. As he tried to swing his weapon up and around, the Knight came across with the toe-end of his boot and hit the man firmly at the hinge of his jawbone. The bone broke, the man's face becoming disproportionate, as his eyes rolled upwards into his head until they showed nothing but white. Then he fell to the floor.

One of the men on Leviticus's side, who had yet to engage, swung his weapon toward Jeremiah, found his mark, and pulled the trigger. Before Jeremiah could unsling his weapon, bullets tore into his thighs, the impacts knocking him off his feet, as if they had been kicked out from under him.

Leviticus raised his weapon and strafed two men with gunfire—the one who shot Jeremiah and the one standing next to him. A series of bullet holes magically appeared along their chests as blooming rose petals.

The force of the impacts drove them back, sending one man through a glass pane of decorative etched glass, the window smashing into tiny beads that reflected like embers against the red light.

The remaining two guards brought their weapons up and fired off a stream of ammunition in Leviticus's direction, the large Knight diving to the side. A bullet struck his shoulder.

The pain was immense. It was as if someone had punched him through with a hot knitting needle. With his good arm, he brought his weapon up and pulled the trigger, waving his rifle from left to right, with some of his shots landing true. A bullet had struck the top of one man's head, sheering it off as gore and pulp, while a second bullet hit the man squarely in the throat and decimated the bony column of his neck.

That left just one.

As Leviticus tried to maintain his ground, his weapon was becoming much too heavy to bear. The point of the suppressed barrel fell to the floor, the man exhausted. He tried to raise it again in his defense but failed.

The soldier was moving forward with his weapon directed on the Vatican Knight, the man screaming obscenities at the top of his lungs. When he was on top of Leviticus and looking down, when Leviticus could see the black opening of the barrel's mouth, he closed his eyes and prayed.

And a shot rang out.

The man stood over Leviticus for a long moment, teetered in his stance, and then fell backward, dead. His eyes were staring ceilingward.

Across the room, a ribbon of smoke was rising from the tip of Jeremiah's weapon.

Both men appeared winded.

And both men were wounded.

But they were alive.

When the battle was over, Gary cautiously entered the salon. Bodies were everywhere.

Jeremiah was moving slowly across the floor in an elbow crawl. And Leviticus was getting to his backside. Of the two, Jeremiah was the more seriously wounded. So, Gary went to his aid.

Letting his back rest against the wall, Leviticus lowered his lip mic. "Isaiah?"

"Yeah."

"The path topside has been cleared. I repeat: the path topside has been cleared. But two men are down."

"Do we have a green light to proceed?"

"That's a Roger. You're good to go." He raised his mic and looked over the carnage they'd left behind.

In the end, he thought, they were lucky to be alive.

CHAPTER FIFTY-ONE

When Kimball heard the volley of gunfire, he stopped in his tracks until the action played itself out. What was most disconcerting, however, was the subsequent silence that always followed. He never knew who was left after an engagement. And this is what gnawed at him.

Did his team become the victor?

Or did he now stand alone?

Feeling a coldness creep over him like a blanket from head to toe, he moved forward until he came to a hatch. Turning the wheel until the clamps pulled back, he opened the door and allowed a strange red light to filter into the corridor.

Stepping out, he found that he had worked his way to the ship's stern, where a battery of heat swirled within the gloom of red lighting. His surroundings wavered with a satanic cast to them.

At the end of this enclosure was a spiral staircase that led up to the upper tiers, to the top levels. Without hesitating, Kimball took the steps two at a time.

Jadran Božanović heard the gunfire and waited until the last shot was fired. Even then he waited longer; making sure that the boat had been secured by his unit.

But when he entered the salon on the top tier, he found what was left of his team either dead, dying, or rendered unconscious.

He did a slow walk-through, stepping over bodies as they continued to bleed out, while others moaned. He looked at his surroundings and noted the bullet holes in the walls, and then the smashed interior of broken glass and destroyed antiquities. This area had become a war zone, with his team on the losing end.

When he stepped out onto the open deck and felt a cool breeze glancing against his skin, he looked down at the docks to see the woman and her husband, and three other men—two of them wounded as they labored in their movements. They were all escorting his products to safety.

From his vantage point, he had lost everything.

"This is just the first step of dismantling your Bridge of Bones," someone said.

Božanović wheeled around to see the shadow of a man standing silhouetted against the backdrop of red light.

The man came forward. "Piece by piece, bone by bone," the man said. And then the light of the docks showered against his face.

Božanović's eyes lit with a marginal flare of surprise. Then, after cocking his head to one side and leaving it there, he said, "Well, if it isn't the priest who is not a priest. I'm impressed. You're the first of five to enter the maze and come out alive. Perhaps there's something to this *urbana legenda* after all."

"You said you wanted more of a challenge. Well, here I am, Božanović." Kimball raised his KA-BAR and directed its point at the Croatian. "Just so that you know, I plan to make a statement of my own."

The Croat smiled. "Ah, I see," he said. "Statements are always good. And it's nice to know that I have influenced you to do the same." He removed his knife and turned it over in his hand, the man staring at it with a sort of twisted admiration. "Do you know why I do what I do? Why I send the messages I do?"

"I don't really care."

"In 1462," Božanović went on, "Mehmed II, the conqueror of Constantinople, was a brilliant tactician noted for his psychological warfare and the impalement of subjugated peoples in the Ottoman Empire. He returned to Constantinople after being sickened by the sight of 20,000 impaled corpses outside of Târgovişte, the capital city of Vlad the Impaler. That message sent by Vlad was so powerful, the invading army retreated without a single warhorse stepping onto Vlad's territory. And *that* is the power and reason behind what I do. I send messages to my opposition to stay away. If they don't, as with your case, then they will suffer the harsh and brutal consequences."

"Have you even looked at the scoreboard, Božanović? Have you even looked around you? Your army is lying in pools of blood."

The corner of Božanović's lip began to move in nervous tics.

"Then, in the end, I guess it comes down to you and me; two men fighting from different ends of the moral spectrum."

"You think I'm different from you, Božanović? I'm not. I've killed women. I've killed children. So, when I look at you, I see myself. My scars may not be visible like yours, but they're still there."

Božanović laughed at this. "You think you're like me? You're nothing like me at all," he said. "Just because we've killed before doesn't make us similar in any way. You and I are separated by one major difference. After what you just told me, it's obvious that you're working under the authority of the Church, hoping to redeem yourself for the things you've done in the past. I, on the other hand, have no delusions of morality at all. None. And that's where we differ, Knight. You're deluded by the hope that there is salvation in the end... I am not."

"Maybe you're right. Maybe you're wrong. But I can't imagine a God who would disapprove the actions of someone who takes out the likes of you."

"So, in the end, if you beat me, you think salvation will be yours? Is that it?"

"I'm counting on it."

Božanović bent his knees and readied himself for combat. "Then let's get this over with so we can both find out the truth," he said.

On the dock, the children gathered by the van that was too small to transport them all. Jeremiah was badly hurt, with gunshot wounds to both legs. Leviticus had a bullet in his shoulder, but neither man was in a life-threatening situation. Gary's face was battered, and Shari's was bruised; their appearances had seen better days.

From their position on the mooring pier, it was Shari who saw Božanović standing close to the stern, in combat-ready position with a knife in his hand. Moving closer and closing the gap with a KA-BAR in his grasp was Kimball, the two men converging until they were in the kill zone.

"Look." Shari pointed, drawing the attention of the Knights. "It's Kimball."

Isaiah grabbed his weapon and began to charge the yacht's gangway when Leviticus called after him.

"Isaiah!"

The Vatican Knight stopped and turned.

Leviticus called him back with a beckoning hand. "We've completed our objectives," he said. "Kimball's last order to us was to get the children to safety. What goes on from this point on, is Kimball's choice. It's his decision."

Isaiah seemed to be caught in the middle of indecision, as he looked toward the stern and then back to Leviticus, trying to settle on a choice. And then the choice was made for him, when Leviticus finally said, "He told us to understand his wish to go after Božanović alone. So, this is not the road you need to go down, Isaiah. Not now, not ever. You even said so yourself: *This is not what we're about.* And we're not. He chose not to follow the rules of engagement. That's why he removed his collar."

Isaiah's shoulders slowly slumped with defeat.

"Kimball will be fine," added Leviticus.

But it wasn't enough to placate Isaiah, as everyone stood ringside watching the two men at the stern of the ship converge on one another with knives slashing.

CHAPTER FIFTY-TWO

Kimball deflected Božanović's jabs and strikes with simple flicks of his wrist. The Croat quickly changed his attack by coming across with horizontal and diagonal sweeps, his blade connecting with Kimball's one more time. Kimball stood back and realized that Božanović was an unskilled practitioner of double-edged weaponry and that he was, at best, a hacker with no true coordination behind the choreography of his attacks.

But Božanović wasn't without his skills of interpretation, either. He immediately read Kimball's body language with a keen eye and noted that the Vatican Knight was favoring his left side, especially his shoulder, which sloped further downward than the right.

And this was all Jadran Božanović needed to understand.

The Vatican Knight was injured.

The Croatian circled Kimball, studying the man while looking for an opportune moment to strike.

And then he found it.

When Kimball squared off with Božanović so that his injured shoulder was no longer held away from the Croat, Božanović struck at Kimball's Achilles heel. He kicked out with his foot and caught Kimball alongside his knee joint, nearly causing the Vatican Knight to buckle to the deck on one knee. The moment Kimball leaned into the fall, Božanović launched into a roundhouse kick that struck Kimball's wound, the gash reopening to its fullest.

Kimball stumbled back with a hand to his injury, gritting his teeth. Then Božanović attacked Kimball with the point of his knife held forward, with every intent to run it through him. But Kimball responded quickly by lashing out with the pommel of his knife, striking Božanović on the bridge of his nose, hard. The strike opened a deep gash, the force behind the blow staying Božanović's momentum.

The Croat staggered on his feet, his eyes trying to maintain focus, the double and triple images of the world eventually working their way back to a single aspect of reality. He then bull-rushed Kimball, the man screaming in primal rage as he hit the Vatican Knight in his midsection with a shoulder. The blow lifted Kimball off his feet. With Kimball in a bear hug with no ground on which to anchor his feet, Božanović carried him to the edge of the stern. He elevated Kimball above and over the transom, then slammed him against the yacht's 45-degree decline, where they held each other by the wrists, with Kimball hanging precariously over churning waters that were driven by the ship's twin screws.

Božanović looked down at him with malicious amusement. "And so, it comes down to this," he said evenly. "To a tenuous hold between two men."

Kimball tried to set the soles of his feet against the stern wall of the yacht. But the surface was too slick, too steep, the man slipping with every effort to find a reasonable purchase.

Within seconds, Božanović allowed their grasps to slip until they were holding each other in an obscene handshake, and then by just the curls of their fingertips.

"It's time to die, priest who is not a priest." Božanović walked along the transom with Kimball being dragged along the skin of the yacht until he was situated directly over the recess that housed a turning screw.

The surface of the water beneath him bubbled and boiled with activity, the propulsion system maintaining at maximum. It was as if sharks were positioning themselves just below the surface, intuiting the chum and bait that was about to fall into their jaws.

Božanović's smile grew wider, which tugged at his scar.

Kimball stopped struggling, resolving himself to the inevitable.

In the long pause between them, both men looked each other in the eyes. Whereas Kimball saw a man in the throes of steaming madness, the Croatian discovered the priest to be a man of inner conflict and smoldering anger.

Without giving any indication of his next action or what he was about to do, Jadran Božanović released Kimball to his fate.

The Vatican Knight slid down the yacht's steep transom toward the shaft that housed the turning screw.

The waters bubbled with anticipation, as he slid toward the path of the churning water, his feet trying to slow the slide and failing. The surface came closer, the tides soon to be red from the dicing of his limbs.

From somewhere in the distance, Kimball heard a cry. It was faint, a warbled scream. But he knew it was Shari, and like him, she understood that his outcome could only be one of finality.

As he hit the surface, and as the waves washed over him and pulled him underneath, the last thing Kimball Hayden heard was the voice of the woman he loved.

Shari watched from the dock as Jadran Božanović held Kimball over the transom at the ship's stern. At the moment of their release and the beginning of Kimball's long slide toward the course of the turning screw, Shari brought her fisted hands to her chest and cried out in a long, banshee-like wail that carried throughout the docks.

The moment he hit the surface, the moment he was carried underneath, she knew that she would never see him again.

Kimball Hayden was finally gone from her life.

Jadran Božanović watched the man slip beneath the churning waves and waited. But the man never resurfaced.

Stepping away from the transom, he looked down at the children that had gathered and the champions that surrounded them. They were products that were forever gone; he knew that. They were profits lost.

Now looking at the woman and seeing the agony within the twisted lines of her features, he brought his hand to his throat and drew his fingers across it in a cutting motion, making sure that she had seen the action.

The message to her was clear: *I'm coming for you.*

Shari was watching Božanović the moment he drew his fingers across his throat in a cutting motion. Given his profile, she knew that she would never escape his pursuit.

Ever.

The world just wasn't big enough for her to hide.

CHAPTER FIFTY-THREE

The propulsion room three decks below Božanović was saturated with gas fumes and uncontainable heat, the engines and turbines running well beyond their capacities. They had been for some time.

Some of the copper leads and connection points inside the engines had grown red-hot, and the area suddenly became volatile. And as waves of gases moved throughout the room, the fumes found themselves to be the perfect combustible gas, as the red-hot coils ignited a simple lick of flame that quickly grew to a fireball eruption that pitched the overhead floors upward.

Wood flooring splintered skyward against the power of boiling flames. They threw Božanović away from the stern and toward the doorway of the salon, which was closer to the midsection. Getting quickly to his feet and seeing fire rise and then mushroom at a height greater than the flybridge, he reacted out of the purest form of instinct: self-preservation.

He ran toward the ship's bow, the stern beginning to rise from the water, the hull becoming misshapen, as cracks and fissures ran along the boat's length, dividing it into separate pieces. More than 9000 gallons of fuel in separate tanks were beginning to fire off.

The stern finally exploded, the ship's rear end rising and then gone, with the fiery debris taking flight in every direction and in a perfect radius.

And then the midsection started to go, the floor cracking around Božanović as he raced forward. The polished wood split with jagged ends poking up dangerously around him, like punji sticks, the points sharp and deadly, as the hull began to come apart from all positions of the ship—front and aft.

And then the remaining fuel tanks began to go off in quick succession.

...Whump...Whump...Whump...Whump...

As the fireballs ripped upward through the decks, Jadran Božanović dove over the side and into water. The final fury of a massive explosion lifted the ship from the surface and divided the remains into three separate pieces. Debris continued to burn freely along the ripples of the Seine, like Japanese water lanterns.

A distance away, Božanović waded, the Croat watching the remnants of the yacht slide smoothly beneath the water.

With lit debris bobbing all around him and with the rush of sirens coming closer, he began to swim away from the pier and to the safety of distant shores.

CHAPTER FIFTY-FOUR

Vatican City, Inside the Papal Chamber
One Week Later

When Monsignor Giammacio entered the papal chamber, he found Pope Pius XIV standing at the balcony overlooking St. Peter's Square. The pontiff was quiet and subdued, and he never turned to acknowledge the monsignor's presence.

"Your Holiness."

Pius raised his head but didn't face the man, afraid that the monsignor would see the agony in his face or the aged lines that had deepened over the week. Or perhaps he would take note of the deeply saddened eyes that held the constant and burning sting of tears.

"Your Holiness," he repeated.

"Yes, Monsignor."

The monsignor held up a manila envelope. "I have Kimball's clinical records, as you requested."

The pontiff nodded and held out a hand to him. The monsignor gave him the envelope, then stepped back. Pius didn't even open it. He simply held it in his hand, which he kept behind the small of his back.

"Shari Cohen and her husband are here for the services as well," the monsignor added.

Pius nodded. "Did you know that this will be the second time that Kimball will be buried in an empty coffin?"

"It came up in counseling, yes."

There was a long pause before the pontiff finally spoke. "Personally speaking, Monsignor, do you think Kimball found the salvation he was looking for?"

"I would like to think so."

"Technically speaking, and by your clinical observations," he held up the manila envelope. "Do you think he found it?"

There was a slight moment of deliberation. Then: "No."

Although the monsignor could not see it, Pope Pius closed his eyes to blink away the tears. "I will file these with his records and archive them," he eventually stated. "Thank you."

The monsignor bowed his head, and quietly left the chamber.

For a long and saddening moment, Pius tried to galvanize himself to commence the service for the Vatican Knights who had fallen in battle, including Kimball. But to find the courage and strength to do so would be hard if not completely difficult. He didn't know how he would manage without breaking before those in attendance. But he also knew that it was not a sin to mourn openly for the one you love. If he did break, surely his actions would be understood.

Unable to hold back the sting any longer, he shed another tear.

He had loved Kimball and tried to give the man the same direction that a father would give his son, by giving him the tools necessary to grow and build. And Kimball had given him the same love and respect as well, seeing him as the loving father he wished he'd had, instead of the given one, who had been cruel and dispassionate.

Feeling a pang in his heart and a sadness he was sure would never end, Pius called upon God to give him strength. And in the end, he knew it would be granted, and the pain would diminish.

Opening his eyes that were red and raw in appearance, Pope Pius XIV raised his shoulders with feigned strength, raised his chin, and went to conduct a burial service over a man he had come to love as his son.

As he made his walk to the ceremonial chamber, he finally broke down and slowly took to his knees, his back heaving and pitching with deep sobbing and tears of anguish.

Kimball should have buried me, he thought. *A son should always bury his father. A father should never have to bury his son.*

He continued to sob, never having felt so empty or so lost in his entire life.

A bishop wearing full vestments opened the door and peeked his head inside a holding room filled with plush furnishings. "Ms. Cohen, Mr. Molin, services are about to begin. We'll send someone to get you in a few moments."

Shari got to her feet. "Thank you."

The door closed softly between them.

Gary got to his feet, went to his wife, and embraced her. When she fell into him, she began to cry. "It'll be all right," he told her without emotion. He knew it was extremely lame, but it was the only thing he could think of to say at the time, to ease her pain.

Deep underneath he was fuming and angry and hurt because he knew—perhaps by the way she had looked at Kimball, or by the shine in her eyes, or the way her face had beamed whenever he was around—that she loved him on some level, deeply or otherwise.

She couldn't even begin to mask it.

"Did you love him?" he finally asked her. It had been a question that had been weighing on him for some time now.

Shari noted the wounded look on Gary's face. "Honey, Kimball was the only one who came to our aid. He risked his life not once, but twice, to put our family whole again. And this time he paid the ultimate price. I think I'm entitled to mourn the loss of a dear friend, don't you?" She had come off much too harsh with the bite of her attitude, far too severe and certainly unwarranted. Perhaps it was something that she did not want to admit to herself. The reality of her words became her enlightenment regarding how she really felt for Kimball, which shamed her into becoming somewhat defensive.

She then reached up to place a hand behind Gary's head. She pulled him close until the tips of their noses were touching. "Kimball was a dearer friend than most," she told him softly, almost apologetically. "I'll admit to that. But it's always been you, Gary. It's always...been...*you.*"

They kissed.

CHAPTER FIFTY-FIVE

Washington, D.C.
Five Weeks Later

The man stood away from the brownstone, watching the family who resided within from a stand of trees across the way.

He had been there for a while, waiting.

And in such a neighborhood as this, where houses were upper-end and the landscape expertly manicured, he did not belong.

Like a shadow, his outline could be determined as someone whose hair was in a wild tangle, his beard unruly and unkempt. And that was why he stayed within the trees, hiding, waiting, and watching.

He had surveyed the family through the windows of the brownstone, seeing the mother and daughters hugging, then laughing, and sometimes arguing. He had seen the woman hug, hold and kiss her husband—the husband then tracing his fingers down along her pretty cheeks in loving fashion.

The man had watched this repeatedly—could feel the love coming from within the home, even from a distance.

Then the man looked skyward at the canopy of stars, noting the gemlike sparkles and thinking that time was getting close.

It had to be.

In the shadows, the man waited.

It was late, and Shari sat alone in the den, nursing a glass of warm milk. It was quiet with Gary and the kids in bed. And she savored these moments alone, a time where she could reminisce without interruption.

Her bruises had faded, but Gary's still lingered, with contusions

211

that had faded to a deep yellow and green. For a few days thereafter, he had spent time in a Parisian hospital for a concussion. He had been released just prior to the commencement of Ceremonial Services at the Vatican.

She closed her eyes and could feel the warmth of the cup clutched within her enfolding hands. She remembered everything.

Pope Pius spoke not with a voice that was strong or powerful or with anything that hinted at an emotional detachment. It was weak and frail with his voice often cracking with emotion too great to control, and the weight of Kimball's loss too heavy to bear.

And she broke as well, Pius's sentiments becoming infectious to all those around them.

When it was over and they had said their goodbyes, the coffins—Joshua and Samuel among them—were taken away to be buried in a place of honor beneath the Basilica.

It was one of the most painful things she had ever endured.

Now, more than a month later, she still wondered about Kimball, praying and hoping that he had found the salvation he had been seeking. Had he seen the Light of Loving Spirits? Or was he somehow caught within his darkness, along with the demons that had always plagued him?

In the end, however, sixty-four families were reunited with their loved ones. Sixty-five, should hers be included in that count.

That was a lot of lives affected by the actions of a few people.

She took a slow sip from the cup, then allowed the cup to rest against her lap, as she sat on the couch with her legs up.

Since their return to D.C., things were somehow getting back to the norm. It was amazing how resilient children could be, she thought. After their ordeal, they were beginning to fall back to the ways of old. They were once again rolling their eyes against authority, house rules were once again 'lame,' and bedroom doors slammed in the wake of teenage angst.

It was good to get back to normal when everything was anything but.

The only one who really changed was Gary, smiling and accepting the girls' attitudes as a momentary way of life because he had daughters who were now safe. No longer did he take things for granted. Instead, even when doors slammed and eyes rolled, he cherished every single moment that they were here to do so.

Shari on the other hand, thanked Kimball with silent prayers, for making their family whole.

Setting the cup aside, and feeling fatigued since the night was getting late, she stood up, stretched, and shut off the light.

Within moments, she was in bed lying next to her husband, who was sound asleep.

In the neighboring rooms, her daughters were also asleep.

She then closed her eyes and smiled.

Thank you, Kimball, for making my family whole again.

CHAPTER FIFTY-SIX

Jadran Božanović had watched the last light turn off inside the brownstone.

Quietly, he removed his knife from its sheath and toyed with it, the same way that a majorette would twirl a baton between her fingers. He would wait an hour before entering. Then he would commence with his butchering, by killing the husband first, and then maiming the wife. He would then relish the kills of the two young girls, before their mother's eyes. He would use his knife as a tool to wonderfully carve out a macabre feature that would serve as a message. It would run far and deep within media circles, stating that no one, not even the FBI's elite, was safe in their twenty-four-carat neighborhood.

The Croatian's hands were visibly shaking, the anticipation of the hunt was beginning to act like a narcotic that was coursing through his veins. The uncontrollable lust and passion behind his eagerness to kill were almost too much for him to handle.

And these were the moments he reveled in, the instances of making a statement with the hallmark brand that was uniquely his for the world to see. In this brownstone, when it was over and done with, the brutal mastery of Jadran Božanović would be shaped by the broad strokes of his knife.

After waiting the required hour, he finally made his approach with footfalls that were silent. And the moment his foot took the first step that led to the first of two doorways of the residence—the entrance and the foyer doors—a voice that was low and even and with all the cold fortitude of a machine sounded off behind him.

"Where the hell do you think you're going?"

The Croat wheeled on the balls of his feet with his knife already poised and leveled. Standing there was a man who was silhouetted against the backdrop of a streetlight, his outline proposing that he was a man with an unkempt and unruly beard, and hair that suggested that it was caught in a wild tangle.

Božanović raised his knife. "You have no idea what you just walked into," he said.

The man remained unmoving.

So Božanović took a step forward, smelling a hint of alcohol coming off this man.

In a flash of movement, the man launched a series of punches, striking Jadran Božanović repeatedly with crushing blows to the face and abdomen. The Croatian's eyes rolled as internal stars orbited around his mind's eye. And when his eyes finally focused, he quickly discovered that he was lying on the turf with his assailant standing over him, the man's head oddly surrounded by a halo of light that shined from a distant lamp.

Božanović slowly got to his feet, his knife aimed directly at his assailant's heart. From under his breath, he said something obscene in his native tongue, but the man remained unmoving and perhaps unconcerned. But Božanović couldn't tell what the man was thinking, since his face was masked by darkness.

Božanović ground his feet and set himself. But his opponent didn't move into any position of self-defense—no bending of the legs, no raising of the arms. He didn't move at all. And because he didn't move, Jadran Božanović found the moment to be an opportune one. He lashed out with a straight jab.

But the man snapped out a hand and grabbed Božanović by the wrist, twisted it, and broke the bones underneath. In an equally fluid move, the man came across with his free hand and grabbed the knife, as it was falling free from the Croatian's grasp. He had sole custody of the weapon.

Božanović's eyes started as he cradled his arm—the man was so quick.

Then, without warning and within the pulse of a single heartbeat, the knife came up and sliced Božanović's unscarred cheek. The Croatian brought his uninjured hand to his face and traced his fingers over the lips of the fresh wound. The gash was wide and deep. He drew back fingertips that were tacky with blood.

This time when the Croat backpedaled, the man followed, matching

Božanović step by step. When the Croat reached the first step that led to Shari's residence, he ascended the stairway while keeping his eyes on his attacker—and the knife the man wielded. Once Božanović reached the landing, he fell to his knees, the pain in his arm and the slice to his face suddenly going white-hot with agony.

The man loomed and leaned over him. With a voice that was cold and detached, he said, "This is for Joshua."

The Croatian gave him a questioning look. *Who?*

And that was when the man punched the knife home, driving it into Božanović's chest.

Stepping back and watching the Croatian trying to register the moment of his death, the man lifted his leg and kicked it forward, hard, the impact of his foot driving the knife through the man's body until the point exited through his back.

The man then watched Božanović as, in his last effort at life, he tried to get to his feet. But with another frontal kick, the man sent the Croatian through the paned glass window of the door and into the foyer, where he lay dead, as shards of broken glass littered the area around him.

Immediately, the lights to the second-floor hallway came on.

The man looked upward.

Then the lights to the stairwell illuminated.

Shari Cohen descended the staircase with her Glock.

Gary descended with a bat.

When they reached the first-floor landing and opened the door that led to the foyer, Shari's heart threatened to misfire in her chest. Jadran Božanović lay dead in her home, with his eyes rolled so far back that nothing but the whites were showing. A knife was buried to the hilt in his chest, so there was no need to check for a pulse that she knew would not be there.

Slowly and cautiously, she made her way to the landing's threshold with the point of her firearm taking the lead.

The night was dark beyond her doorway. Whoever had left Božanović behind was making a statement of his own: *You're safe now.*

She looked over the landscape that was barely lit by the phase of a crescent moon. It was a big world out there, she considered, with endless places to hide.

Whoever killed Jadran Božanović did so with a penchant for justice rather than following the letter of the law. Whereas the law would have brought Božanović before the leading principals of international courts, simple justice was to send him to Hell.

She looked down at Božanović, feeling an undeniably one-sided effect that she was glad the man was dead. She knew he had finally come for her and her family.

And from this she became overjoyed. Not because Jadran Božanović lay dead at her feet, but because he lay dead by the hands of the man who had become her savior so long ago.

She then looked out into the darkness and into the shadows, her eyes spying for a shape. And then she realized that the night was a dark and lonely place that harbored many secrets, some that would never be solved or understood. But there was no mystery here tonight with Božanović lying in her doorway. In fact, it was all too clear: her savior had come once again.

She lowered her firearm. Then with the corners of her lips beginning to arc into a smile, and with the onset of tears beginning to sting, she had a single thought:

Thank you, Kimball.

EPILOGUE

Washington, D.C.
The Following Morning

"All right, buddy. Let's go. No one's allowed to sleep on a public bench." The officer tapped the bottom of the homeless man's shoes with the tip of his ASP baton. "C'mon, move! If you need a place to sleep, then get yourself to the shelter on Concorde."

The man, with his hands tucked beneath his armpits for warmth, labored into a sitting position with narrowed eyes that were still on the cusp between awake and sleep.

"C'mon, buddy, let's go."

The homeless man nodded.

"You might want to grab yourself a shower, too. You could definitely use a good once over to get that stink off you."

After the officer walked away, the man held his gloved hands out in front of him. But they weren't gloved at all. They were covered with blood that had dried to the color of burgundy. In a nearby puddle where pigeons cooed along its edges, the man took the full liberty of washing away the wine-colored flakes until the water became a blend of whatever color black and burgundy made. Once the surface settled, the man appraised his mirrored image.

His hair was in a wide mess, with pointed licks and tufts going everywhere. His face was smudged, the lines of his crow's-feet caked with grime, which made them look deeper and more pronounced. And his beard was completely unruly, with loops of curly hair standing out in all different sizes and lengths. The only constants were his cerulean blue eyes—those lonely orbs that spoke of a man who had served as the fulcrum between sinner and saint, who constantly seesawed from one side to the next in turmoil.

..eturning to the bench, he raised and rotated his left shoulder and arm. Over the past few weeks, the pain had subsided, and his strength returned. And with his strength had come agility. And with his agility had come a particular set of skills that had made him one of the world's elite as a killer. Or in the eyes of others, a savior.

When he'd slid down the ship's transom and toward the turn of the screw, he had conceded to his fate, believing that the mystery of what laid beyond this life was about to be answered with either the realm of the Light of Loving Spirits, or by him becoming the centerpiece of some dark orgy in Hell. But as soon as he hit the water, the power of the screw kicked him away from the ship with a punch that was like a blast from a fire hose, hard and ramming. The force pushed him into the pilings beneath the docks, where he slipped in and out of consciousness.

What happened thereafter remained a blur, his memory not as keen.

But he did remember Jadran Božanović was a man of reciprocity, who knew no boundaries when it came to retaliation. If nothing else, the man had considered, the Croat was predictable and would remain true to his psychological profile. And since people were by nature creatures of habit and fell in love with a certain lifestyle, he knew that Božanović would be no different.

So, he had to make the world believe that he was dead. If Božanović thought otherwise, then he would have sliced his way through the Vatican to get at him. And should that have been the case, a lot of lives would have been lost as a consequence of allowing the Croat to live.

So, the dead man waited in the copse of trees across the way from the brownstone, knowing that Božanović would someday arrive. And as he stood there night after night, when temperatures plummeted to near freezing, he would watch the family go through the paces of life... Then he wished he had a family of his own.

When Božanović finally showed up with his knife, it was all he needed to do to make everything wrong in the world right again. He had chosen justice over law. And by doing so, he literally deposited the man's body at Shari's doorstep, letting her know that she and her family would now be safe.

The world was once again right, at least for the moment.

This, the dead man was sure of, as he took note of the park's surroundings, watching people walk their dogs along the grass that

219

was perfectly manicured. To the east, streamers of morn¡
beginning to show in colors of reds and yellows, perha¡
another beautiful day with a uniform blue sky peppered
scudding clouds.

Everything is so peaceful, he thought.

So…

…calm.

I like being dead.

He then reached into his shirt pocket and removed a Roman
Catholic collar that was soiled and stained. He had removed it a long
while back, knowing the Vatican would never condone his actions
when it came to Jadran Božanović. He had chosen free will over the
objectives of the Church.

And for that, he had damned himself for eternity.

Then with all the tenderness of treating something as the greatest of
holy relics, he placed the soiled collar against the bench, and with the
blade of his hand tried to smooth away the creases, but he failed
miserably with the effort.

Holding the collar before him, he remembered in kind the memories
it brought him. So, he kept it, tucking it away in a shirt pocket that had
the embroidered emblem of a powder-blue shield with a silver Pattée
at its center.

The insignia of the Vatican Knights.

The dead man stood, stretched, and allowed his eyes to trace the
walkway that wended through the park. With freshly-cleaned hands,
he followed the winding path to see where it would lead him.

Read an excerpt from Book #6 six of the Vatican Knights series:

CROSSES to BEAR

PROLOGUE

Paris, France. One Year Ago.
The Day After The Election Of Pope Gregory XVII.

Ezekiel sat at an outdoor eatery with a small cup of latte before him. In his hands was the *Le Parisien*, a Parisian newspaper.

After escaping Necropolis all bloodied and fatigued, he was able to find his way to a hack doctor who healed his wounds for a nominal fee on top of an upfront charge to keep him quiet. But when the doctor hinted that he would renege out of the deal unless Ezekiel came up with more of the original sums agreed upon, Ezekiel grabbed a scalpel and threw it across the room, impaling a cockroach that was scaling the wall.

Point made!

After that, the doctor said nothing more and attended to the assassin.

Once Ezekiel was able to travel, he made his way to France and kept a low profile.

Now, almost three months to the day after the battle inside Necropolis, Ezekiel's heart grew heavy inside his chest.

On the front page of *Le Parisien* was a glorified obituary regarding the death of Amerigo Anzalone, Pope Pius XIII. It covered the man's life, such as his rise to the papal throne and his final days as a servant to Christians around the world.

How I must have disappointed him in the end, he thought. *How deeply saddened he must have been.* He had respected the pontiff on so many levels that he hoped that Pius, at least in the end, had forgiven him for his betrayal against the Church as a Vatican Knight.

Please forgive me.

He lowered the newspaper slowly to the white-clothed tabletop and

watched the pigeons gather close to his feet—the birds p
and cooing.

And then the birds took flight with their wings beati
panic, the world around him becoming a wall of feather.
they were gone.

In their place stood a well-built man of fair complexion, raven hair,
and a wedge of pink scarring beneath his chin. "Disgusting creatures,
don't you think? I believe you Americans refer to them as 'rats with
wings.'"

Ezekiel just stared at the man who pointed to an empty chair at the
table opposite Ezekiel. "May I?"

"Do I know you?"

The man took the seat without waiting for Ezekiel's invite. "In a
way, I believe you do," the man said.

Really. How so?

As the waiter approached the man waved him off, crossed his legs
in leisure, and cupped his hands over a knee. "We've never met face to
face, but I'm sure you've heard of me," he told him. "In your circle,
you would know me as Abraham Obadiah."

Ezekiel started to reach for a weapon.

Obadiah immediately raised his hand as a statement to Ezekiel to
stay his action. "Don't," he said evenly. "Do you really think I would
sit at this table without the proper resources backing me up?"

"I'd kill you before they had time to react."

"I hardly doubt it," he returned. "Look at your chest."

Ezekiel found three red spots from laser sightings directed to the
center of his body mass, all kill shots. But he couldn't spot the
assassins in hiding.

Ezekiel could feel his anger stewing. A few years ago, this man
sitting before him was responsible for the kidnapping of Pope Pius and
the executions of several bishops within the Holy See. Of Obadiah's
entire team, which included military elitists, he was the only one to
escape after the Vatican Knights defeated them in close combat.

"Why are you here?"

Obadiah stared at him briefly before digging a photo out of his
pocket and placing it on top of the open pages of the *Le Parisien*. The
photo was aged, but still in excellent condition, not grainy. It was a
photo of a much younger Cardinal Bonasero Vessucci. Beside him
stood a man wearing black fatigue pants, a military beret, boots, and a

's shirt with a Roman Catholic collar. It was an earlier moment when Kimball had become a Knight.

"When the blood relative of a superior American senator is taken in by the State of the Vatican, it draws attention." Obadiah tapped the photo. "This was taken a day after papers were filed for your release into their custody with no questions asked by state agencies. The people I work for take notice of things like that."

"What's your point?"

He pointed to Kimball. "This man," he said. "Who is he?"

"Why?"

The man's tapping became more adamant. "Who . . . is . . . he?"

The two squared off against one another with hardened gazes. Then with measured calm, Ezekiel said, "His name is Kimball Hayden."

Obadiah fell back into his seat. "Kimball Hayden," he uttered distantly. He now had a name. "And what does Kimball Hayden do?"

"Why do you want to know?" Ezekiel asked harshly.

Obadiah leaned forward. "Let's just say that my team keeps an eye on things globally for the welfare of humankind."

Ezekiel smirked. "Espionage," he said. "The word at the time of the pope's kidnapping was that you worked for Mossad."

"You can believe whatever you want," he returned. "If that was the 'word,' then that was the 'word.'" The man leaned further forward, as if in close counsel. "Now tell me, who is this Kimball Hayden? And what was his interest toward you, the only surviving relative of a powerful American senator?"

Ezekiel did not draw close to Obadiah. Instead, he tented his hands together and placed them over the photo. "He is a Vatican Knight," he told him. "As I was."

Obadiah fell back once again. "A Vatican Knight?"

He nodded. "The Vatican has its own team of elite commandos," he returned. "It was the Vatican Knights who took down your team the day the pontiff was freed . . . And it was Kimball Hayden who led the team."

Obadiah raised his arm and showing off a ragged scar. "He did this to me."

"He should have killed you."

"But he didn't." A pause, then: "Tell me. Why his interest in you?"

Ezekiel maintained a look of hard determination. "To become a Vatican Knight, you must be without family and someone who is

orphaned. From a young age, you are trained to be lear.
in combat."

"Fascinating," he murmured. "Taking pages directly .
legacy by rearing a child to become an elite soldier. And ᴸ
saw these latent skills within you as a young boy? That's ʷ ⌐ ᴜe took
you in?"

He shook his head 'no.' "It was because he murdered my
grandfather."

"While working under the auspices of the Church?"

"No. At that time he was an assassin for the United States
government. He was ordered to terminate my grandfather."

Obadiah's eyes suddenly detonated with the shock of surprise. This
type of information was incredibly damaging—the murder of an all-
powerful political figure sanctioned by major principals within the
White House. "And your role?"

"I was chosen by Hayden because of his reasons."

Obadiah smiled. "For redemption," he said. "He raised you for his
redemption."

"You're very perceptive."

"The man has a conscience that cannot be pacified, so he serves the
Vatican in order to achieve salvation. But for him to do that, he
believed that saving you after he destroyed your life was a way to
make amends."

He nodded.

"Then you were nothing more to him than his puppet?"

Ezekiel looked down at the photo. "He tried to save me."

"Sure he did." Obadiah removed several photos from his jacket
pocket and spread them over the tabletop. They were postmortem
shots of the members from the Pieces of Eight. "I'm impressed with
your handiwork," he told him. "Our intelligence knew about the Pieces
of Eight, but we could not determine who these people were or what
their role was. But when we were informed that they were being
terminated, our sources had to find out why ex-GI officials were being
eradicated, whether the reason was political or otherwise." He tossed
another picture on top of the others, this one taken through the lens
with NG capability. It was a photo of Ezekiel leaving the ranch house
moments after he killed Hawk. And then another photo was laid down
by Obadiah, this one showing Ezekiel on the rooftop with a sniper rifle
moments before he shot one of the Hardwick brothers with pinpoint

.uracy.

"And then we realized that this had no political implication behind it at all—that this was nothing more than a vendetta." Obadiah tossed the third photo down, this one of Kimball Hayden taken from a distance. "It was this man that you wanted dead, wasn't it?"

Ezekiel stared at the photo but said nothing.

"When I saw this photo, I recognized him right away. I knew it was the man at the depository who freed the pontiff and took out my team. I never thought I'd ever see him again." Obadiah picked up the photo and examined it. "Kimball Hayden was a member of the notorious kill squad the Pieces of Eight, and now serves as a warrior for the Church. Talk about extremes."

"What do you want, Obadiah?"

"My own redemption," he quickly told him. "When I realized that this man, for whatever reason, was being targeted by the grandson of a once-powerful senator, that's when I saw the opportunity for my own salvation. So, I waited, hoping that you would fulfill your goal of terminating Kimball Hayden from both our lives." He laid the photo down and sighed. "But you failed."

"I have not forfeited my goals," he told him. "Kimball Hayden is one of the best in the world at what he does."

Obadiah rubbed the scar on his arm. No one knew better regarding that statement than he did.

"He'll be waiting for me, which will make my agenda more difficult to achieve."

Obadiah stopped rubbing his old wound. "And that is why I'm here," he stated. "It appears that Kimball Hayden has become our white whale. So, I would like to offer you a proposal."

"A proposal?"

"Work with my group," he simply said. "Kimball Hayden may become a liability in future ventures. Therefore, he must be taken out of the equation. Against one of us, the odds are even; but against two, then the odds are skewed in our favor."

"Why would I want to join with a man who tried to assassinate the pope?"

"What I did was purely business with political aspirations behind the motive. But in the end, when I realized the mission was over, I was the one who cut the bonds of the pontiff's chains and set him free. I may be a fanatic in my duties to my organization, but I also recognize the fact that if the journey is over, then it's over. There w~~ killing the pope."

"But your team tried."

"And they suffered the ultimate cost at the hands o~ Hayden and the Vatican Knights." He held up his arm, the ~ar was still ugly and purple. "Including myself."

"Looks like a small price to pay considering that others had paid with their lives."

"True. But he hampered my skills somewhat. But nevertheless, I'm still skilled."

The men measured each other carefully from across the table for a long moment.

And then, from Obadiah, "Do we have an alliance, Mr. Cartwright?"

"I go by Ezekiel."

Obadiah smiled, and then lifted his hand as an offering. "Fine," he said. "Then do we have an alliance, Ezekiel? Shall we hunt the white whale together?"

Ezekiel looked at the proffered hand, then at Obadiah, noting stoicism on his face.

The former Knight lifted his hand and joined it with Obadiah's to form a new alliance. Then: "Are you Mossad?"

Obadiah smiled. "Perhaps," he returned. He then waved his free hand and the three red dots disappeared from the center of Ezekiel's chest. He fell back into his seat bearing all the smugness of achieving a great victory. "I will train you. And then I will give you guidance. In a year's time, maybe longer, I'll need you to return to the United States. More specifically, to Atlanta."

"For what?"

"There's a new technology being created deep inside a chamber, a powerful weapon. And I want it."

"So, get it."

"If it was only that easy," he said. "But it's not. I need someone with your particular skills to manage my team. Someone who has *hutzpah*. Training will be long and difficult, but I have confidence in your abilities."

"And what do I get in return?"

"All the resources you need to bring down Kimball Hayden. And I promise you, Ezekiel, this time you will not fail."

preamble of a smile started to make its way at the corner of Ezekiel's lips.

He was in.

Printed in Great Britain
by Amazon

23813199R00126